Invisible Fire

Sara West

Published by Sara West, 2024.

This is a work of fiction. Similarities to real people, places, or events are entirely coincidental.

INVISIBLE FIRE

First edition. October 26, 2024.

Copyright © 2024 Sara West.

ISBN: 979-8227396259

Written by Sara West.

Chapter 1: "A Job I Never Wanted"

The car door opened with a whisper, as if the vehicle itself knew to be cautious. I stepped into the cool air of early autumn, leaves rustling in a lazy ballet across the sidewalk, the scent of pumpkin spice and impending rain mixing in the breeze. I had half a mind to walk away, to let the moment pass like a fleeting dream, but curiosity snagged me in its net. It was as if the universe had put a finger on my shoulder, urging me forward.

The interior of the car was swathed in leather that smelled faintly of sandalwood, and the quiet hum of the engine added a reassuring thrum beneath the silence. I took a moment to adjust to the luxurious cocoon before me, fighting the instinct to slide back into my comfort zone, the modesty of my office filled with therapeutic books and cozy throw blankets. Instead, I found myself across from him—a figure poised like an untamed storm, tall and angular, with dark hair that fell across his forehead in a way that was both stylish and slightly unruly. He wore a tailored suit that seemed to breathe wealth and power, but it was his eyes, sharp and restless, that pulled me in like a moth to a flame.

"Dr. Lane," he said, his voice smooth as aged whiskey, carrying a hint of something dangerously enticing. "I'm glad you accepted the invitation."

"Did I have a choice?" I shot back, unable to help myself. I prided myself on my directness, especially when faced with someone who likely thrived on the mystique of power. The sharp lines of his smile suggested he appreciated my candor.

"True," he replied, his gaze unwavering. "But I'm hoping we can make this an enjoyable collaboration."

I raised an eyebrow, silently challenging him. The truth was, I didn't want this job, not even a little. I was a healer, not a corporate pawn. I spent my days delving into the lives of others, peeling back their layers of pain, trauma, and hope. The thought of working with a billionaire—one known for his ruthless business tactics—made my skin crawl. Yet, beneath my apprehension lay a pulse of intrigue. Who was this man behind the polished exterior? What darkness lurked behind those calm, cool eyes?

"You know my background," I said, folding my arms defensively, trying to summon an air of authority in this unfamiliar terrain. "I specialize in rehabilitation, not damage control."

"Precisely why I reached out to you." His eyes flashed with something that could have been admiration, or perhaps challenge. "I need someone who understands the intricacies of the human psyche, someone who can help me navigate... the consequences of my actions."

I leaned back, digesting his words. "And what makes you think I'm interested in your consequences?"

He chuckled, the sound deep and rich. "Because you're curious, and I can see that you're not afraid of the truth. I can also offer you a generous salary, along with the opportunity to change lives—your expertise could help countless people. Just think about it: if you could influence a person like me, imagine the ripple effect."

I suppressed a shiver at his words. His proposition was steeped in allure and risk, like standing at the edge of a cliff with a view of the ocean crashing below. "What's your name?" I asked, as if learning it would unlock some hidden part of him.

"Oliver Blackwood," he replied, his gaze unwavering. "And I'm not asking for forgiveness, just a chance to become something better."

That name was familiar, a whisper of scandal lingering in the air of New York City. I had read the headlines, the murmurs of his empire built on tech and the waves of controversy that seemed to follow him like shadows. I felt my heart race—not with fear, but with the thrill of possibility. Who could resist a chance to dive into the depths of such complexity? The idea of transforming someone, or at least attempting to, sent an exhilarating rush through my veins.

The car slipped into traffic, the city's heartbeat pulsing all around us. I turned to watch the world blur by, buildings rising like titans, and for a moment, the noise faded. I was grappling with something far more significant than my daily routines, and it was intoxicating. Oliver's presence, however unsettling, sparked a dormant part of me that craved challenge, adventure, and a glimpse into the darker corners of human experience.

"You realize this isn't just about your brand, right?" I said, shifting the conversation back to safer ground, though the allure of the unknown loomed large. "This could get messy."

"Messy is what I do best," he replied, a hint of mischief in his voice. "And I'm counting on you to help me find a way to make it worthwhile."

I sighed, half-exasperated and half-amused by his audacity. "What does that even mean? How do you plan to make this worthwhile?"

He leaned in, an intensity in his demeanor that momentarily silenced the world outside. "By not just cleaning up my mistakes, but by making sure that the work we do together has lasting impact. I want to show people that change is possible, even for those who seem irredeemable."

The warmth of his words clashed with the chill that skittered down my spine. I could feel the threads of tension weaving between us, a strange mixture of reluctance and excitement tugging at the corners of my heart. This was no ordinary job; this was a tempest waiting to unfold. I realized, as the skyline flickered past, that I was standing on the precipice of something vast and unpredictable.

"What's the catch?" I asked, my tone playful, but my heart pounding in my chest.

"Only that you might find yourself in over your head," he replied, a hint of challenge dancing in his eyes. "But then again, that's where the real magic happens, isn't it?"

In that moment, as the city sprawled endlessly ahead of us, I felt the first inkling of an adventure begin to stir within me. With Oliver Blackwood, it seemed I was not just embarking on a new job, but a journey that could lead to transformation—for both of us.

As we drove through the city, the rhythm of New York thrumming beneath us like a heartbeat, I couldn't shake the feeling that I had just stepped onto a tightrope. The skyline glimmered under the waning afternoon light, a labyrinth of glass and steel that both invited and repelled. I found myself caught between the lure of adventure and the nagging apprehension that perhaps I was tumbling into a world that would swallow me whole.

"Where are we headed, anyway?" I asked, breaking the silence that had settled between us. My voice came out steadier than I felt, but Oliver's gaze remained fixed ahead, the contours of his jaw tightening ever so slightly as he concentrated on the road.

"Just a small gathering," he said, his tone casual, though the tension in his shoulders hinted at something more significant lurking beneath the surface. "You'll be meeting some of my closest associates, those who have been instrumental in my... projects."

"Projects?" I echoed, intrigued and wary. "You mean the ones that involve throwing money at problems instead of, I don't know, actually solving them?"

He turned to me, a glimmer of amusement dancing in his eyes. "Ah, you've already done your research. It's refreshing to meet someone who isn't intimidated by the glittering facade."

"Intimidated? No. Disgusted? Absolutely." I shot back, relishing the slight challenge in our back-and-forth. "The last thing I want is to end up being your personal PR crisis manager, mopping up the messes left by your 'projects.'"

"Rest assured, I'm not looking for a scapegoat," he replied, his lips twitching as if he fought against a smile. "More like a partner who can help me navigate the fallout of my choices. Trust me; I have more than enough self-inflicted mess to deal with. You'll be diving into something deeper than a mere PR issue."

"Are we talking about a swimming pool or an abyss here?" I couldn't resist asking, my curiosity piqued despite the warning bells ringing in my mind.

"More of a whirlpool," he quipped, shooting me a sidelong glance that sparkled with mischief. "But I promise you, it can be exhilarating."

The car pulled to a stop outside a striking building that loomed like a modern fortress against the dusky sky. The exterior was an interplay of dark glass and concrete, the kind of place that whispered of power and ambition. I felt a flutter of nerves but quickly pushed it down. There was no time for hesitation. After all, this was the moment I had agreed to, no matter how much I had tried to convince myself otherwise.

As I stepped out, the air was cooler, the bite of approaching winter tangling with the remnants of a warm day. Oliver followed closely behind, the low murmur of voices spilling from within the building as we approached. He gestured to the entrance, his expression shifting to one of determination. "Welcome to my world."

The lobby was awash in warm tones, a stark contrast to the cool exterior. Plush seating arrangements filled with artful accents invited conversation, and the soft glow of pendant lights overhead cast a golden hue on the polished marble floors. A bar stretched across one corner, offering a tantalizing array of drinks that promised to loosen the tension of the evening.

"You clean up nice," I remarked, glancing down at my own ensemble—simple yet elegant, as I had tried to play it safe. I had chosen a fitted navy dress that hugged my curves without being too provocative. But Oliver, in his tailored suit, exuded an effortless charisma that made me feel like an amateur in an art gallery.

"Just wait until you see the real show," he replied, his tone teasing, but there was an edge of sincerity behind it.

As we moved further into the space, I spotted a group of people congregated near the bar, their laughter mingling with the clinking of glasses. Each face held an air of polished sophistication, with sharp suits and stunning gowns, embodying the wealth that swirled around us like an unseen force. It was easy to feel like an outsider here, yet my resolve steadied as Oliver introduced me to his inner circle.

"Everyone, this is Dr. Lane," he announced, his voice smooth and confident. "She'll be working with us moving forward."

A chorus of greetings followed, each person extending a hand in welcome. Their smiles were warm, yet I sensed an undercurrent of scrutiny beneath the pleasantries. They were sizing me up, trying to figure out how I fit into their carefully crafted puzzle.

One woman stepped forward, her confidence radiating as she extended a hand. "I'm Sophia. If you need anything, just let me know. We're all here to support Oliver, and it's great to have a fresh perspective." Her charm was disarming, but there was a spark in her eyes that hinted at ambition.

"Right. Fresh perspectives," I muttered under my breath, feeling the weight of their expectations.

The evening unfolded like a well-rehearsed performance, each interaction dancing between cordiality and competition. I tried to keep my wits about me, engaging in conversation while glancing at Oliver, who seemed at ease, exchanging banter and ideas with the others. There was an undeniable chemistry in the air, a mixture of camaraderie and underlying tension that kept my senses on high alert.

Eventually, the crowd began to shift, and I found myself cornered by a particularly boisterous man named Jacob, who clearly took pride in his bravado. "So, Dr. Lane, what exactly do you think you can do for Oliver? Heal him, perhaps?" He laughed, the sound booming in the sleek space.

I smiled, choosing to deflect his jabs. "Well, I can certainly offer some therapy, but I doubt it will be as effective as a multi-million dollar PR campaign."

"Touché," he said, raising an eyebrow. "But don't let him fool you. Oliver is a tough nut to crack. He has a reputation, and not all of it is flattering."

"Careful, Jacob," Oliver interjected, stepping into the fray with a knowing smirk. "You're speaking of my only hope for redemption here."

"I'm just saying, it's a tall order," Jacob replied, shrugging nonchalantly. "But hey, if anyone can pull it off, it's you, right? The two of you might just become the power couple of the century."

At that, I nearly choked on my drink. The notion of being linked to Oliver—my nemesis and my unexpected ally—sent a shiver down my spine. My eyes darted to Oliver, whose expression was a mix of amusement and something deeper.

"Don't let him get to you," Oliver said, leaning closer as if to shield me from the weight of Jacob's words. "We're just here to disrupt the status quo."

"Right," I said, my voice tinged with sarcasm. "Nothing like stirring the pot to make friends."

He chuckled softly, and for a moment, the intensity of our earlier conversation faded into the background, replaced by an unexpected warmth that left me wondering what exactly I had stepped into. It was exhilarating and terrifying, a cocktail of emotions that I wasn't entirely prepared for.

The evening wound on, laughter and conversation swirling around us, the air thick with ambition and secrets. I could feel the pulse of the city outside, a constant reminder of the stakes at play. As

I engaged with more of Oliver's associates, I started to glimpse the complex network of relationships that defined this world—alliances forged in ambition, rivalries hidden behind charming smiles.

But through it all, one thing was becoming clear: stepping into this arena with Oliver Blackwood was not just about the work; it was about untangling the threads of a life that was as messy as it was compelling. And somehow, I knew that unraveling that knot would lead me somewhere unexpected.

As the evening wore on, the atmosphere shifted subtly. The laughter and clinking glasses mingled with the murmur of whispered secrets, and I could sense an undercurrent of tension that electrified the air. Oliver moved among his guests with an ease that belied the weight of the stakes at play. I watched him engage with each person, charm radiating from him like heat from a flame, and yet I couldn't shake the feeling that beneath that polished exterior lay a maelstrom of conflict.

"Tell me, Dr. Lane," Sophia leaned closer to me, her gaze appraising. "What exactly do you think you can do that the others haven't? Change his mind about life, or perhaps change the world?"

I paused, considering her question. "I'm not here to change anyone's mind. I'm here to help guide a process, perhaps help people see things differently."

"Very diplomatic," she replied, a hint of challenge in her tone. "But are you prepared for the chaos that comes with it? Change rarely comes without a fight."

I shrugged, a flicker of defiance sparking within me. "I'm not afraid of a little chaos. It's where the best stories unfold."

Her lips curled into a smile, and I sensed she respected my spunk, though I also recognized her willingness to protect her territory. In this sea of confidence and ambition, I had to tread carefully. I turned to scan the room, watching as Oliver animatedly discussed plans with Jacob, gesturing with his hands, the glint of determination in his eyes. I felt a swell of admiration mixed with apprehension. Who was he really beneath that magnetic exterior? What depths would we have to explore together?

"Let's just hope you're ready for whatever storm Oliver brings," Sophia said, her voice low, almost conspiratorial.

I nodded, my curiosity about the storm that loomed ahead growing by the minute. The idea of navigating this journey alongside Oliver was both thrilling and terrifying, a conundrum wrapped in an enigma.

As the evening progressed, I found myself cornered by one of Oliver's business associates, a wiry man named Lucas, who seemed to embody the essence of a tech-savvy hawk. "You're stepping into dangerous waters, Dr. Lane," he said, his voice edged with something I couldn't quite place—was it concern or something more sinister? "You have no idea what you're getting into with Oliver."

"Everyone seems to think I need a warning," I replied, my tone dry. "Maybe I'm just that good at swimming."

His lips curled into a knowing smile, though his eyes were serious. "It's not swimming you should be worried about. It's the undertow."

Before I could respond, Oliver strode over, placing a firm hand on Lucas's shoulder, an unspoken message passing between them. "Don't scare her off, Lucas. We need her."

There it was again—the sense of camaraderie tinged with something darker. As the evening pressed on, the conversations became more heated, discussions weaving in and out of topics ranging from new tech innovations to ethical dilemmas, each voice raising the stakes. I found myself pulled into debates, my passion igniting as I argued the importance of compassion in technology, the need for ethics amidst the chaos of innovation.

"Interesting point," Oliver remarked as I wrapped up a particularly fervent response. "But are you ready to get your hands dirty?"

"Dirty? You should see my office. I have post-it notes stuck to the walls like some kind of abstract art installation. It's a mess," I shot back, enjoying the playful banter that had developed between us.

He laughed, a sound that reverberated through the room. "I like your style, Dr. Lane. Just know that this ride will test your resolve."

Just then, the atmosphere shifted dramatically. The lights flickered overhead, a faint crackle of electricity whispering through the air, and a sudden hush fell over the crowd. Conversations sputtered out as eyes darted toward the source of the disruption. I caught Oliver's gaze, and the playful facade melted into something sharp and alert.

"What was that?" I asked, instinctively moving closer to him.

"Nothing we need to worry about," he said, though the tension in his voice betrayed him. I could see the gears turning in his mind, strategizing, calculating.

The power flickered again, plunging us into semi-darkness, the murmurs of confusion rising. "I think we might have a problem," Oliver said, his expression hardening.

Suddenly, the doors burst open, and a figure clad in dark clothing stormed into the room. The atmosphere shifted once more, tension coiling tightly, and I felt a jolt of fear. This was not the moment I had signed up for.

"Oliver!" the newcomer shouted, their voice sharp and demanding. "We need to talk. Now."

A murmur of shock rippled through the crowd, eyes darting between the intruder and Oliver. The man's expression was grim, a storm cloud hanging over him. I could see Oliver tense, his muscles rigid as he moved forward, an imperceptible shift in his stance that indicated he was ready for anything.

"Excuse us," Oliver said, his voice low and controlled, but I could sense the undercurrents of urgency. He motioned for me to stay back, and in that instant, the gravity of the situation settled heavily on my shoulders.

"Who is that?" I whispered to Sophia, my heart racing.

"Someone who doesn't care for the image Oliver is trying to project," she replied, her eyes wide, a cocktail of fear and intrigue mixing in her expression.

I felt the urge to lean closer, to understand the unfolding drama, but I was rooted to the spot, watching as Oliver stepped into the fray, his confident demeanor intact but his eyes glinting with something unspoken.

"Whatever you think you know, it's not what it seems," Oliver said to the intruder, his voice measured yet low, each word laced with tension.

"I think you're underestimating how far this can go," the figure shot back, their tone filled with menace. "You don't want to take this lightly."

A chill ran down my spine as the crowd shifted uneasily, the energy in the room morphing from playful banter to palpable fear. I could feel the air thickening, a storm brewing on the horizon, and just like that, I realized I was no longer a mere observer in this world. I was entwined in a web of intrigue and uncertainty, and the stakes were higher than I had ever anticipated.

"Get out," Oliver said, his voice steady but his eyes fierce, a silent challenge radiating from him.

I stood frozen, heart pounding, wondering how quickly this gathering could unravel. The shadows of Oliver's world loomed large, and as the intruder stepped closer, the threat felt undeniable. Suddenly, a loud crash echoed through the space, and the lights flickered violently before plunging us into darkness.

In that moment, everything changed.

Chapter 2: "A Fortress of Glass"

The air crackled with unspoken words as I stepped into the glass fortress, a space so meticulously designed that it felt more like an exhibit than a home. Each wall, a transparent declaration of wealth and isolation, reflected the city's heartbeat below—a thrum of chaos juxtaposed against Adam Hawthorne's carefully sculpted existence. I stood at the threshold, my shoes tapping softly on the polished floor, the sound swallowed by the cavernous silence that enveloped us.

Adam's gaze pierced through me, assessing, calculating. His eyes were a stormy gray, flecked with hints of warmth that seemed to flicker just beneath the surface, elusive and enigmatic. He was a man carved from granite, a statue of power and control, yet there was something undeniably human hidden in the crevices of his demeanor. The kind of man who had likely never been told "no," whose world operated in shades of black and white, leaving no room for the nuances of life.

"Why are you here, exactly?" His voice, deep and resonant, sliced through the silence, compelling yet cautious, as though he were trying to decipher my intentions.

I had rehearsed my response a dozen times, each version more polished than the last. "I'm here to help you," I replied, forcing a lightness into my tone that I didn't entirely feel. The truth was, I was just as drawn to the mystery of him as I was to the task at hand. He needed saving from himself, but could I really be the one to accomplish that?

"Help?" The word lingered in the air, dripping with skepticism. He arched an eyebrow, an action so subtle yet so commanding that I momentarily lost my train of thought. "Help implies that I need it. Do I seem like a man who requires assistance?"

"Not at all," I said, a small smile tugging at my lips, "but even a fortress needs a good architect every now and then. I'm here to see if

I can help you with... renovations." I motioned vaguely to the space around us, the carefully chosen sculptures and paintings, each one a testament to his impressive, albeit sterile, taste.

He crossed his arms, a move that turned his body into a taut line of resistance. "Renovations imply something is wrong," he countered, the corners of his mouth curling slightly, as if amused. "Are you suggesting my life needs an overhaul?"

I stepped forward, daring to bridge the distance between us. "Not an overhaul. Just a little... adjustment. Your life is a masterpiece in the making, Adam, but the canvas seems a bit too... pristine. Where's the chaos? The color?"

He regarded me with a mixture of intrigue and wariness, as though I were a puzzle piece that didn't quite fit into his grand design. "You have an interesting way of looking at things."

"Interesting is just a euphemism for 'troublemaker,'" I quipped, letting the weight of my words linger for a moment. "I like to think of myself as a spark plug in the engine of life. A little jolt can create some real movement."

"Then I suppose I should be careful not to let you in," he replied, a smirk finally breaking through his stoic facade. "Who knows what kind of chaos you might unleash?"

In that moment, I saw a flicker of warmth in his eyes, a glimpse of the man beneath the polished exterior. The tension in the room began to shift, like a tide rolling in, filled with uncharted possibilities. Perhaps, just perhaps, I could peel back the layers of his carefully constructed façade.

"Let me show you," I said, my heart racing at the audacity of my own words. "What's the harm in a little chaos? It might even be fun."

He tilted his head, studying me, and I felt the weight of his scrutiny like a tangible thing. "Fun is a dangerous game, and I don't play with fire."

"Then perhaps it's time to learn," I shot back, emboldened by the challenge in his eyes. "Fire can warm a cold fortress, you know. And trust me, I'm not as reckless as I seem."

"Is that so?" His lips twitched as if he were fighting a smile. "And how do you plan on convincing me of that?"

"Let's start small," I suggested, my mind racing with ideas. "Let's have a drink. I'll share a secret about myself, and you can reciprocate. It's a bonding exercise."

He chuckled softly, and the sound sent a ripple of triumph through me. "A bonding exercise? Is that your professional method of persuasion?"

I shrugged, grinning. "Call it a warm-up. Besides, I have a few secrets of my own that might intrigue you."

"Very well," he said, finally uncrossing his arms, the slightest hint of vulnerability cracking his fortress. "But if we're going to play this game, I expect you to keep up."

With that, I followed him deeper into his glass sanctuary, where the city below pulsed with life, a vibrant tapestry woven with stories that seemed to echo through the walls. The bar was an oasis of smooth lines and sleek finishes, and I couldn't help but admire how even the simplest elements of his home reflected his desire for perfection.

As he poured two glasses of an amber liquid, I felt a thrill of anticipation—this was where our worlds would intersect, where the rigid walls he had erected would begin to soften, if only a little. The first sip was rich and warm, the flavors mingling with the tension that still lingered in the air.

"Okay, my turn first," I said, leaning back against the cool granite of the counter. "When I was a kid, I wanted to be a storm chaser."

He raised an eyebrow, his interest piqued. "A storm chaser? That's unexpected."

I grinned, pleased to have caught him off guard. "I loved the idea of chasing storms, feeling the rush of the wind, the thrill of nature's power. I used to fantasize about standing on the edge of a tornado, feeling invincible."

Adam's expression softened, curiosity flickering in his eyes. "And did you ever chase one?"

"Not yet," I replied, leaning forward. "But it's on my bucket list. What about you? What did you dream of as a child?"

He paused, and for a moment, the fortress around him seemed to crack just a little. "I wanted to build things. Towers, bridges... something that would last."

The revelation hung between us, a fragile thread connecting our disparate worlds. I could sense the weight of his ambition, the burden of his expectations. "And have you?"

"Yes," he replied, his tone laced with a hint of pride. "But I've built walls instead."

The honesty in his admission was disarming, a chink in the armor I hadn't expected to find. "Well, maybe it's time to start building bridges," I suggested, my heart racing at the thought of what lay ahead. "Life's too short to live in a glass fortress, don't you think?"

He met my gaze, and in that moment, I knew we were standing on the precipice of something profound, a connection forged in vulnerability and the promise of chaos. The city below pulsed with life, and I felt a rush of excitement at the possibility of what might unfold next.

The moment lingered, charged with an electricity I couldn't quite grasp. Adam's expression remained inscrutable, yet something flickered in the depths of his eyes—a glimmer of curiosity that hinted at an untold story just beneath the surface. The glass walls surrounding us refracted the light of the setting sun, casting a kaleidoscope of colors across the room, a stark contrast to the dark brooding of his demeanor. It was as if the world outside was desperate to break through his fortress, a vibrant reminder of life that he seemed intent on keeping at bay.

"Okay, your turn," I prompted, taking a sip from my glass, the amber liquid igniting a warmth that coursed through me. "What's your secret?"

He set his drink down and leaned against the counter, arms crossed again, a posture that spoke of both defensiveness and intrigue. "You expect me to just spill my life's story like some cheap novel?"

I laughed, the sound bouncing off the glass walls, making the fortress feel just a bit less imposing. "Well, if we're going to build a bridge, we should start with something sturdy. Besides, I'm pretty sure you're more than just a wall of glass."

He chuckled softly, the sound surprisingly rich against the backdrop of his sterile environment. "All right, but don't expect a heartwarming tale. My life is more a series of strategic moves than serendipitous moments."

"I'll take strategic over boring any day," I shot back, feigning a serious expression. "Go on, Mr. Strategic. I promise I won't yawn."

He smirked, his eyes glinting with a hint of mischief. "Fine. When I was younger, I was obsessed with chess. I would spend hours playing against anyone willing to sit across from me, plotting every move, anticipating the next."

"Chess? Is that why you seem so intent on controlling everything around you?" I teased, raising an eyebrow. "You see life as a game to be won?"

"Perhaps," he admitted, the amusement fading slightly from his voice. "Or perhaps I just learned early on that the best way to navigate chaos is through strategy."

"Ah, the mind of a master tactician," I mused, swirling my drink in my glass. "But tell me, did you ever lose?"

"Of course. Many times." His voice dropped, becoming more serious. "Losing teaches you more than winning ever could. It's the moments of defeat that shape you."

The weight of his words settled between us, shifting the mood in the room. There was a vulnerability in admitting his losses, a softness I hadn't expected from the man who so carefully curated his life. I leaned in, sensing an opportunity. "So, what's the grand strategy behind this glass fortress? You're clearly a man of ambition, yet you've chosen isolation."

He sighed, the brief flicker of vulnerability extinguished. "Isolation is safer. Control is easier when no one else is involved."

"But isn't it lonely?" I pressed, my heart pounding as I risked peeling back another layer of his carefully constructed armor. "Building walls to keep people out must be exhausting."

"I prefer the term 'boundaries,'" he countered sharply, but there was an edge of defensiveness in his tone. "It's a different game when the pieces start moving on their own."

"Are you really so afraid of the unexpected?" I challenged, a spark of defiance igniting in me. "You've built this fortress, but it looks like you're missing out on everything that makes life interesting."

"And what makes life interesting, exactly?" He leaned forward slightly, intrigued but cautious, as though I were revealing a strategy he hadn't considered before.

"Risk," I replied, the word rolling off my tongue like a sweet melody. "Adventure, spontaneity! Life is a series of unpredictable moments. You can't just sit in your fortress and expect everything to stay in perfect alignment."

His brow furrowed as he considered my words, a flicker of something—fear or maybe longing—crossing his features. "And what would you suggest? That I throw open my doors and invite chaos in?"

"Why not?" I laughed lightly. "What's the worst that could happen? You might discover something about yourself you never knew. Besides, chaos can be fun. Haven't you ever danced in the rain?"

His expression shifted, a blend of skepticism and amusement. "Dancing in the rain is for children."

"Exactly!" I exclaimed, my enthusiasm bubbling over. "When was the last time you felt like a child? Free and alive? You're missing out on all the joy because you're too busy calculating your next move."

"Joy isn't calculated. It's chaotic," he said, his tone almost defensive now. "And I've made my peace with that."

"Have you?" I challenged gently, my heart racing with the intensity of our conversation. "Or is it just easier to convince yourself that chaos is a weakness?"

A silence fell over us, heavy and laden with unspoken truths. The city continued to pulse beneath us, vibrant and full of life, while we remained locked in our battle of wits. Adam's fortress, once an impenetrable barrier, now felt like a fragile structure teetering on the edge of collapse.

Finally, he spoke, his voice lower, almost contemplative. "Perhaps chaos isn't as frightening as I thought, but it requires a level of trust I'm not accustomed to."

"And that's where I come in," I said, my pulse quickening at the realization that I was beginning to weave a thread of connection between us. "I can help you find that trust. Together, we can step outside this glass box."

He studied me for a long moment, his expression inscrutable, but the tension in the air had shifted yet again. "You're quite bold, aren't you?"

"Only when the situation calls for it," I replied, mirroring his earlier posture of crossed arms. "It's part of my charm."

Adam shook his head, amusement breaking through the tension once more. "Charm and chaos. A dangerous combination."

"Only if you let it be," I said with a wink, feeling the lightness of our exchange push against the heaviness of his world. "Imagine this: one spontaneous night, you let go of the reins. We could try a new restaurant, go dancing—"

"Dancing?" he interrupted, incredulous. "I don't dance."

"Exactly! This is the point," I insisted, leaning closer, my excitement bubbling over. "You have to step outside your comfort zone. Think of it as... field testing a new strategy. Who knows? You might find you have a hidden talent for tango."

He scoffed but couldn't suppress a grin. "Tango? You might be reaching a bit there."

I laughed, feeling the walls between us continue to crumble. "Reaching for greatness, perhaps! But I can settle for a small step. Just one night of letting go. Think of it as a little experiment."

He hesitated, and for a moment, the air thickened with anticipation. "One night," he finally conceded, the corners of his mouth twitching upward. "Just to prove you wrong."

"Deal!" I exclaimed, my heart soaring at the prospect of finally breaking through the barriers he had so carefully constructed. "And I promise you won't regret it."

"Regret is my specialty," he replied, a playful glint returning to his eyes. "But I'm willing to risk a little chaos for now."

And with that simple agreement, the first crack in his fortress felt monumental, like a chisel striking stone. I could see the possibility of something transformative flickering between us, a promise of adventure woven into the fabric of our growing connection. It was a small step, perhaps, but every monumental journey begins with a single, audacious move.

With the ink of our agreement still fresh in the air, a challenge hung between us like the scent of rain before a storm. I sensed the flutter of something new, a spark that dared to illuminate the shadows of Adam's carefully constructed world. As the sun dipped lower, casting an orange glow across the glass walls, the city below began to twinkle to life, a chaotic canvas of lights beckoning us to join its symphony.

"What's your ideal idea of a spontaneous night?" I asked, my curiosity piqued. "If we're throwing caution to the wind, I need to know what I'm working with."

He straightened, the playful glimmer in his eyes quickly replaced by that familiar calculating gaze. "Spontaneity is not something I typically indulge in. But if we're breaking down walls, I suppose we could start small. Dinner at a restaurant that doesn't require reservations?"

I could hardly suppress my excitement. "Yes! Let's aim for a little unpredictability. How about we choose the first place we see?"

He narrowed his eyes, skepticism written all over his face. "You really think that's wise? The city is full of... interesting establishments."

"Interesting is precisely what we want!" I grinned, feeling as though I'd cracked open a door to a world of endless possibilities. "You need to trust me. I promise I won't lead you astray."

"I'll hold you to that," he replied, his voice laced with an undertone of both challenge and intrigue. "But I have my own ideas about how this little adventure should proceed."

"Such as?" I leaned in, eager to catch a glimpse of his thoughts, his plans.

"Let's start with something easy," he suggested, a sly smile creeping across his lips. "How about a simple wager? Whoever loses pays for dinner."

"A wager?" I feigned indignation, raising an eyebrow. "What are we, ten years old?"

"Let's say a casual bet," he said, folding his arms with the kind of confidence that made it clear he was ready to play. "We'll each ask the other a question. If you answer incorrectly, you pay. If I answer incorrectly, I pay. Simple."

The thrill of the game electrified the air. "Alright, I'm in," I agreed, ready to match his intensity. "You go first."

"Fine." He considered his question, the light from the city catching in his eyes, giving him an almost predatory gleam. "What's your biggest fear?"

I hesitated, the question striking a chord I hadn't expected. "That I'll never fully live," I finally admitted, my voice softer than intended. "I mean, I don't want to wake up one day and realize I've let fear dictate my life."

He nodded slowly, as if digesting my words. "Interesting choice. And here I thought you'd say something more conventional, like spiders or heights."

"Those don't scare me," I laughed lightly, grateful for the sudden shift in mood. "I'll take a thrilling hike over a calm day at home any time."

His smile returned, and I felt the distance between us shrink another fraction. "Very well. My turn."

"Go for it," I challenged, leaning forward.

"Who was your first crush?"

"Oh, come on!" I exclaimed, rolling my eyes. "That's a cliché."

"Cliché or not, it's your turn to answer," he replied, crossing his arms, a smirk playing on his lips.

I bit my lip, recalling the awkwardness of middle school. "Fine. It was Jason Reynolds. He had the best smile and the most terrible haircut."

"Really?" Adam's laughter was deep and genuine, a sound that reverberated through the room. "What a travesty! I'd have thought you'd pick someone more... sophisticated."

"Sophisticated?" I scoffed. "We were twelve! What did I know about sophistication?"

He leaned in, his tone teasing but earnest. "You may be underestimating yourself, you know."

"Touché," I said, my heart quickening at his unexpected compliment. "Your turn again."

"Right. What's one thing you've always wanted to do but haven't?"

The question hung in the air, weighted with possibility. "I've always wanted to travel to New Zealand. There's just something about the landscapes, the culture. It seems like a place where adventure could really happen."

"Why haven't you?" he asked, genuinely intrigued.

"Life, work, the usual excuses," I shrugged, attempting to mask the ache in my heart. "But I plan to go someday. Just not yet."

He leaned back, considering me for a moment. "And how much longer do you plan to wait? Life has a funny way of slipping through your fingers if you let it."

"More wisdom from Mr. Fortress of Glass?" I teased, my pulse racing. "Next thing I know, you'll be giving me quotes from some self-help book."

He chuckled, the tension easing between us, but I sensed a deeper layer beneath his amusement. "And yet, here we are. Two people stepping outside their comfort zones."

"Speaking of stepping outside," I began, feeling a surge of boldness. "Let's finish this round. What's your biggest regret?"

The lightheartedness of our game evaporated, leaving behind a silence so thick it could be cut with a knife. Adam's expression turned serious, shadows dancing across his features. "That's a dangerous question."

"Maybe, but it's part of the game," I insisted, my voice steady.

He inhaled deeply, wrestling with something that lay just beneath the surface. "Regret is a hard thing to carry," he finally admitted. "I once lost someone because I didn't have the courage to fight for them. I was too consumed by my own plans."

My heart sank, the gravity of his words weighing heavily in the room. "I'm sorry. That sounds... painful."

He shrugged, dismissing my sympathy with a wave of his hand. "Painful but also necessary. It's shaped me into who I am."

"I can't help but wonder if you might have another chance," I said, my tone gentle yet hopeful. "People can change. Maybe there's still time."

"Change requires vulnerability," he replied, his voice barely above a whisper. "And vulnerability is a dangerous game."

"Isn't everything in life a game?" I asked, feeling an uncharacteristic boldness surge within me. "What's the worst that could happen if you tried?"

"Death?" he replied dryly, but there was a flicker of something in his eyes that told me he didn't quite believe it.

"Let's not jump to conclusions. You know what I mean," I shot back, my pulse racing at the thought of pushing his boundaries. "One night, one risk. It could change everything."

He regarded me with a blend of respect and caution. "Fine. But if I agree to your plan, I expect you to hold up your end of the deal."

"Deal," I replied, feeling a rush of triumph. "Just promise you won't bail on me at the last minute."

"Let's just say I've never backed down from a challenge."

"Good! Then we're set." I couldn't help but smile, the thrill of our newfound connection invigorating. "So, let's pick a time. When are we doing this?"

Adam leaned back against the counter, the shadows of uncertainty still lingering in his eyes. "Let's make it soon. A week from today."

"Perfect! I'll hold you to it," I said, feeling a warmth radiate from the prospect of the adventure ahead.

But just as I was about to suggest we plan the details, the atmosphere shifted. A sudden, loud crash echoed from the hallway beyond the glass walls. My heart lurched, and I turned to see a figure looming just outside the entrance, silhouetted against the dimly lit corridor.

"Adam," I whispered, my pulse quickening as uncertainty spiraled within me.

He stiffened, his expression transforming into one of focused intensity. "Stay back."

Before I could comprehend the gravity of the situation, the door swung open with a force that sent my heart racing, and a woman stormed into the room, her eyes ablaze with a fury I had never encountered.

"Where is he?" she demanded, her voice sharp like shattered glass.

Adam stepped forward, an air of authority enveloping him. "You shouldn't be here."

"What's happening?" I interjected, my instincts kicking in as I glanced between them, the tension crackling like electricity.

The woman's eyes narrowed, and for a moment, I felt as if the entire world had condensed into that single moment, suspended in time. I stood on the precipice of something I couldn't yet understand, the air thick with secrets and danger.

"Adam, this isn't over," she hissed, the intensity of her gaze locking onto him, leaving me feeling like an intruder in my own moment of discovery.

And in that instant, with a heartbeat echoing in my ears, I realized that the fortress was far more than just a structure of glass. It was a labyrinth of emotions, buried histories, and unresolved conflicts. I had only just begun to scratch the surface, and the shadows lurking within its walls were ready to reveal themselves.

Chapter 3: "The First Crack"

I perched on the edge of my chair, the leather creaking beneath me, feeling an odd mixture of excitement and trepidation. The office was a sanctuary of muted colors and soft light, a carefully curated oasis designed to coax emotions out from their hiding places. The scent of chamomile hung in the air, mingling with the faintest hint of citrus from the candle flickering on the shelf, casting dancing shadows on the walls. I had prepared for this session with him the same way I always did—notes meticulously organized, a soothing playlist on standby—but nothing could have prepared me for the moment his demeanor shifted.

He sat across from me, a fortress of composure in a tailored navy suit, every inch of him exuding the kind of confidence that turned heads and stopped conversations. Yet, when I broached the subject of family, something cracked. His eyes, normally bright with mischief and cleverness, dulled as he looked away, fixing his gaze somewhere beyond the window. I could almost hear the gears turning in his mind as he constructed his usual defenses, but there was a tremor in his chin, a hint of vulnerability that whispered he was considering something he had long buried.

"How did your family influence who you are today?" I ventured, my voice as gentle as the breeze that ruffled the curtains. I leaned in slightly, an unspoken invitation, hoping he might take a step closer to truth.

For a heartbeat, silence wrapped around us like a thick blanket. The air grew heavy with the weight of unspoken words. He sighed, a deep, shuddering breath that felt like the first crack of thunder before a storm. "Family is... complicated," he said, the words tumbling out with the reluctance of a child forced to eat their greens.

"Complicated how?" I pressed, intrigued by the hint of pain lacing his tone.

"Let's just say," he began, a shadow flitting across his face, "the ones who are supposed to protect you can sometimes be the ones who hurt you the most."

A knot twisted in my stomach. I was accustomed to hearing tales of woe, the chronicling of lost dreams and broken hearts, but his revelation carried a different weight. This wasn't a mere recounting; it was a glimpse into a wound, deep and festering. "I get that," I replied, my voice steady, wanting him to see the understanding in my gaze. "But those experiences can also teach us resilience."

He scoffed lightly, the sound laced with irony, and I noticed a flicker of defiance in his posture as if he were testing the waters, gauging whether he could trust me with the truth. "Resilience? Sure, but at what cost? I mean, look at me." He gestured toward himself, the tailored suit an emblem of success, yet the tension in his shoulders spoke volumes. "I've built this perfect façade, but underneath..."

"Underneath, there's something else," I finished, holding my breath as the silence stretched between us.

His gaze flickered back to mine, searching for something he hadn't quite found. "You think you know me?" he challenged, but there was an edge of curiosity in his voice, as if the question were a dare.

"I think I see the man behind the suit," I replied, my heart racing at the boldness of my words. "What you show the world is only a part of who you are. The rest is buried somewhere, waiting for the right moment to break free."

He stared at me, something akin to surprise dancing in his eyes. The armor he wore so effortlessly began to crack further, revealing the raw edges beneath. "And what if I'm not ready to let that part out?"

"Then that's your choice," I said, leaning back slightly, letting the space between us breathe. "But you should know that there's strength in vulnerability. It doesn't mean you're weak; it means you're human."

A flicker of something—hope? Skepticism?—crossed his face. "You really believe that?"

"I do." The conviction in my voice surprised me, but as I looked into his eyes, I realized I was no longer just speaking to him. I was addressing every wall I had ever built, every fear that had ever held me back. "You're not alone in this. We all have our demons."

There it was again, that moment of vulnerability I craved to explore. He shifted, crossing his arms tightly over his chest as if physically barricading himself against the emotions I hoped to draw out. "You have no idea what my demons are," he muttered, a hint of defensiveness creeping back into his tone.

"Try me."

He hesitated, and in that moment, I sensed an invisible thread of connection weaving itself between us, fragile yet strong. "What if I told you," he began slowly, "that my family's love came with strings? That every gesture felt like a negotiation rather than an act of kindness?"

"That's a heavy burden to carry," I said softly, feeling the weight of his words settle over us like a heavy fog.

"It made me question everything," he confessed, the vulnerability raw and unpolished, "including my worth. I thought if I could just be perfect, if I could be what they wanted, then maybe I'd be worthy of love."

His admission hit me like a splash of cold water. I could almost feel the remnants of his childhood, the unrelenting pressure and the desperate need for approval, swirling around us. "You are worthy, regardless of anyone's expectations. You deserve to be loved for who you are, not what you accomplish."

He looked at me then, truly looked, and in that moment, I glimpsed the truth—a man caught between the past that had shaped him and the future he feared.

The air in the room felt charged, as though each word exchanged ignited a spark that danced between us, and I could hardly believe I had managed to coax out that glimpse of humanity. My fingers drummed against the armrest, the rhythm echoing my pulse as I weighed my next words carefully. I had always been adept at reading people, but this—this was a different beast entirely. I felt like an explorer inching into uncharted territory, every step taken with the delicate balance of curiosity and caution.

"Tell me about the last time you felt... free," I ventured, hoping to shift the conversation from the painful past to something lighter, perhaps even joyful.

He ran a hand through his meticulously styled hair, a gesture that betrayed a hint of discomfort. "Free?" he echoed, as if the word itself were foreign to him. "That's not something I think about often."

"Why not?" I pressed, intrigued. "You seem like the type who could pull off a spontaneous adventure—dive into the ocean, dance under the stars, maybe even try karaoke."

A flicker of a smile danced at the corners of his lips, and for a moment, the stoic facade slipped. "Karaoke? Not my style," he said, amusement lacing his tone. "The only thing I'm proficient at is embarrassing myself."

"Embarrassing yourself? That sounds like a prerequisite for living. Besides, everyone has a hidden talent. Mine is a slightly off-key rendition of 'Livin' on a Prayer' after a couple of glasses of wine."

He chuckled, the sound warm and unexpected, illuminating the shadowed corners of the room. "I can't imagine that would sound good at all. Wine only enhances the bad notes, I'm afraid."

"True," I conceded, leaning forward, emboldened by his response. "But it's about the experience, not the execution. Besides, what's the point of being perfect? That just sounds exhausting."

"Exhausting is an understatement." He sighed, a wistful expression crossing his face. "I've spent years chasing perfection. It's like a mirage; the closer I get, the further away it seems."

There was a heavy weight in his admission, an echo of something profound. "What if you let go of the need to chase it?" I suggested softly, hoping to create a space for him to breathe. "What if you allowed yourself to just... be?"

He shifted uncomfortably in his seat, as if my words had pricked at something tender beneath his skin. "You make it sound so simple," he countered, his voice low, but there was a glimmer of interest there, like a flicker of light teasing the edge of a darkened room.

"Simple? No. But worthwhile? Absolutely."

A pause hung between us, a silent dialogue of uncertainty and budding trust. "I remember one summer, years ago," he said slowly, the memories unfurling like the petals of a flower blooming in slow motion. "We spent the whole week at a cabin by the lake. My brother and I would swim until we were pruney, laugh until our stomachs hurt, and we didn't care about anything else."

The nostalgia in his voice painted vivid images in my mind—a sun-drenched lake shimmering under a cloudless sky, laughter echoing across the water, a boyhood friendship untouched by the demands of adulthood. "That sounds beautiful," I said, savoring the sweetness of his recollection. "What happened to that boy?"

The smile faltered as he met my gaze, the weight of the question heavy in the air. "He got lost in the chaos of expectations. Life moved on, and I forgot how to be that carefree version of myself."

"Maybe he's still there, waiting for you to remember him."

"Maybe," he mused, his eyes distant, reflecting an inner battle between hope and skepticism. "But the world isn't kind to those who choose to remember."

I felt a pang of empathy for the man before me, the layers of hurt woven into his very being. "True," I admitted, "but it's also not kind to those who never try."

The tension shifted, his expression morphing into something more contemplative. "What if I told you that trying has always felt like standing at the edge of a cliff?"

"And what if I told you that sometimes the only way to discover your wings is to jump?"

He regarded me, an eyebrow arched in mock skepticism, but I could see the spark of intrigue dancing in his eyes. "You really think I can learn to fly?"

"Not if you stay rooted in fear," I countered playfully. "You have to take the leap, or you'll never know what it feels like to soar."

"Leaps and bounds, huh?" He chuckled, and for the first time, I felt the barrier between us begin to melt. "You make it sound so easy, yet here I am, a captive audience."

"Captive, huh? That sounds a little dramatic. I was going for inspirational."

He laughed, the sound genuine, and it echoed in the small space like a spark igniting a flame. "Inspirational, sure, but only because you're here to lead the charge. What's your secret?"

"Persistence," I said, meeting his gaze. "And the belief that everyone has a story worth telling."

His expression shifted, something unguarded flickering across his features. "Maybe it's time I told mine," he said quietly, a thread of resolve weaving into his tone.

"Whenever you're ready," I replied, offering him the space he needed. The unspoken bond between us felt palpable, an uncharted territory waiting for exploration.

The conversation drifted like a leaf on a gentle stream, finding its way through twists and turns, revealing pieces of him I hadn't anticipated. He shared snippets of his childhood—the hidden joys, the burdens of expectation—until the weight of his words filled the room like a dense fog.

As he spoke, I leaned closer, utterly captivated by the way his stories unfurled. There was a raw honesty in his voice, a willingness to peel back the layers that had long been shielded from view. "And what about you?" he asked, his eyes searching mine. "What's your story?"

A smile crept onto my face, playful yet introspective. "Oh, mine's not nearly as dramatic. I've had my share of ups and downs, but I've learned to embrace the chaos. Life is a rollercoaster, and I'm just trying not to lose my lunch."

"Now that sounds like a talent worth pursuing," he said with a grin, and for a moment, the world outside faded away, leaving just the two of us suspended in this newfound intimacy.

With each word exchanged, the cracks in his armor widened, revealing a man who was not just a polished surface but a landscape of depth and complexity. And as we continued to navigate the intricate dance of vulnerability and connection, I couldn't shake the feeling that perhaps this was the beginning of something profound, a journey that would lead us both to places we had yet to imagine.

The connection between us, tenuous yet electric, transformed the confines of the small room into a world of its own. I could sense the thoughts swirling in his mind, a tempest barely contained by the walls of his carefully constructed persona. Each word I uttered felt like a key, and I was beginning to wonder if, perhaps, I could unlock the door to whatever lay behind his guarded heart.

"I know it's hard to peel back those layers," I said, leaning forward, my tone earnest. "But sometimes, sharing your story can be the first step toward healing. It's like pulling off a Band-Aid; it stings at first, but once it's gone, you can let the wound breathe."

He considered this, his brow furrowing as if my words were a puzzle he was trying to solve. "A wound? Is that how you see it?"

"More like a scar," I corrected gently. "Something that may always be there, but it doesn't have to define you. It can be a reminder of strength, of survival."

"Survival, huh?" he mused, a smile ghosting his lips, though his eyes remained thoughtful. "I like the sound of that. But sometimes, I wonder if I'm just existing instead of living."

"Existence is the first step toward living," I replied, my voice infused with encouragement. "You're here, aren't you? Engaging in this conversation, exploring the depths of who you are. That's a choice most people don't dare to make."

His gaze flicked to the window, as if searching for answers in the passing clouds. "Maybe. But what if I don't know how to take the next step?"

"Then we'll figure it out together," I assured him, letting the warmth of my conviction wash over the space between us. "It's not a race. It's a journey, and every step counts, no matter how small."

"I appreciate that," he said softly, though I could hear the doubt still clinging to his voice. "But what if the journey leads me to places I'm not ready to face?"

I smiled, recognizing the fragile vulnerability behind his bravado. "That's the beauty of it. You can choose your pace. You're in control here."

His laughter rang out, a sound that felt like a refreshing breeze breaking through the thick tension in the air. "In control, huh? That's a new one for me. Usually, I feel like I'm a marionette on someone else's strings."

"Then it's time to cut those strings," I replied, my heart racing at the intensity of our exchange. "No one should hold that power over you."

He turned to me, a spark igniting in his eyes. "And how do I go about that? I mean, it's easy to say, but..."

"But it's hard to do," I finished, nodding in agreement. "I get it. I've had my own share of battles with the puppeteers in my life. But it starts with recognizing your worth."

"Worth." The word hung in the air like a delicate thread. "That's a concept I've struggled with for as long as I can remember."

"Then let's redefine it together," I suggested, wanting to pull him further into the warmth of our shared moment. "You have every right to determine your own value. It's not based on accomplishments or family expectations."

His expression shifted, the guardedness melting away like frost under the sun. "I don't even know where to begin."

"Start by acknowledging the things that bring you joy," I replied, a flicker of inspiration igniting in my mind. "What makes you laugh? What makes you feel alive?"

"Good question." He tapped a finger against his chin, a playful glimmer returning to his eyes. "You might be surprised, but I do enjoy a good pun. The worse, the better."

"Ah, a connoisseur of dad jokes. I should have known," I teased, a smile spreading across my face. "Hit me with your best one."

"Okay, here goes. Why don't scientists trust atoms?" He paused, eyes twinkling. "Because they make up everything!"

I laughed, the sound spilling into the room and creating a bubble of lightness that momentarily shielded us from the heaviness of earlier discussions. "Okay, that was bad. But it's great. I can see why you keep that one in your pocket."

"See? I'm not all serious," he said, his demeanor shifting, his laughter infectious. "I promise I have more where that came from."

"Then I'm looking forward to the next session," I quipped, leaning back, enjoying this newfound rhythm we'd established. "We'll go from therapy to a comedy club in no time."

But as the playful banter continued, a subtle tension prickled at the edges of our conversation, a reminder that beneath the surface, there were currents pulling us in different directions.

"Okay, but seriously," he said, his expression growing earnest again. "I don't know how to shake off the feeling of inadequacy that's been my shadow for so long."

I leaned closer, empathy coursing through me. "You don't have to do it alone. It's okay to lean on someone else while you find your way."

His gaze held mine, a silent battle waging within him. "That's the hardest part, isn't it? Allowing someone to see your flaws, to help you carry the weight."

"Perhaps, but it's also incredibly freeing," I said, my heart racing. "To let go of the façade and allow someone to help you pick up the pieces."

"Maybe you're right," he admitted, the vulnerability of his admission echoing in the room. "But what if those pieces are too shattered to be put back together?"

"Then we'll build something new. A mosaic, if you will." I grinned, embracing the metaphor. "Imperfect, but beautiful in its uniqueness."

He chuckled, and I could see the tension ease from his shoulders. "You've got a way of spinning things, don't you? Making them seem less daunting."

"That's my superpower," I replied with a wink, but beneath the lighthearted exchange, I felt the flickering spark of something deeper growing between us.

Just then, a knock at the door interrupted our moment, sharp and unwelcome. I exchanged a glance with him, the mood shifting as an unspoken question passed between us. "I'll get it," I said, trying to shake off the nagging feeling that had settled in my stomach.

As I stood, the warmth of our conversation lingered in the air, but a sense of foreboding crept in. Opening the door, I found a colleague standing there, her expression unusually grave. "I'm sorry to interrupt," she said, glancing past me to where he sat. "There's been an emergency. I need to speak with you."

A wave of anxiety washed over me. I turned back to him, uncertainty clouding my thoughts. "Just a moment," I said, stepping into the hallway to speak privately.

"What's going on?" I asked, my heart pounding.

"There's been a situation at the center," she replied, her voice low. "We might need you on standby."

"On standby? For what?"

"Some clients are struggling, and we need all hands on deck."

I glanced back toward the room, where he was sitting, alone with his thoughts. "Can't it wait? I was in the middle of something important."

She hesitated, glancing back toward him again, her eyes filled with a mixture of concern and urgency. "I'm afraid it can't. You know how unpredictable these situations can be."

Reluctantly, I nodded, the tether connecting me to him pulling taut. I wanted to be there, to support him as he began to unravel his story. "Fine," I said, forcing calm into my voice. "I'll be right there."

As I turned to walk back into the room, I felt a swirl of conflicting emotions—a knot of fear and protectiveness, a desire to shield him from the chaos that threatened to disrupt our fragile connection. But the moment I opened the door, my heart sank.

He stood, his expression shifting from relaxed curiosity to something darker, eyes wide with uncertainty. "What's wrong?"

My breath caught in my throat, the weight of the impending storm pressing down on us. "There's—"

Before I could finish, a phone buzzed violently on the table, cutting through the silence. He glanced down, and the color drained from his face as he picked it up. "No. It can't be."

The moment hung, suspended like a fragile breath caught in a gale, the air thick with unspoken words and looming fears. And just like that, the safety of our conversation shattered, leaving us teetering on the precipice of an unknown future.

Chapter 4: "Crossing the Line"

The city sprawled beneath me, a mosaic of twinkling lights and bustling streets, alive with the hum of life that pulsed through its veins. Each flicker from the windows of distant apartments told a story I could only imagine, while the distant echo of laughter and the honk of taxis filled the air. I leaned against the cold metal railing of his balcony, a dizzying sense of freedom mingling with the thrill of my predicament. I should have turned away; I should have tucked my feelings neatly back into the box marked "professionalism," but standing there beside him, with the wind teasing my hair and the night stretching out endlessly before us, I couldn't summon the will to move.

His presence was magnetic, a force field I didn't know I needed. It was the way he held himself—confident yet unguarded—as if every word we exchanged was a shared secret, a flicker of intimacy threading through the space between us. When he spoke, his voice was low, a rich timbre that wrapped around me like a well-worn blanket. "Do you ever let anyone in?" he asked, and for a moment, the world faded away, leaving just the two of us suspended in the night.

I swallowed hard, a lump forming in my throat. The question struck me like a bolt of lightning, illuminating the dark corners of my heart I had long kept hidden. Did I let anyone in? The answer echoed in my mind—a cacophony of memories, of faces that had blurred into the backdrop of my life. My past relationships had always been filtered through a lens of caution; I had worn my armor like a second skin. Trust had become a currency I hoarded, unwilling to spend it even when it was desperately needed. I glanced sideways at him, at the way his dark hair caught the light of the city below, framing a face that was both familiar and enigmatic. "No," I replied, the word a whisper that felt heavier than it should.

He was silent for a heartbeat too long, and I could feel the weight of his gaze as it studied me. "Why not?" he pressed, his curiosity a velvet rope pulling me closer, wrapping around my thoughts and tangling them into knots. I was used to controlling the narrative, shaping conversations with deft maneuvering, yet with him, I felt vulnerable and raw, as if I was peeling back the layers of my carefully constructed facade. I should have laughed it off, should have changed the subject, but instead, I found myself leaning into the discomfort.

"Because it's easier this way," I finally admitted, surprising even myself with the honesty. "Less risk. Less pain." The words hung in the air, a stark contrast to the music of the city below. I turned away from him, my eyes searching the skyline, but I could feel his presence—intense, probing, as if he could see the truths I hid behind closed doors.

"And what if I told you," he said, his voice a soft rumble against the backdrop of distant traffic, "that you're missing out on something beautiful? Something that could change everything?"

His words were like honey dripping into the crevices of my doubts, sweet yet heavy with implication. My heart raced, a wild animal trying to escape a cage I had built around it. I turned back to him, my mind racing, the city lights reflecting the storm brewing inside me. "Are you suggesting I throw caution to the wind? Let down my guard for a stranger?" I said, my voice teasing yet edged with seriousness.

"A stranger?" He chuckled softly, his eyes sparkling with a playful defiance. "I think you underestimate the power of connection. We're not strangers, not really. We're just two people standing on the edge, afraid to jump."

My breath hitched at the unexpected truth of his words. There was a thrill in what he said, a challenge that sent a rush of adrenaline coursing through my veins. But jumping meant surrendering, and surrendering was something I had sworn never to do. I crossed my arms over my chest, a protective gesture that was almost reflexive. "You make it sound so easy."

"It can be, if you let it," he said, stepping a fraction closer, the warmth of his body almost palpable. "What's the worst that could happen?"

I opened my mouth to respond but faltered. In the chaotic spiral of my thoughts, I had to confront the truth: the worst that could happen was exactly what I feared—falling into something so deep it would swallow me whole, leaving me gasping for breath. But standing on that balcony, with him so close, the air heavy with unsaid words and unfulfilled desires, I felt a flicker of something I hadn't dared to acknowledge in years—hope.

I inhaled sharply, the cool night air filling my lungs, swirling with the scent of jasmine from the nearby trees. "You really think it's worth the risk?" I asked, my voice barely above a whisper.

"More than you know." He met my gaze, his expression earnest, sincerity etched into the lines of his face. "But you have to be willing to take that leap. You have to let someone see you."

His words wrapped around me, drawing me in. It was an invitation to vulnerability, a path I had avoided for too long. But as I looked into his eyes, something shifted. It was a connection deeper than mere attraction, a tether pulling us closer until the city around us faded into a blur of lights and sounds. Maybe—just maybe—crossing the line wouldn't lead to disaster. Maybe it could lead to something beautifully unexpected.

Before I could second-guess myself, I took a step forward, the space between us evaporating, and with it, the barrier I had so carefully constructed. The tension crackled in the air, electric and intoxicating. I was on the precipice of something terrifying and exhilarating, and as his gaze held mine, I could feel the universe shifting, aligning in ways I never thought possible. In that moment, I made a choice. I chose to jump.

The decision hung in the air, palpable and potent, like the electric charge before a summer storm. I felt my heart thumping loudly against my ribs, each beat a reminder of the risk I was about to take. As he leaned closer, the world around us shrank until it felt like the two of us were the only inhabitants of the universe. The city, with its shimmering lights and restless energy, faded into a soft murmur, a distant backdrop to the intense connection building between us.

"Let someone see me?" The words slipped from my lips, a challenge wrapped in curiosity. "What if they don't like what they find?"

His expression softened, a knowing smile curling the corners of his mouth. "And what if they do?" He paused, allowing the question to linger. "Isn't that worth it?"

His gaze held mine, and I felt the weight of his sincerity envelop me like a warm embrace. I was used to being seen as the composed, unflappable professional, the one who navigated life with poise and precision. But in that moment, with the cool breeze playing with the strands of my hair and his eyes searching mine, I could feel the carefully constructed walls begin to tremble. The thrill of danger ignited a fire within me, and I yearned to let go, even just a little.

"You're awfully confident for someone who just met me," I quipped, attempting to inject a note of humor into the tension. "What if I'm just a charming disaster waiting to happen?"

He chuckled, a deep, rich sound that sent ripples of warmth through me. "Then I guess I'm in for a wild ride. But let's be honest; charm can be quite the alluring disaster."

I couldn't help but laugh, the sound bubbling up from somewhere deep within me. It felt freeing, like a dam breaking after a long drought. "I'll have you know that I'm usually much more composed. A complete disaster would involve tripping over my own feet or accidentally setting something on fire."

"Then let's avoid the fire, shall we?" His grin was infectious, and the way he leaned into the banter made it feel like we were both dancing on a tightrope, the thrill of the moment threatening to tip us into the abyss of something exhilarating. "But if you trip, I'll be right there to catch you."

There was a sincerity in his words that made my pulse quicken. The idea of falling—literally or metaphorically—was terrifying. But the way he spoke made it seem less like a hazard and more like an adventure. I found myself wondering what it would be like to abandon my cautious nature, to embrace the spontaneity that seemed to vibrate in the air around us.

"Okay, fine. Let's say I let you in," I said, testing the waters. "What happens next?"

He stepped closer, and I could feel the warmth radiating off him, a contrast to the cool night air. "Next, we share a story," he replied, his voice dropping to a conspiratorial whisper. "And in return, I'll let you into my world."

A story. I could do that. I could let him see a piece of me. But what part? The part that had been buried under layers of expectation, the part that still believed in fairytales despite knowing the world was full of cynicism? "You go first," I challenged, raising an eyebrow. "If I'm going to spill my secrets, you'd better not be holding back."

He chuckled, a low rumble that sent a thrill through me. "Alright, but be warned—my secrets may not be as charming as yours." He paused, his expression shifting into something more serious. "I grew up in a small town, and I was the kid everyone forgot. You know, the one sitting alone at lunch, the one who faded into the background?"

My heart squeezed at the vulnerability in his words. It was a side of him I hadn't expected to see—the fearless man I had first encountered now stripped of bravado, revealing a tender heart that had once been overlooked. "That sounds... lonely," I murmured, my own experiences flashing through my mind.

"Lonely is a kind word," he said, a hint of bitterness creeping into his tone. "It taught me how to become invisible. I learned to blend into the scenery, to adapt. But at the same time, it made me crave connection, crave a place where I could belong."

I could see the raw honesty in his eyes, and it struck me deep within. We were two souls navigating the murky waters of existence, searching for a way to be seen and heard. "And now?" I asked, genuinely curious. "What changed?"

His gaze grew distant for a moment, as if he were plucking memories from the air. "I moved to the city, thinking it would be my escape, my chance to reinvent myself. But I quickly learned that blending in was just as easy here. I found my footing in work, in achieving, but it still felt hollow at times."

"So you're telling me you're a success story who still feels like a shadow?" I teased, trying to lighten the mood, though my heart ached for the boy he had been.

He smirked, the corners of his mouth quirking upward. "I guess so. But every shadow needs light, right? It's just a matter of finding it."

I found myself leaning in, captivated by the depth of his words. "And what if you find it?"

His eyes locked onto mine, intensity radiating from him. "Then I guess we'll see how brightly I can shine."

There was a promise in his words, a challenge that danced tantalizingly in the space between us. And just as I opened my mouth to respond, the sound of laughter broke through the atmosphere, sharp and jarring. I turned to see a group of friends across the street, their joyous energy spilling out into the night, reminding me of everything I had tried to escape.

"See?" I gestured toward them. "Those people have the kind of connection we dream of. They don't have to fight to be seen."

"Or maybe they're just as lost as we are," he countered, his gaze unwavering. "Connections come in many forms. They just take courage to cultivate."

The unexpected wisdom of his words resonated deep within me. Perhaps he was right; maybe it wasn't just about being seen but about seeing others, allowing ourselves to be vulnerable in a world that often felt so detached.

"Alright, Mr. Philosopher," I said, crossing my arms playfully. "What's your plan for cultivating that connection?"

He moved a fraction closer, a challenge sparking in his eyes. "Let's start by breaking down the barriers between us. Let's be real for once."

I bit my lip, feeling the thrill of his proposition wash over me. "Real?"

"Yeah. No pretense, just us." His sincerity was disarming, and I could feel the boundaries I had carefully maintained begin to dissolve.

The night stretched on around us, a canvas waiting to be painted with our truths, fears, and dreams. And for the first time in a long time, I felt the stirrings of something daring—an adventure waiting just beyond the horizon of my carefully planned life. With him by my side, perhaps I could finally learn to embrace the chaos of connection.

As we stood on the balcony, the weight of his gaze still pressing against me, I felt an exhilarating tension knotting itself tighter in my chest. Each heartbeat resonated with the pulse of the city beneath us, a symphony of life echoing through the night air. I was caught in a moment of rare clarity, where every fear and every longing collided like stars in a brilliant constellation.

"I can't promise it'll be easy," he said, his voice a soothing murmur that wrapped around me like the softest blanket. "But I can promise it'll be real. And real is often messy."

"Messy is my middle name," I shot back, feigning bravado while my heart raced. "I excel at disasters, thank you very much."

"Then consider this a challenge. Let's turn that disaster into something a little more... magnificent."

His smile was infectious, pulling me further into his orbit. I bit my lip to hide my grin, resisting the urge to laugh at the absurdity of it all. Here I was, a straight-laced professional teetering on the edge of chaos, and he had the audacity to make it sound like an adventure. "And how exactly do you propose we achieve this magnificent disaster?"

He stepped closer, our bodies nearly touching, and I could feel the warmth radiating from him, pulling me in. "By sharing a little more of ourselves. You tell me a secret, and I'll tell you one in return. It's the perfect recipe for a disaster, wouldn't you say?"

"Very clever," I replied, trying to keep my voice steady, despite the butterflies taking flight in my stomach. "I suppose you think you're quite the charming rogue, don't you?"

"Charm is my superpower." His eyes sparkled with mischief, and I felt a tug of something raw and exciting. "But it's not the charm I'm interested in right now; it's what's underneath."

I hesitated, the weight of his words settling around me like a heavy cloak. What lay beneath my own surface was a tangled mess of dreams, insecurities, and aspirations. Did I really want to pull back the curtain and reveal it all? "Alright, fine. I'll go first," I said, steeling myself. "But you might regret it."

He tilted his head, his curiosity piqued. "I doubt it. Lay it on me."

I took a deep breath, summoning the courage that had always eluded me. "I once dreamed of being a novelist. I spent years crafting stories that never saw the light of day, afraid of what people might think if they read them."

"Why didn't you pursue it?"

"Fear, mostly. The fear of failure, the fear of being judged. I convinced myself that my career was safer—more respectable." I shrugged, the admission tasting bittersweet on my tongue. "But every time I sit down to write, it feels like I'm slipping away from myself."

He absorbed my words, his expression shifting to one of understanding. "That's powerful. You have a gift, and hiding it only does you a disservice."

I smirked, a little incredulous. "Wow, you should be a motivational speaker. But wait, you haven't shared your secret yet."

His eyes darkened with a hint of something serious. "Alright. Here goes. I've always wanted to be an artist, but my family pressured me into a corporate career. So I traded in my paintbrush for a suit, thinking I could find fulfillment in the boardroom."

"Turns out the paintbrush suits you better?" I teased, but the gravity of his words weighed heavy in the air.

He sighed, a deep, almost pained sound. "Let's just say I've painted my own prison. I'm trapped in a cycle of expectations, and it feels suffocating."

The vulnerability in his voice struck a chord within me, resonating with my own hidden struggles. "So what now?" I asked, genuinely curious. "Are you going to break free?"

"Maybe. If I can find the courage to take that leap." His gaze lingered on me, the intensity of his stare sending shivers down my spine.

A moment passed between us, charged with an electricity that threatened to spark into something more. The connection we had forged felt tangible, as if I could reach out and touch it. "You know, we could both escape together," I suggested lightly, attempting to inject a bit of humor back into the conversation.

"Oh, really? And how do you propose we do that?" he asked, amusement flickering in his eyes.

"By making a pact. A commitment to pursue our passions—no matter the consequences."

"Sounds dangerously adventurous."

"Dangerous is my middle name," I replied, winking playfully.

His laughter danced through the night, wrapping around us like a warm embrace. But then, as if sensing the fragility of our moment, the air shifted. The carefree atmosphere tightened, and suddenly the world around us felt heavy with unspoken tension.

"Hey," he said, his expression turning serious again. "I mean it. If you're willing to take that leap, I'll be right there with you."

"Are you sure you're ready for that?" I asked, a flutter of uncertainty creeping into my chest.

"Let's just say I've never been more certain of anything."

Just then, a loud crash erupted from the street below, shattering the moment like glass. We both jumped, instincts kicking in as we turned toward the sound. A group of partygoers had knocked over a trash can, and the ruckus drew the attention of passersby. The laughter and shouting filled the air, breaking the intimate bubble we had created.

"Ah, the enchanting sound of urban life," I said, forcing a lightness into my voice as I gestured to the chaos below. "How delightful."

He laughed, but I could see the glimmer of disappointment in his eyes. "I was hoping for a more profound moment," he quipped, masking his disappointment with humor.

"Don't worry; we can always recreate it," I suggested, my heart racing with the thrill of spontaneity.

"Alright, then. We'll have to find our moment again." His tone turned earnest as he met my gaze. "But we can't keep dodging what's right in front of us."

Just as I opened my mouth to respond, the ground beneath us trembled, the sound of heavy footsteps echoing against the concrete. My heart sank as I turned to see a group of men in dark clothing moving swiftly through the streets, their faces obscured by the shadows. There was something unnerving about their presence, an energy that radiated danger.

"Do you see that?" I whispered, my pulse quickening.

He nodded, tension tightening his features. "Yeah, I see it."

"What do you think they want?"

Before he could answer, one of the men looked up, locking eyes with us. A chill raced down my spine as recognition flickered across his face, and in that instant, the connection we had built felt precariously fragile.

"Run," he said, urgency lacing his voice.

We didn't hesitate. I grabbed his hand, and together we bolted into the night, hearts racing as we plunged into the chaos that awaited us.

Chapter 5: "The Mask Slips"

The clock on the wall ticked in a steady rhythm, a metronome counting down the moments as Adam and I sat in his dimly lit study, an oddly comforting cocoon of leather and wood. I could smell the faint hint of sandalwood from the candle flickering on the desk, its flame dancing gently, casting playful shadows that seemed to reflect the turmoil swirling in my mind. Each evening spent in this space felt like we were on the precipice of something monumental—both exhilarating and terrifying. As I glanced at Adam, the man who had once been untouchable, now vulnerable and exposed, I couldn't help but wonder how we had reached this point.

He leaned back in his chair, fingers laced behind his head, his tousled hair catching the light like spun gold. There was a softness in his gaze that was both unfamiliar and intoxicating. I had spent months dissecting his carefully curated persona, a façade built on charm and bravado that began to fracture the deeper we delved into his past. I could see the artist behind the mask, a man haunted by the shadows of his own making, and yet I was becoming entranced by the very vulnerability I had set out to heal.

"Do you ever think about what your life would look like if the world didn't know who you were?" he asked suddenly, his voice low and contemplative.

The question hung in the air, heavy with the weight of his meaning. I considered it, shifting in my chair, the leather creaking beneath me. "All the time," I confessed, my own façade slipping just slightly. "I mean, imagine a life where your every mistake isn't scrutinized. Where you can just... breathe."

His lips curved into a wry smile that made my heart flutter, a breath of warmth in the chilly room. "Breathing sounds nice. I seem to have forgotten how."

There was a moment of silence, the kind that vibrated with unspoken truths. In that silence, I felt a crack in my own defenses, a fissure revealing my desire to pull him from the abyss he was spiraling into. I had become more than just a therapist; I was a confidante, a friend, and somewhere deep inside, I realized I wanted to be more than that.

"Tell me," I urged, leaning forward, resting my elbows on my knees. "What's the worst thing you think would happen if you let go of the mask?"

His expression darkened, the playfulness evaporating like mist in the morning sun. "What if I let it slip and they don't like what they see? What if they see the real me and decide I'm not worth their time?"

The air felt thick with tension, and I could sense the internal battle raging within him. "I think you'd be surprised, Adam," I said, my voice barely above a whisper. "The real you might be exactly what they need."

He shifted in his seat, and I caught the glimmer of unshed tears in his eyes, a storm brewing just beneath the surface. My heart ached at the thought of this man, once so confident and carefree, now teetering on the edge of despair. It wasn't fair. He didn't deserve to carry the weight of everyone's expectations on his shoulders. And yet, I found myself enmeshed in his turmoil, wanting to share the load.

"Maybe," he murmured, breaking the silence again. "But what about you? What about the walls you've built?"

I was taken aback. "What do you mean?"

He met my gaze, unflinching. "You come here, night after night, peeling back layers of me, but you never show me your own scars. What's behind your mask?"

I hesitated, the words catching in my throat. The truth was, I had crafted my own barriers to keep the world at bay, a well-honed defense mechanism to protect my heart from the chaos that had marked my past. In helping Adam confront his demons, I had unknowingly cast a light on my own.

"Okay," I breathed, the admission tumbling out of me like an unexpected wave. "I guess I'm afraid too."

His eyes widened slightly, surprised by my candor. "Afraid of what?"

"Of losing control," I confessed, the words tasting bittersweet. "Of being vulnerable. What if I open up and I'm not enough?"

He leaned forward, elbows resting on the desk, an intensity in his gaze that made my pulse quicken. "What if you are?"

The question hung between us, laden with implications. I felt an inexplicable connection pulse in the air, a thread binding our two souls together. Just then, he reached across the desk, his fingers brushing mine, sending an electric jolt through my body. My heart raced, a wild stallion escaping its pen, and I could see the moment he realized the implications of that touch—what it meant for both of us.

In that instant, the carefully constructed walls around me began to tremble, the barriers I had erected crumbling under the weight of an undeniable truth: I was not just here to help him; I was here to confront my own fears, to risk it all. The fear of losing myself in this man was almost suffocating, yet the allure of stepping into the unknown felt like a siren's call I could not ignore.

"Maybe we both need to let our masks slip," I whispered, a challenge lacing my tone.

His gaze held mine, fierce and unwavering, and in that moment, I knew we were on the cusp of something extraordinary—something that could either heal us or shatter us completely. And I was terrified, yet exhilarated at the thought of diving into that abyss together.

As Adam's fingers lingered against my skin, a tremor of awareness rippled through me, a spark igniting a mixture of dread and exhilaration that I had never encountered before. This was no longer a mere therapeutic endeavor; it was a delicate dance on the edge of something profoundly intimate. The study, once a sanctuary of professional boundaries, felt like a stage where our secrets began to unravel under the spotlight of unspoken feelings.

"Do you think vulnerability is contagious?" I asked, trying to break the thick tension enveloping us. My voice was light, but my heart raced as I navigated this uncharted territory.

He tilted his head, his expression thoughtful. "If it is, then we're about to create a pandemic." There was a flicker of mischief in his eyes, the corner of his mouth lifting slightly, and for a moment, the gravity of our situation lightened.

A laugh bubbled up from my throat, unexpected and joyful, but it was quickly followed by a pang of reality. "It feels more like a wildfire," I quipped, attempting to regain control. "One spark could set everything ablaze."

"Or," he countered, leaning closer, "it could be the warmth we've both been searching for."

Our laughter faded, replaced by the quiet hum of uncertainty. It was as if the walls of the room had shrunk, pulling us closer together, amplifying every breath and heartbeat. Suddenly, I felt uncomfortably aware of my own vulnerability. What if this conversation spiraled beyond the realm of professional discourse? What if we ignited a fire that consumed everything we had built so carefully?

"Okay, so let's pretend for a moment that I don't have the faintest idea what I'm doing," I said, attempting to play it cool, even as my palms grew clammy. "What's your plan for escaping the wildfire?"

He grinned, a roguish charm shining through the cracks in his carefully constructed persona. "I could use some help extinguishing it. Or maybe just a fire extinguisher on standby."

"Or perhaps a bucket of ice water," I replied, rolling my eyes playfully, even as my heart soared at his banter.

Our exchanges were laced with the tension of unacknowledged emotions, an electric current that danced between us. I had to remind myself that this was still work, a delicate process of untangling his demons. Yet every time I caught a glimpse of the real Adam, the one who was more than just a public figure or a broken man, I wanted to dive deeper.

"Let's do this," I declared, surprising even myself with my boldness. "If we're going to explore these vulnerabilities, we should do it properly. No masks, no pretenses."

He raised an eyebrow, the teasing light in his eyes flickering back to intensity. "What are you proposing?"

"Tell me something real. Something you've never shared with anyone." The challenge hung between us, heavy yet exhilarating.

Adam's gaze softened, and for a moment, he seemed lost in thought. "Okay, but only if you do the same. No backing out."

"Deal," I said, a thrill racing through me.

He took a deep breath, his vulnerability palpable. "When I was a kid, I was obsessed with drawing. I used to sit for hours sketching my favorite superheroes. But there was a part of me that always wanted to create my own characters, ones who weren't limited by the roles others expected of them. I never showed anyone, though. I was too afraid they'd think I was silly."

I felt the corners of my mouth lift, both proud and sympathetic. "You should've shared them. I bet they were amazing."

His smile faltered, revealing a flicker of the boy he used to be, a dreamer hidden beneath the layers of fame and expectation. "Maybe. But I was terrified. What if they laughed? What if they saw me as just a pretty face?"

"Funny," I replied, a playful smirk tugging at my lips. "I thought the same thing about my own writing. I kept journals filled with stories, but I never let anyone read them. Too scared of judgment."

"Why not?"

"Because what if they didn't see me as anything more than a therapist? What if my words were the masks I was wearing? It feels safer to stay behind the scenes."

He leaned back, contemplation etched on his features. "So, we're both hiding behind our own masks then, huh?"

"Seems like it," I said, the realization settling heavily in the air between us.

For a moment, we sat in silence, the weight of our confessions lingering like the smoke from the candle that flickered weakly on the desk. It was strange how liberating sharing such intimate truths could feel. But I was still acutely aware of the distance between our hearts, even as our words bridged the gap.

"Okay, your turn again," he said, a sudden determination flaring in his eyes. "What's something you're afraid of? Not just in this moment, but in life?"

The question caught me off guard, and my mind raced. Fear was an old companion, one I was all too familiar with. "Honestly?" I hesitated, searching for the right words. "I'm afraid of never being enough. That I'll give everything I have to help others, and when it comes to my own happiness, I'll still fall short."

Adam's brow furrowed, and he leaned forward, his voice dropping to a conspiratorial whisper. "That's a lot to carry. But I think you underestimate your impact. You help people see their own worth, but who helps you see yours?"

My heart skipped a beat. He had a way of piercing through my defenses, laying bare the insecurities I had tucked away. "I guess I don't have a great answer for that," I admitted, my voice wavering slightly.

"Then let's work on it together," he suggested, an earnestness in his tone that was impossible to ignore. "I could use someone like you to help me find my footing again."

The sincerity of his words struck me, filling the air with a promise that felt almost tangible. Could we really be each other's anchors in this storm? As I searched his gaze, I saw the flicker of hope, the possibility of connection that transcended our professional roles.

Before I could respond, the moment shifted. The door creaked open, shattering our bubble of intimacy. In strode Lucy, his assistant, her presence a stark reminder of the world outside this sanctuary. The tension snapped like a tightrope, leaving behind an aftershock that rippled through the room.

"Sorry to interrupt," she said, a quick glance of surprise darting between us. "But Adam, there's a press briefing in ten."

His expression shifted from vulnerability to a practiced mask of poise in the blink of an eye. I felt the weight of our exchange slip away as he composed himself, reshaping the pieces of his identity as quickly as he could.

"Right, of course," he replied, the warmth in his gaze dimming as he leaned back in his chair.

I swallowed hard, the thrill of connection dimmed by the return of reality. In that instant, I realized we weren't ready to face the world outside. Not yet.

The moment Lucy entered, it was as if the air had shifted, carrying with it the distinct aroma of professionalism and urgency. I watched as Adam's demeanor morphed seamlessly, his vulnerability slipping away like a shadow retreating from the dawn. He straightened in his chair, rolling his shoulders back with the practiced grace of a man who had spent years in the spotlight. The warmth of our conversation evaporated, replaced by the chill of expectation.

"Of course, I'll be right there," he said, his voice smooth and authoritative, almost unrecognizable from the man who had just shared his fears with me. Lucy nodded and retreated, casting one last curious glance in my direction. I could almost hear the gears in her mind whirring, trying to piece together the moment she'd just interrupted.

As the door clicked shut, I felt the walls of the study close in around me. "I guess that's my cue to leave," I said, my voice a blend of disappointment and self-preservation. The connection we'd just forged felt too raw, too fragile to withstand the weight of the outside world.

"Wait," Adam said, his tone slicing through the quiet like a blade. He stood abruptly, leaning against the desk, eyes searching mine with an intensity that sent shivers down my spine. "Can we—can we not let this be the end?"

His plea hung in the air, heavy with implications. I could see the conflict etched on his face, a mix of longing and fear that mirrored my own. "What do you want from me, Adam?" I asked, my heart pounding against my ribcage like a caged bird desperate to escape.

He hesitated, biting his lip as he considered his words. "I want you to keep being honest. With me and yourself. I don't want to retreat back into my mask, and I don't want you to either."

"I don't know if I can do that," I admitted, the words spilling from my lips unfiltered. "This is a complicated situation. If we start crossing lines—"

"Crossing lines is all I seem to do lately," he interrupted, a wry smile creeping onto his face, masking the storm brewing beneath. "But this time, I want to choose where I land."

The sincerity in his eyes caused my heart to flutter, a warmth spreading through me, battling against the chill of uncertainty. "And what if I don't want to be the reason you crash?" I asked, challenging him even as a part of me desperately craved that connection.

"Then let's make a pact," he said, stepping closer, his presence overwhelming in the best way. "We both confront our fears and be honest with each other, whatever that may lead to."

I mulled it over, feeling the weight of his words settle around us like a thick fog. There was something intoxicating about the idea of facing our fears together, of stripping away our masks and exposing the raw truth beneath. But fear was an unyielding beast, and I wasn't sure I was ready to wrestle with it.

"Okay, I'm in," I finally said, my voice steadying as I met his gaze. "But we have to promise to keep this professional. No expectations."

His grin was infectious, a spark igniting in his eyes. "No expectations. Just honesty."

Just as I began to relax into our newfound understanding, the door swung open again, this time with far less subtlety. A tall figure burst in, his expression a storm cloud that darkened the room instantly. My stomach dropped as I recognized him as Oliver, Adam's manager, a man whose reputation for being all business made me instinctively bristle.

"Adam, we need to talk now," Oliver said, his voice tight, as he glanced between us, a sharpness in his gaze that suggested he wasn't thrilled with the cozy atmosphere we'd created.

"Is everything okay?" I asked, the question slipping out before I could catch myself. This felt like a misstep; I had no right to intrude on their conversation.

Oliver turned his full attention to me, an eyebrow arched in mild irritation. "This isn't really a discussion for you, Sophia," he replied coolly. "I'd prefer to keep it between us."

I felt a flush creeping up my neck, an urge to retreat into myself. "Right, of course. I'll just…" I trailed off, taking a step back as the tension in the room thickened. But Adam wasn't having it.

"No, she stays," he said, his tone surprisingly firm. "Whatever this is, it involves her too."

The air crackled with unspoken tension as Oliver squared his shoulders, his expression hardening. "This isn't just about you anymore, Adam. The board is getting restless. They want results, and they're not satisfied with the 'new you' angle. They want the old Adam back—the one who was fearless in front of the camera, not this version who's wallowing in self-pity."

The words hung in the air, heavy with implications. I watched as Adam's face transformed, the playful spark extinguished, replaced by a storm of emotion. "Self-pity?" he echoed, disbelief lacing his voice. "You think I'm wallowing? I'm trying to be better. I thought that was the point."

Oliver shrugged, his expression indifferent. "Better doesn't sell. They want a story, not some sob story about how you're finding yourself. This is the entertainment industry, Adam. You can't afford to be weak."

"Then what do you suggest I do?" Adam shot back, frustration coloring his words.

"Get back on that stage, remind them of who you were," Oliver insisted, crossing his arms defiantly. "Charm them, engage them, make them remember why they fell in love with you in the first place."

I could feel the tension spiraling, like a tightly coiled spring ready to snap. "You can't force someone to be who they're not," I interjected, stepping forward, unwilling to let Adam shoulder this alone. "If he's trying to change, he deserves the chance to do so."

Oliver's gaze flickered toward me, surprise crossing his face, but it quickly hardened again. "This isn't your decision, Sophia. Adam has a reputation to uphold. If he doesn't meet expectations, he could lose everything."

Adam looked between us, his eyes alight with conflict. "What do you think I should do?" he asked, his voice barely above a whisper.

Before I could respond, the weight of uncertainty crashed over me. The fragile connection we'd forged felt at risk of shattering, and the sense of impending chaos surged like a tidal wave. I wanted to tell him to choose the path of honesty, to follow his heart. But would that lead to ruin?

Oliver's eyes narrowed, his impatience palpable. "Time's ticking, Adam. Make a decision."

Adam's gaze landed on me, and in that moment, I felt the gravity of our choices hanging between us. I could see it in his eyes: the plea for support, the desire for authenticity clashing with the crushing weight of expectations.

As I opened my mouth to speak, a loud crash resonated from somewhere outside, followed by a frantic shout. My heart raced, and all thoughts of our discussion faded as a wave of chaos washed over us.

"What was that?" I exclaimed, panic creeping into my voice.

Adam turned toward the door, his expression shifting to one of concern. "I don't know, but it doesn't sound good."

Before we could react, another sound reverberated through the air—a scream, high-pitched and filled with terror. My stomach dropped as I exchanged a terrified glance with Adam.

The world outside our sanctuary had turned chaotic, and in that moment, I realized our fragile connection was about to be tested in ways none of us had anticipated. The masks we had just begun to peel away felt more necessary than ever, and yet, somehow, we were drawn to face whatever lay ahead together.

Chapter 6: "A Storm Brews"

The air was thick with an electric charge, crackling with unspoken words and tangled emotions as we drove deeper into the hills. The trees, tall and stoic, seemed to lean toward us, their branches whispering secrets in the breeze. I glanced at Adam, his hands tight on the wheel, knuckles pale against the dark leather. He was a tempest contained, every line of his jaw carved from resolve, yet I could see the shadows lurking in his eyes, the ones he tried so hard to shield from me. I had always prided myself on my ability to read people, but Adam was an enigma wrapped in mystery. Each smile he flashed could flip on a dime, and I found myself torn between wanting to unravel him and the instinct to preserve the beauty in his chaos.

"Do you ever wonder what's at the end of these roads?" I asked, my voice breaking the silence, each word drifting into the cabin like a timid bird.

He glanced at me, a flicker of surprise crossing his features before he returned his gaze to the winding path ahead. "Only when I'm driving aimlessly." There was an edge to his tone, something defensive, as if I had touched on a raw nerve. I took a breath, the weight of unspoken thoughts filling the space between us like fog rolling in off the water.

"Maybe it's about the journey, not just the destination," I suggested lightly, hoping to lighten the mood. But I felt the air grow heavier, thick with an unsaid tension that felt palpable, almost tangible. I wished he could see that I wasn't just a distraction. I wanted to be his refuge, but he was guarding himself like a fortress.

The road twisted like a snake, revealing glimpses of the valley below, a vibrant tapestry of greens and golds, punctuated by the occasional flash of a blue sky peeking through the clouds. It should have been beautiful, but the scene outside only amplified the turmoil brewing inside the vehicle. I wished I could reach into his mind, peel back the layers of his history like pages in a well-worn book, but each time I came close, he withdrew, fortifying the walls that separated us.

"We all have our pasts, don't we?" I ventured, trying to breach the silence. "You don't have to share if you don't want to. I just think—"

"I don't want to talk about it." His voice was a low rumble, and I felt it settle heavily in my chest. It was a simple sentence, but it carried with it the weight of a thousand unspoken fears. I could see that my curiosity only exacerbated the shadows in his heart. I leaned back in my seat, stifling the impulse to press him further. His pain was a dark cloud hovering over us, threatening to unleash a storm.

The car slowed as we approached a quaint little town nestled at the foot of the mountains. The wooden storefronts exuded charm, their painted signs swaying gently in the breeze, inviting us to stop and explore. I felt a flicker of hope, a chance to break the tension. "Let's grab some coffee. I think we could both use a little pick-me-up," I suggested, my voice more confident than I felt.

He hesitated for a moment, brow furrowed, but then nodded, turning into the gravel parking lot. As we stepped out, the air was cooler, refreshing against my skin. The scent of pine mingled with the rich aroma of roasting coffee, creating an intoxicating blend that made my heart race. I led the way into the café, my senses awakening to the cozy atmosphere—a warm glow from the vintage light fixtures and the soft murmur of patrons lost in their own worlds.

The barista flashed a friendly smile, and I placed my order, hoping the simple act of sharing something as mundane as coffee would ease the tension coiling between us. As we waited, I could feel Adam's eyes on me, assessing, contemplating. "What's your go-to order?" I asked, trying to draw him into conversation.

"Black coffee. Simple." He replied, his gaze unwavering, but I could sense the walls starting to crack.

"Ah, a man of few words and fewer frills. I should have guessed." I smirked, and for a moment, the corners of his mouth twitched upward, almost teasingly.

"You've got me all figured out, don't you?" He returned, a note of playfulness threading through his words.

I shrugged, feigning nonchalance. "Only the basics. You've got a mystery vibe going on, and I'm all about solving puzzles." I leaned in closer, lowering my voice conspiratorially. "But I can promise you, I don't bite."

"Not yet," he shot back, a mischievous glint in his eyes that sent a thrill through me.

Our drinks arrived, and as I took a sip, the heat of the coffee radiated through me, melting away some of the ice that had formed around my heart. "So, tell me about your favorite book. If you have a favorite, that is," I challenged, trying to pull more from him.

"Why would I share that? It's like giving away a piece of myself." He sipped his coffee, his expression turning contemplative.

"Exactly! And I'd never share my favorite, not until I know it will be cherished." I leaned back against the counter, savoring the moment. "You see, if I tell you, I'm handing over a tiny fragment of my soul. You'd better be prepared to reciprocate."

He chuckled, the sound low and rumbling, filling me with warmth. "That's quite the negotiation tactic."

"I've had to learn a thing or two about negotiating over the years," I replied, grinning. "But it's worth it for the right story."

The moment hung between us, a fragile thread woven from the laughter and the unsteady honesty that lingered just out of reach. I could sense the storm still brewing, but in this small café, it felt like we were momentarily sheltered from the rain.

As we settled into a small, rustic booth, the café wrapped us in its warm embrace, almost shielding us from the tempest outside and the turmoil inside. I could still feel the tension rippling between us, but the coffee—dark and robust—served as a balm, smoothing over some of the sharp edges. I took a sip, letting the warmth fill my chest, hoping it might coax Adam out from behind his fortress of silence.

"So, are you going to tell me what book is worth that fragment of your soul?" I probed, leaning forward with a playful grin. The café was alive with the clatter of cups and muffled conversations, and I felt an unexpected thrill at the intimacy of our little world, even as the shadows of his past loomed larger.

Adam regarded me with a mixture of amusement and caution. "You really want to know?"

"Absolutely. I promise I won't judge. Unless it's something truly embarrassing, like a self-help book or a poorly written romance novel," I teased, narrowing my eyes playfully.

He laughed, a genuine sound that cut through the heaviness that had enveloped us. "Well, you'd be surprised. I enjoy a good mystery now and then, something that keeps me guessing. But to give you a piece of my soul, I'd need something in return."

"I can do that." I leaned back, crossing my arms in mock defiance. "But let's set some ground rules first. No spoilers, and it must be something you loved as a child."

He raised an eyebrow, intrigued. "A child? Well, that certainly narrows it down. But I think I can manage."

With a dramatic sigh, I leaned in closer, the scent of cinnamon and fresh coffee swirling around us. "Then I'll go first. My favorite childhood book was The Secret Garden. The idea of finding a hidden paradise always enchanted me. Plus, I was convinced that if I found one, I could make all my problems disappear."

"Classic choice," he nodded, his eyes sparkling with a hint of recognition. "I think I read it five times, but for the sake of the rules, I'll stick to one. I was obsessed with The Adventures of Tom Sawyer. That boy knew how to have fun—and avoid chores. There's something so liberating about living a life on the edge of mischief, don't you think?"

"Are you saying you were a little hellion?" I laughed, picturing a young Adam, mischief glinting in his eyes. "I can't quite see it."

"Trust me, I was. Not all of us were the well-behaved types. Some of us had to add a bit of chaos to our lives to keep things interesting." He smiled, and for a moment, it was as if the storm clouds had shifted, revealing a little sunlight.

"I can relate to that," I said softly, the shared laughter drawing us closer. "Chaos is my middle name. Not that I've ever had a traditional life, but who needs one of those, right?"

"Right." He looked at me intently, as if he could see the hidden layers of my own story. "What kind of chaos have you stirred up?"

"Oh, you know, just the usual—unplanned road trips, spontaneous dance parties in my living room, and once, I nearly bought a one-way ticket to Paris on a whim." I leaned back, folding my arms, allowing the thrill of the memory to wash over me. "But it all led me here, to this moment, and I wouldn't trade it for anything."

For a second, his gaze softened, and I could almost feel the warmth of connection glowing between us. "So, what are you doing with that freedom? Besides prying into my past?"

"Honestly?" I leaned forward again, lowering my voice conspiratorially. "I'm searching for something that feels real. Something that makes sense in this chaotic world."

His expression shifted, the shadows flickering back into his eyes. "Not everything needs to make sense. Some things are just... messy."

There it was again—the darkness that shadowed his thoughts. I wanted to reach out, to pull him from that abyss, but the last thing I wanted was to push him further away. "Messy can be beautiful, you know. Like art or a wildflower garden. Sometimes the best stories come from the most unexpected places."

"Or the worst mistakes," he countered, his tone more serious, but I detected a hint of vulnerability beneath it. "Like letting someone in only to have them leave."

The weight of his words settled heavily in the air, pulling the laughter from the café and leaving a poignant silence in its wake. I felt a sharp ache in my chest, a flicker of recognition for the scars we both carried. "I get it, Adam. But isn't it worth the risk? What's life without a little bit of mess?"

He hesitated, his gaze wandering to the window, where dark clouds loomed on the horizon. "Maybe. But there's a fine line between chaos and destruction."

As if on cue, the wind howled outside, rattling the windows and sending a shiver through me. I couldn't help but smile at the irony. "You know, they say storms bring cleansing. Maybe what you see as destruction could be a new beginning."

He turned back to me, the hint of a smile breaking through the storm cloud that hung over him. "You're quite the optimist."

"And you're quite the skeptic," I shot back, unable to resist the urge to tease. "Maybe we balance each other out."

"Or we're both just a little too stubborn for our own good," he replied, a glimmer of challenge dancing in his eyes.

"Touché," I said, holding his gaze. The air around us hummed with an electric charge, anticipation crackling like static before a storm. There was something exquisite in the way he pushed and pulled, the way his walls began to tremble, as if he were testing the limits of what it meant to let someone in.

"Okay, let's make a deal," I proposed, trying to keep the atmosphere light despite the tension simmering below the surface. "I'll tell you one secret about me if you tell me one about you."

He considered my offer, his expression thoughtful. "Alright, but if I go first, I get to choose the secret."

"Deal." I held my breath, excitement and curiosity thrumming in my veins.

"Fine, but it has to be something you've never shared with anyone." He leaned in closer, eyes locked onto mine, as if searching for the truth behind my playful demeanor.

"Deal," I echoed, my heart racing.

The moment hung between us, charged with the promise of secrets yet to be revealed. As the café buzzed around us, I couldn't shake the feeling that, like the storm brewing outside, something was shifting between us—something powerful and unpredictable, and perhaps just a little bit dangerous.

The moment hung between us like the silence before thunder, electric and heavy with anticipation. I could feel the weight of his gaze, a mix of curiosity and trepidation, daring me to step further into the depths of our connection. The café, with its warmth and comforting smells, felt like a cocoon, sheltering us from the brewing storm outside. I was determined to unravel whatever tension lay beneath the surface, to dig deeper into the beautiful mess we were creating.

"Okay, I'll go first," I declared, my heart racing as I leaned closer, reveling in the thrill of sharing something intimate. "I once took a road trip to a small town just because I saw a sign for a pancake festival. Yes, you heard me right—pancakes." I paused for dramatic effect, the corners of my mouth curling into a mischievous grin. "I may have even tried to convince a few friends to join me, but let's just say, it was a solo venture."

His brow arched, a mix of amusement and disbelief dancing across his features. "A pancake festival? And here I thought you were all about deep, philosophical conversations."

"Hey, pancakes are serious business!" I laughed, lightening the mood. "But what's life without a little whimsy, right? Now it's your turn."

He hesitated, a flicker of uncertainty shadowing his eyes. "Alright, I'll bite. Once, I tried to impress a girl by climbing the tallest tree in my neighborhood. I got stuck, of course, and had to be rescued by a fireman. Let's just say my tree-climbing days were over after that."

I burst into laughter, my drink nearly spilling as I leaned back. "Oh, I can just picture that! A fireman and an awkward kid stuck in a tree—it sounds like the beginning of a rom-com!"

"Not my finest hour," he chuckled, shaking his head. But I noticed the way his smile faded slightly, the light dimming as the shadows returned.

"Come on, that's classic. At least you have a memorable story," I encouraged, sensing the deeper layers of his discomfort. "We all have our embarrassing moments. It's what makes us human. I mean, the pancake festival was a low point for me, too."

He studied me, the tension ebbing and flowing between us like the tide. "You're good at this," he said softly, almost reluctantly. "Unraveling layers. But there are some layers I'd rather leave untouched."

"Why do you keep pushing me away?" I leaned in closer, the challenge ringing in my voice. "I'm not afraid of the mess. In fact, I find it fascinating. It's what makes us real, and isn't that what we're searching for?"

Adam sighed, and the weight of his past hung heavily in the air. "It's not that simple. Not everything can be fixed with a cup of coffee and a few laughs. Some things are broken beyond repair."

"Then let me help," I urged, my heart racing as I searched his eyes. "Let me in. I want to understand."

For a moment, I thought he might relent. He opened his mouth, then closed it, the battle within him palpable. "You don't know what you're asking for," he finally replied, his voice barely above a whisper. "I'm not what you think I am."

The storm outside rumbled ominously, and I felt a shiver skitter down my spine. "Then show me who you really are," I challenged, my pulse quickening. "I can take it. I promise."

He held my gaze, a thousand unsaid words crackling in the air between us. Then, as if summoned by my plea, the power flickered, and the café was briefly plunged into darkness. Gasps echoed around us, followed by the flickering of emergency lights. My heart leaped into my throat, a blend of excitement and dread stirring within me.

"Is this part of your chaos?" Adam asked, his eyes wide, revealing a glimpse of vulnerability.

"Maybe," I joked, trying to mask my unease. "Or maybe it's just the universe reminding us how unpredictable life can be."

The lights flickered back to life, casting a warm glow over the café. But the momentary darkness had shifted something between us. Adam's expression hardened, and I sensed a storm brewing—not just outside, but within him.

"Let's step outside," he said abruptly, his voice low and urgent.

I nodded, my heart racing with curiosity and concern. We pushed through the café doors, the chill in the air wrapping around us like an unwelcome embrace. The wind howled, sending leaves spiraling through the air, and I felt the tension between us escalate, thick and palpable.

"What's going on, Adam?" I asked, trying to keep my tone steady as I faced him. The clouds overhead swirled ominously, mirroring the tumult in his eyes.

"I told you I'm not what you think," he said, his voice hoarse. "You see the mystery, but you don't know the darkness that comes with it."

I stepped closer, my breath visible in the crisp air. "Then let me in. Share it with me, please. I can handle it."

He hesitated, the storm brewing around us growing in intensity. "You don't know what you're asking for," he repeated, but there was a tremor in his voice that hinted at his internal struggle.

Suddenly, a loud crack of thunder shattered the air, making me jump. The sky darkened, and I felt a surge of adrenaline course through me. It felt like an omen, a warning of the chaos that lay ahead.

"Tell me, Adam!" I urged, my voice barely audible over the roaring wind. "What are you hiding?"

He looked away, his expression shifting, and in that moment, I saw the flicker of something raw and vulnerable beneath his guarded exterior. "You deserve the truth. But the truth might destroy what we have."

My heart raced, the words hanging between us like a fragile thread. "Then let it destroy it. I'd rather know than live in the dark."

He stepped back, a tempest swirling in his eyes. "You think you want to know, but once you do, there's no going back."

I opened my mouth to respond, but before I could speak, the wind howled louder, and the first raindrops began to fall. I looked up, the sky erupting into a cascade of dark clouds, and felt a sense of foreboding settle over me. Just as I was about to say something—anything—to bridge the widening chasm between us, a distant scream pierced the air, pulling my attention away.

"What was that?" I whispered, the hairs on the back of my neck standing on end.

Adam's eyes widened, fear flashing across his face. "I don't know, but we should check it out."

As the rain began to pour, drenching us in seconds, we turned toward the sound, the storm closing in on us as we raced into the unknown, the echoes of his secrets trailing behind like a distant thunderclap.

Chapter 7: "Falling for the Enemy"

The warmth of his body enveloped me, a heady mix of surprise and exhilaration. For a moment, time unraveled. I had always imagined that if I ever found myself in a moment like this, it would feel like stepping off a cliff, plummeting through the air with nothing but an adrenaline rush to keep me company. But standing there, tangled in Adam's arms, it felt more like floating. My heart raced, thundering in my chest as I pulled back, searching his dark eyes for any sign of mischief or doubt. Instead, I found an unexpected vulnerability that nearly took my breath away.

"What was that?" I asked, my voice unsteady, more a whisper than a question, as if saying it aloud might shatter the illusion of the moment.

His lips curled into a smirk, and I could see the devilish glimmer lurking beneath the surface. "Just a little verbal sparring, don't you think? Nothing more than a friendly competition." He brushed a thumb across my cheek, and I nearly melted.

We were enemies, or at least that's how I had labeled our tumultuous relationship. I had been hired to fix the mess that was Adam Hawthorne's public image. The billionaire recluse, a man shrouded in scandal and secretive whispers, had quickly become more than just an assignment; he was a challenge wrapped in a puzzle, and I had never been one to back down from a challenge. But the moment we had sparred—no, flirted—across the conference table, I had known this battle would be different.

"Right," I replied, forcing a laugh that was shaky at best. I stepped back, creating space between us as I attempted to regain my composure. "But you know I'm not just here for fun and games. I have a job to do."

"Oh, I know," he replied, his voice low and teasing. "You're here to save me from myself."

"More like save you from your bad decisions," I quipped, trying to mask the wild thumping in my chest with bravado.

The air crackled between us, alive with an unspoken tension that had been simmering just below the surface. It was more than a playful rivalry; it was a slow burn that left me wondering if I had made a grave mistake by allowing myself to feel this way.

I turned away from him, focusing on the pristine view outside his office window. The city sprawled out below us, a symphony of chaos and beauty, but all I could see were the emotions swirling within me like a storm. The high-rise buildings gleamed in the late afternoon sun, casting long shadows across the street, yet all I could feel was the weight of Adam's gaze on my back, steady and intense.

"Can you really fix me?" he asked, and I could hear the sincerity behind the casual tone.

I hesitated, the air thick with uncertainty. "That's the plan, but it's not going to be easy. You're not exactly the poster boy for rehabilitation, you know."

He chuckled, the sound rich and genuine. "I'm aware. But I have to admit, the prospect of having you as my guide is... intriguing."

Intriguing was an understatement. I could feel the very ground shifting beneath me as I considered what it would mean to delve deeper into this complicated relationship. I had spent weeks battling the allure of his charm and the dangerous thrill of our banter, and now I found myself teetering on the brink of something both exhilarating and terrifying.

"Stop looking at me like that," I said, my heart racing as I met his gaze. "You're going to make me forget everything I know about professionalism."

"I could say the same about you," he shot back, his voice dropping an octave, sending a shiver down my spine. "You have a way of getting under my skin."

"Oh, please. If anyone is getting under anyone's skin, it's you," I retorted, crossing my arms defensively. "You're like a high-end puzzle—stunning on the outside, but an absolute headache on the inside."

"Careful, or I might just take that as a compliment," he said, his grin widening, and in that moment, I realized how easily he had turned my annoyance into something else entirely—something more dangerous.

Yet, as I fought to keep my resolve intact, my phone buzzed loudly on the desk, a jarring reminder of reality. The screen lit up with a text from my boss, reminding me of our impending deadline.

"Duty calls," I said, retreating toward the door. The moment was already slipping through my fingers like grains of sand, and I was not prepared for the fallout that would follow.

"Is it so wrong to want to enjoy this? To want to—"

"Adam," I interrupted, my heart racing with urgency, "this isn't just about us. There are consequences here. You know that."

He leaned back in his chair, an unreadable expression crossing his features. "So, you're saying I should just walk away? Ignore what just happened?"

"Not what happened—what could happen," I replied, my voice firm, but inside, I felt like I was trying to contain a wildfire.

Silence fell between us, thick and heavy, as I wrestled with the rising tide of emotions threatening to drown me. I had come here to do a job, not to fall into a web of attraction that could ensnare us both. I turned to leave, but as I grasped the doorknob, I felt the weight of his presence behind me, a magnetic pull that held me in place.

"Tell me you don't feel anything," he said, his voice a low murmur that sent a ripple of anticipation through me.

I hesitated, the truth caught in my throat. I had never been one to shy away from admitting what I felt, yet with him, it felt like admitting defeat. And in that moment, I realized I wasn't just wrestling with my attraction to him; I was wrestling with the very real possibility that I was on the verge of something entirely new—something terrifying and exhilarating all at once.

The echoes of our kiss lingered in the air, a palpable reminder that I was no longer just a professional on a mission. Adam Hawthorne had shifted the dynamics of our relationship, turning it into something that could no longer be neatly categorized. I pressed my palms against the cool, polished surface of the desk, grounding myself in reality, but my mind was swirling like the leaves caught in an autumn gust outside his skyscraper office. Each breath felt electric, sending little sparks of confusion through my veins.

"Look," I said, steadying my voice, "this isn't how it's supposed to go. We have an agenda, remember? My job is to help you regain your image, not... not whatever this is."

He leaned forward, elbows resting on the desk, eyes glimmering with mischief and something else—something more vulnerable. "And what if this is part of the agenda? What if I need to be... understood?"

"Understood? Adam, we barely understand each other." The absurdity of it all bubbled to the surface, igniting my irritation. "One moment, you're throwing out razor-sharp jabs at me, and the next, you're sweeping me off my feet. How am I supposed to navigate this?"

"Isn't that what makes it interesting?" His smirk was infuriating and undeniably charming, a combination that made me want to scream and laugh at the same time. "Think of it as a... real-time case study in complexity."

I rolled my eyes, though I couldn't help the slight smile creeping in. "You know, there are less complicated ways to conduct a case study. Maybe a book? A lecture series? A reality show?"

"Don't tempt me. I'd make a fortune off watching you squirm under the glare of the cameras," he shot back, a playful twinkle in his eyes.

"Hard pass," I replied, trying to maintain my composure, but I could feel the tension tightening in my chest. "We need to refocus here. We're a week away from the gala, and I have to put together a plan to overhaul your image—fast. This isn't just about you; it's about the stakes involved."

"Ah, the stakes." He leaned back, feigning a thoughtful pose. "So, you really do care about my reputation?"

"Of course I care," I snapped, suddenly more defensive than I intended. "You might be a billionaire, but that doesn't give you the right to play with people's lives."

His expression shifted, and I could see the weight of my words settle over him. "You're right," he conceded, his voice softer now. "And you're not just some pawn in this game. I get that."

I shifted my gaze to the view outside, the sprawling city below buzzing with life. "Good. Because I'm not here to be a part of your scandalous lifestyle. I want you to succeed, but it has to be on your terms, not just because of the chaos we've created between us."

"Then let's make a deal," he suggested, a hint of determination creeping back into his tone. "If I help you with this plan, will you agree to stay? No distractions, just business."

"Deal?" I asked, arching an eyebrow. "What makes you think I'd trust you?"

"Because I'm just as interested in this as you are. We have a common goal." He straightened up, his demeanor shifting back to that of the confident CEO. "And besides, I think you're more than capable of handling me."

"Handling you?" I laughed, the sound slightly nervous. "I'm not sure anyone has ever succeeded in that endeavor."

"Challenge accepted," he said, a gleam of mischief in his eyes.

As we exchanged banter, I couldn't shake the feeling that we were stepping onto a tightrope, one with no safety net below. Yet, in the heart of this chaos, I felt a spark of excitement—a chance to confront not just the challenge ahead but also the magnetic pull that had drawn us together in the first place.

We spent the next few hours mapping out strategies and brainstorming potential angles for his public relations overhaul. The light shifted in the room as the sun dipped lower in the sky, casting a golden glow through the window. I lost myself in the details, the thrill of the game taking over, the seriousness of our situation blending into the background.

"Okay, let's say we go with the 'mysterious billionaire' angle," I proposed, scribbling ideas across a notepad. "We can create a narrative that emphasizes your philanthropic endeavors while still keeping a touch of intrigue. It's all about controlling the narrative."

"Sounds like a personal brand that could rival the best of them," Adam said, leaning in closer, his gaze intent on my scribbles. "I like where you're going with this."

"And we need to prepare for the press at the gala. I can help you rehearse your speeches—"

"I thought we agreed on no distractions," he interrupted, but the grin on his face betrayed him.

"Let me finish," I said, mock exasperation coloring my tone. "We also need to keep the press at arm's length while ensuring they catch just enough to create buzz. That means a strategic appearance—mysterious, yet approachable."

He raised an eyebrow. "You really think I can pull that off?"

"Absolutely. You're already half there with that brooding look of yours. Just add a touch of charm, and you'll have them eating out of your hand."

As the words tumbled from my mouth, I felt a flicker of something deeper pass between us, a recognition of our respective strengths in the madness we were creating. He leaned back in his chair, an easy confidence settling in.

"Fine, I'll play the role of the charming enigma. But only if you promise to keep the press off my back during the actual gala."

"Deal."

We locked eyes, and for a fleeting moment, the air was thick with unspoken promises. It felt like we were not just plotting a public relations strategy, but also dancing around something much more intimate. I broke the gaze first, knowing I needed to stay focused.

But as the hours wore on, the lines of our roles began to blur, and I found myself drawn to him in ways I never anticipated. Beneath the surface of his guarded exterior lay a man yearning for connection, battling shadows that I suspected ran deeper than his public persona. My resolve, once solid as steel, began to crack, and I couldn't help but wonder what it would mean to truly open that door.

Yet, as laughter and strategy flowed between us, I felt the creeping fear of where this path might lead. Could I be the one to help him heal, or would I end up as just another chapter in his complex story? As the sun dipped below the horizon, casting a blanket of stars across the night sky, I realized I was standing on the precipice of something I couldn't fully comprehend. But I knew one thing: I was all in, whether I wanted to be or not.

As the evening wore on, the atmosphere in Adam's office transformed into something more intimate, charged with the electric current of unspoken words. The golden light from the desk lamp illuminated the scattered papers and half-empty coffee cups, casting elongated shadows that danced along the walls, reminiscent of the tension that hung between us.

"Okay, Mr. Hawthorne," I said, reclaiming my professional demeanor as I jotted down notes. "Let's talk strategy for this gala. We need a clear plan to navigate the media while still making a statement."

He leaned back, his posture relaxed but his expression attentive. "What kind of statement? I don't want to come across as just another charity case in a tuxedo."

"Exactly. You need to be more than just a billionaire with deep pockets. You want them to see the real you. We need a hook, something to set you apart." I tapped my pen against my chin, considering the possibilities. "What if we highlighted your recent investments in local startups? It shows you're not just in it for the money."

He nodded, a hint of admiration flickering in his gaze. "That's good. It gives them a story to latch onto—something relatable."

"And it puts you in a position of strength," I continued, buoyed by his enthusiasm. "You'll be showcasing your interest in uplifting others while subtly hinting at your own challenges. It's humanizing."

"Humanizing," he repeated, his voice a low rumble. "Is that what you think I need?"

I looked up, locking eyes with him. "You've built a fortress around yourself, Adam. Sometimes, letting people see the cracks can make you stronger. Vulnerability is powerful."

"Perhaps," he mused, his expression turning contemplative. "But isn't it also dangerous?"

"Risky? Absolutely. But aren't we already in a risky situation?" I shot back, my heart racing. "You're already in the spotlight for all the wrong reasons. This could turn the tide."

The silence stretched between us, thick with tension and possibility. I could see the wheels turning in his mind, the calculated thoughts behind those piercing eyes. "You're right," he finally said, his tone heavy with realization. "But it's not just about the gala. There's something more at stake here."

"What do you mean?" I leaned forward, curiosity piquing my interest.

"I've been working on something behind the scenes—an initiative that could change everything for me, for the people I want to help. But it's a double-edged sword. If it fails, it could ruin everything I've built."

"Then let's make sure it doesn't fail. We'll prepare, we'll strategize, and we'll make it work." I felt the fervor rising within me, a blend of professional duty and personal attachment that I couldn't ignore. "Tell me more about it."

Adam's demeanor shifted as he began to share his vision, the shadows fading away as the light of his ambition took center stage. He spoke passionately about the impact he hoped to achieve, the lives he wanted to change, and the legacy he wished to leave behind. Each word he spoke drew me closer, unraveling the layers of his persona and revealing a man driven not just by ambition but by a genuine desire to connect with the world around him.

"I've been developing a mentorship program for underprivileged youth," he confessed, his voice steady but laced with vulnerability. "I want to help them find their footing in the business world, to show them that success isn't reserved for the elite."

"Adam, that's incredible," I said, genuinely moved by the sincerity of his vision. "You're not just trying to save your own reputation; you're trying to save lives."

He looked at me, an intensity in his gaze that made my heart flutter. "And if I can pull this off at the gala, it could be the turning point I need. But I can't do it alone."

"No one can do it alone," I replied, my voice firm with conviction. "You've got me in your corner, and I won't let you fail."

The moment lingered, charged with the weight of promises and possibilities. I could see a flicker of hope in his eyes, a glimmer that ignited something deep within me. But before I could dwell on the implications of our connection, the shrill ring of my phone shattered the spell.

I glanced at the screen, frowning at the name flashing in bold letters. My boss. The one person I didn't want to hear from right now.

"Great," I muttered, trying to hide my irritation. "Just when things were getting interesting."

"Go ahead, take it," Adam urged, though I could see the slight tightening of his jaw.

I hesitated, glancing at him, but the urgency of the call weighed heavily on me. "I'll be right back," I promised, stepping out into the hallway.

The conversation was brief but heated. My boss was frustrated—there had been whispers about Adam's recent behavior, and they wanted immediate results. I could feel the pressure mounting, tightening like a noose around my resolve.

"Just remember, this isn't just about the gala," he said, his tone brusque. "If this falls through, it's not just your reputation at stake—it's ours."

I ended the call, a storm of thoughts swirling in my mind as I returned to Adam's office. He was standing by the window, silhouetted against the city lights that flickered like stars beneath us.

"What's wrong?" he asked, turning to face me, his expression a mix of concern and something else—was it fear?

"They're getting restless," I admitted, my heart racing. "They want results, and they want them fast. If we don't pull off a miracle at the gala, this whole thing could collapse, and I might be left holding the bag."

"Then we can't allow that to happen," he replied, determination blazing in his eyes. "We need to tighten our plan and ensure everything goes flawlessly. No room for error."

I nodded, inspired by his tenacity. "Exactly. We'll map out our moves, anticipate the questions, and have answers ready. This is our moment, Adam."

As we dove back into strategy mode, the clock ticked steadily towards the gala, each second a reminder of the impending pressure. I could feel the weight of our ambition, our intertwined fates, bearing down on us.

Just as we finalized our ideas, my phone buzzed again, a notification flashing across the screen. A news alert.

I glanced down, my breath hitching in my throat as the headline stared back at me, bold and accusatory: "Billionaire Hawthorne's Past Catches Up—New Allegations Surface!"

Adam's face paled as he stepped closer to see the screen. "What does it say?" he demanded, the calm exterior shattering like glass.

"It's bad, Adam," I whispered, my heart racing as I read the details. "Very bad."

The air crackled with tension, and for a brief moment, everything else faded away. The stakes had just been raised, and I could feel the ground shifting beneath our feet.

Adam's jaw clenched, a fierce determination igniting in his eyes. "We have to get ahead of this. I won't let them control the narrative. Not now."

"No, but we need to move fast. This could ruin everything we've worked for." I could feel the urgency clawing at my insides, the looming threat of a public relations nightmare.

He nodded, resolve etched across his features. "Then let's fight back. Together."

But as we stood there, ready to confront the chaos that awaited us, a shadow flickered across the office door, and I turned, instinctively holding my breath. The door swung open, revealing a figure I never expected to see.

"Sorry to interrupt," said a familiar voice, cool and confident. "But I believe we have a problem."

And just like that, the air shifted again, a new tension curling around us as I realized the battle was far from over.

Chapter 8: "The Secrets We Keep"

Every time I caught a glimpse of Adam, my heart seemed to do a little dance, fluttering and twisting like a butterfly caught in a spring breeze. It was maddening, really, the way he drew me in with his easy charm and that enigmatic smile that hinted at secrets buried deep beneath his surface. We'd spent countless hours together, the kind that slipped by unnoticed, wrapped up in shared laughter and stolen glances. Yet, as our connection grew, I couldn't shake the feeling that there were layers to him—hidden depths I had yet to plumb.

I sat on the balcony of my apartment, the warm summer air wrapping around me like a favorite blanket. The city buzzed below, a cacophony of laughter, honking horns, and the distant strains of music drifting from nearby bars. I sipped my wine, savoring the rich flavor as it danced on my tongue, but the taste felt tainted, overshadowed by the questions swirling in my mind. I had noticed Adam's late-night absences, the way his phone would buzz with urgent messages when he thought I wasn't looking. Each time, my heart sank a little lower, each unanswered question pulling me deeper into a spiral of uncertainty.

He had a knack for deflection, changing the subject with effortless charm whenever I probed too closely, his laughter like a shield, sparkling and bright yet so painfully fragile. I wanted to believe he was just a private man, someone who guarded his past with the ferocity of a lion protecting its cub. But instinct told me there was something more, something lurking in the shadows of his life, something that made the air crackle with tension every time he arrived at my door, a heartbeat after dusk.

That night, when I decided to confront him, the moon hung high in the sky, casting silver beams over the world, illuminating the dark corners that felt all too familiar. I arranged the cushions on the balcony, creating a cozy haven for our discussion, wanting to make the moment inviting yet serious. I could feel the anticipation thrumming in my veins as I replayed the conversations in my mind, weighing my words like precious jewels, trying to craft the perfect inquiry.

When he arrived, looking effortlessly handsome in a fitted shirt and jeans that hugged his form in all the right places, I nearly lost my nerve. The way he smiled at me, all warmth and mischief, made my stomach flip. I motioned for him to sit, and as he settled in, I couldn't help but notice the way his fingers tapped rhythmically against his thigh, a tell I was beginning to recognize. The weight of his secrets hung in the air between us like a heavy fog, and I knew I had to cut through it.

"Adam," I began, my voice steady despite the racing of my heart. "There's something we need to talk about."

His expression shifted subtly, the glint of mischief fading just a touch. "Sounds serious. What's on your mind?"

The challenge in his tone was clear, a dare that made me both anxious and resolute. "You know that I care about you, right? But I can't shake the feeling that you're hiding something from me."

He leaned back, arms crossed, the slight furrow in his brow deepening. "I'm not hiding anything. Just... managing my life, like everyone else."

I held his gaze, refusing to be dissuaded by his practiced charm. "Late-night calls, unexplained meetings. This isn't just managing life; it feels like there's something darker at play."

The air shifted, the playful atmosphere turning tense. Adam's eyes flickered, a shadow crossing his face that made my heart race with apprehension. "You don't know what you're asking for, Emily," he replied, his voice low, gravelly.

"Then make me understand," I pressed, feeling the heat of determination surge through me. "I can't keep pretending everything's fine when I can feel the weight of whatever it is bearing down on us."

He ran a hand through his hair, a gesture of frustration that only fueled my resolve. "You think you want to know the truth, but sometimes the truth is more dangerous than the lies. I'm not trying to protect myself; I'm trying to protect you."

The sudden shift in his tone sent a shiver down my spine. My pulse quickened as I processed his words, each syllable heavy with implications. "Protect me? From what, Adam?"

He hesitated, the silence stretching between us like an unbridgeable chasm. Finally, he sighed, his shoulders slumping. "I can't tell you everything. Not yet. But trust me when I say, I'm trying to keep you safe."

"Safe from what?" I pressed, frustration boiling to the surface. "I don't need you to shield me from your past. I want to stand beside you, to face whatever it is together."

Adam's eyes bore into mine, a storm of emotions swirling within them. "You don't understand, Emily. This isn't just about me. There are forces at play that are bigger than both of us. And if you knew, it would change everything."

The intensity of his words wrapped around me like a vise, squeezing the breath from my lungs. I wanted to push further, to claw at the barriers he had erected, but an insistent voice in my mind warned me of the danger that lay ahead. I took a deep breath, steadying myself, wrestling with the churning chaos inside.

"I refuse to live in a world of shadows, Adam," I finally said, my voice barely above a whisper. "If there's a monster lurking in the dark, I want to face it, not cower behind your walls."

His expression softened for a moment, as if he were seeing me anew. But just as quickly, the armor returned, and I could see the indecision swirling in his eyes, a tempest brewing beneath the calm surface.

"Then prepare yourself," he murmured, his voice low and serious. "Because when the truth comes out, it may shatter everything we've built."

My heart raced at his words, a cocktail of fear and exhilaration surging through me. I had never been one to back down from a challenge, and the thought of unraveling the tangled web of secrets between us was too enticing to resist. Yet, deep down, I could feel the unease clawing at my insides, the ominous weight of the truth looming just out of reach.

As the city lights flickered to life around us, I realized that this moment was just the beginning. The secrets Adam kept were threads woven into the fabric of our lives, and as we both sat in the growing darkness, I knew the night was far from over.

The air was thick with anticipation, heavy with the tension that lingered after Adam's revelation. I could feel my heart racing, each beat echoing the unspoken questions that hung between us like a storm waiting to break. I took a moment, gathering my thoughts, trying to make sense of the swirling chaos in my mind. I had always been the type to dig for answers, to uncover truths, but the weight of Adam's words made me question everything I thought I knew about him—and about myself.

As I peered into his eyes, searching for the hidden depths I sensed within him, I couldn't shake the feeling that I was standing at the edge of something monumental. "What kind of forces are we talking about?" I asked, trying to keep my voice steady, though I could feel it trembling at the edges. "What are you so afraid of?"

He leaned forward, a mixture of urgency and hesitation etched across his handsome face. "You have to understand, Emily, that some truths can't be unlearned. You might think you want to know, but there are shadows in my past that could swallow us whole."

"Swallow us whole?" I echoed, incredulous. "You're not talking about a bad haircut or an embarrassing high school crush, Adam. What could possibly be so terrible?"

The corner of his mouth quirked up, the ghost of a smile that felt out of place. "Those are pretty traumatic, you know," he teased lightly, but the warmth in his voice was quickly overshadowed by a deeper darkness. "I can't give you specifics. Not yet. You deserve to be safe. But believe me, if I reveal too much too soon, it could put you in danger."

"Danger?" The word tasted bitter on my tongue. "Are we talking about bad Yelp reviews or something a bit more... serious?"

He shot me a look that combined exasperation and amusement, and I saw a flicker of the man I had fallen for behind the mask of caution. "I wish it were just bad reviews. It's much messier than that."

His vulnerability pulled at my heartstrings, a reminder that beneath that charming exterior lay a man grappling with demons I couldn't even begin to understand. "Fine," I said, softening my tone. "Let's say I believe you. What can I do to help? You don't have to go through this alone."

Adam's eyes softened, a flicker of gratitude sparking within them. "You're too good for your own good, you know that? But this is something I need to handle myself. Just... trust that I'm doing everything I can to keep you safe."

"Trust? It's hard to trust when I feel like I'm wandering through a fog. You've built walls around you, and I'm outside, banging on the door." I took a deep breath, frustration bubbling beneath the surface. "If you care about me at all, let me in."

His gaze held mine, the weight of his indecision pressing down on us. "You really want to know?" he finally asked, his voice low, almost hesitant.

"I do," I replied, a resolve settling in my chest. "But only if you're ready to share."

After what felt like an eternity, he nodded slowly, the tension in his shoulders easing just a fraction. "Okay. But if I tell you this, there's no going back. You'll have to decide if you still want to be part of my life after."

"Try me," I said, my heart racing. "I promise, whatever it is, I can handle it."

He took a deep breath, his fingers intertwining in front of him as if summoning the strength to share his truth. "I've been involved in some... business ventures that aren't exactly above board. I was trying to escape a life that was dragging me down, but the people I worked with have a way of tying you to them, even when you think you're free."

"Business ventures?" I echoed, the realization dawning on me that I had opened a can of worms far larger than I anticipated. "Are we talking about illegal activities?"

Adam nodded, the weight of his confession hanging in the air like a thick fog. "I got in too deep, made choices I thought would protect me, but now I'm finding it harder to break away. It's like trying to shake off a shadow that refuses to let go."

As the implications of his words sunk in, a chill ran down my spine. "So, what? You're in some kind of trouble? Is that why you've been so distant?"

"Yes," he admitted, his voice barely a whisper. "I'm trying to get out, but every time I think I've found a way, they pull me back in. It's messy, and I never wanted you to be part of this world. I thought I could keep it separate, but the truth is, it's all intertwined."

"What about the late-night calls? The meetings?" I pressed, the pieces of the puzzle beginning to fall into place, each one revealing a more complicated picture. "Are you involved with dangerous people?"

He grimaced, a look of regret crossing his features. "Yes. There's a reason I've been vague. I've had to tread carefully, and keeping you in the dark felt like the safest option. But now..."

"Now you're dragging me into the light," I finished for him, the realization hitting me with a painful clarity. "What happens if they come for you? What happens to me?"

"I'll do everything in my power to protect you," he vowed, his eyes intense, filled with a mix of determination and fear. "But you need to understand—there are no guarantees. These are not people you can negotiate with. They don't take kindly to betrayal."

"I don't plan on betraying you," I said, my voice steadier than I felt. "But I can't just sit back and wait for you to handle this alone. I'm in this with you, Adam. Whether you like it or not."

His gaze softened, and for a moment, I could see the flicker of hope shining through the storm clouds of uncertainty. "You're really something else, you know that?"

"Yeah, well, I've always been a bit of a troublemaker," I replied, trying to lighten the mood despite the gravity of our conversation. "Just ask my parents. They thought I'd end up in juvie for sure."

A smile tugged at the corners of his mouth, momentarily banishing the shadows that loomed between us. "I believe it. You've got that wild spirit, and it's both terrifying and amazing."

"Glad to know I'm not the only one who feels like a walking contradiction," I quipped, allowing the moment of levity to linger between us. "So, what's the plan? I mean, besides sitting around and waiting for the drama to unfold?"

He chuckled softly, the sound a balm against the tension. "I need to get my affairs in order. This might require some... unconventional methods."

"Unconventional methods? You mean like dressing up as a ninja and sneaking around?" I asked, trying to keep the mood light, even as my heart raced at the thought of what lay ahead.

"Exactly. I've always wanted to be a ninja. Think it would suit me?"

"Only if you come with a cool mask and some sweet throwing stars," I teased, but beneath my playful banter was an undercurrent of anxiety.

As we sat there, the city pulsing with life around us, I felt a sense of resolve solidifying within me. Adam was tangled in a web of shadows, but I would do everything in my power to help him find the light. Together, we would face whatever darkness lay ahead, and for the first time, I felt a flicker of hope amidst the uncertainty, a feeling that perhaps we could navigate the storm together.

The night stretched on, each minute a reminder of the storm brewing just beneath the surface of our lives. The laughter we had shared felt like a distant echo now, overshadowed by the weight of Adam's revelations. Yet, amidst the chaos swirling in my mind, I felt a fierce determination building within me, a steely resolve to help him navigate the tumult ahead.

"Okay, so we need a plan," I said, my voice steady despite the racing thoughts in my head. "How do we start untangling this mess? I mean, besides you becoming a ninja."

Adam leaned back, his expression shifting from amusement to contemplation. "I need to figure out who is still in my corner. There are people I trusted who may have turned against me, and I can't let them know I'm looking into it."

"Great," I replied, my fingers drumming against the table, trying to process the enormity of what lay ahead. "So, reconnaissance it is. What's the next step? We can't go charging in without a game plan. That's how you end up in a sitcom—laughing one minute, in a hostage situation the next."

His laughter rang out, a sound I desperately wanted to keep echoing in the quiet of my apartment. "You'd make a terrible hostage," he said, grinning. "But seriously, I need to make a few calls and figure out who's still trustworthy. If you could—"

"Hold down the fort?" I interjected. "Of course. I'll just sit here twiddling my thumbs while you do all the fun stuff."

He shot me a look that was half-exasperated, half-amused. "You know it's not like that. I want you to stay safe while I work this out."

"Safe? Please," I scoffed, waving a hand dismissively. "I'm in this with you now, whether you like it or not. If someone comes after you, they'll have to deal with me. And I'm not exactly the most pacifistic person on the block."

He chuckled again, though there was an edge of tension in it. "You're really something, you know that? I've never met anyone quite like you."

I smiled at the compliment, but the unease lurking in his eyes dampened the moment. "Flattery will get you nowhere if you don't let me help. What about your contacts? The ones you've been avoiding?"

He nodded, a shadow crossing his features. "I need to reach out to Marco. He's the last of the original crew, but he's also got a knack for getting into trouble. I can't guarantee he'll give me any straight answers."

"Marco?" I raised an eyebrow, curiosity piquing my interest. "Sounds shady. Should I be worried?"

"Worried, yes. But also ready for anything." He paused, staring into the distance as if he could see the threads of fate weaving themselves into a tapestry of chaos. "He might have information about the people I'm dealing with. I just need to be careful how I approach him."

"And how do you plan to do that? Send him a postcard?" I teased, trying to lighten the mood even as apprehension gnawed at me.

"I'll meet him in person. Old-school, face-to-face."

I felt a shiver run down my spine at the thought of Adam stepping back into that world, especially when he was already teetering on the edge of danger. "And what about me? Are you really going to leave me here while you dance with the devil?"

He sighed, rubbing the back of his neck. "I'll do my best to keep you out of it. I don't want you caught in the crossfire."

"Too late," I shot back. "You've already dragged me into the deep end. But if you think I'm going to sit on the sidelines, you've got another thing coming."

"Okay, okay," he relented, a hint of a smile returning to his lips. "But you need to promise me you'll stay out of sight. I don't want Marco knowing anything about you until I can figure out how deep the rabbit hole goes."

I held up my hands in mock surrender. "Fine. I'll be your covert operative. I'll blend into the background like a chameleon at a paint factory."

"Just try not to get yourself into more trouble than you already are," he warned, the corners of his mouth lifting into a smirk. "I'm pretty sure you've already hit your quota."

"Challenge accepted," I replied, raising an eyebrow, feeling the thrill of defiance bubbling up. "Just promise to check in with me, will you? I don't want to feel like I'm sitting here twiddling my thumbs while you're off having your clandestine meetings."

"I will. I swear it," he said, reaching across the table to squeeze my hand. The warmth of his touch sent a cascade of emotions rushing through me, a mix of gratitude and unease swirling together. "Now, I really should get going."

"Right. Ninja business awaits," I quipped, trying to keep the mood light as he stood, ready to leave.

"Stay safe," he said again, a hint of worry etched across his brow.

"Always. Just remember, I'm not the damsel in distress you might think I am."

As he stepped out into the night, I felt a strange mix of pride and anxiety knotting in my stomach. I was ready to fight for him, to step into the unknown alongside him, but the shadows whispered warnings I couldn't ignore. With each second that ticked by, the weight of his secrets pressed down harder, and I could feel the storm gathering in the distance.

Alone in my apartment, I took a deep breath, forcing myself to remain calm. I needed to prepare, to think through my next steps. I pulled out my laptop and began to search for any information I could find on Adam's past, on Marco, and the elusive "business ventures" he had hinted at. The keys clicked beneath my fingers, each stroke fueling my determination.

But just as I was starting to gather threads of information, the sound of my phone buzzing shattered the silence. It was an unknown number, but curiosity propelled me to answer. "Hello?"

"Emily," a low, gravelly voice responded, sending chills racing down my spine. "I hear you've been asking questions."

Panic surged through me, and my pulse quickened. "Who is this?"

"Let's just say I know more about Adam than you do," the voice continued, oozing with a sinister calm. "And if you care about him at all, you'll want to be very careful from now on."

The call ended abruptly, leaving me breathless and staring at my phone in disbelief. A rush of adrenaline coursed through me, and I felt the walls of my apartment closing in. I had stepped into a world far darker than I had anticipated, and I realized that the secrets we kept could very well lead to our undoing.

With my heart pounding in my chest, I glanced at the door Adam had just walked through, a sense of urgency and dread washing over me. I couldn't just sit back and wait anymore; I had to take control of my destiny. Grabbing my jacket, I resolved to find him before it was too late. As I reached for the doorknob, a loud crash echoed from outside, shattering the stillness.

I froze, my heart racing. Whatever was happening, it was about to change everything.

Chapter 9: "Shattered Illusions"

I should have seen it coming. The signs were there, in the whispered phone calls, the distant look in his eyes when he thought I wasn't watching. But I had convinced myself that it didn't matter. That what we had—whatever it was—could survive anything. The truth crashed down on me like a tidal wave when I saw the headline. Adam's past, the secret he'd buried deep beneath the layers of his carefully crafted life, was now splashed across every news outlet in the country. A scandal, a betrayal, something that felt too big to comprehend. And I realized, in that moment, I had fallen for a man I didn't really know.

It was a Sunday, the sun drenching my little apartment in warm hues, but the light felt cruel now, mocking my naïveté. I sat on the edge of my too-small couch, cradling a lukewarm cup of coffee in my trembling hands, its bitter scent somehow overshadowed by the acrid tang of betrayal. The screen of my phone was a gaudy display of flashing notifications, headlines that screamed Adam's name with wild accusations. The words blurred together: fraud, embezzlement, former partner speaks out. My heart sank deeper with each line, as if the very fabric of my world was unraveling, leaving behind only a tattered thread of who I thought I knew.

I leaned back, my mind racing to piece together the moments that now felt so fraught with deceit. The way Adam had laughed when I playfully asked about his past, deflecting with charm and that disarming smile that had initially drawn me to him. There was always something evasive in his demeanor, a flicker of something dark behind those kind eyes, but I had ignored it, lulled by the intoxicating rhythm of our late-night talks, the warmth of his embrace that felt like coming home after a long, weary journey. I could still feel the ghost of his touch on my skin, but it was tinged now with bitterness, a reminder that love is never the perfect sanctuary we want it to be.

I pushed myself up from the couch, pacing the room as if movement could somehow shake the weight of reality from my shoulders. The walls, decorated with splashes of color that once brought me joy, now felt like a prison, closing in on me with every breath. I reached for the remote, flicking the television on, half-expecting to find more evidence of Adam's betrayal in the gleeful news anchors' voices. Sure enough, there they were, chattering animatedly, their faces betraying a gleeful anticipation of the chaos unfurling. The footage of Adam's public appearances—his charming smile, the way he commanded attention—was juxtaposed against damning testimonies from former colleagues. I was helplessly drawn into the maelstrom, unable to look away as the pieces of my life crumbled around me.

The phone buzzed again, vibrating insistently on the table. It was Mia, my best friend, the one person I had confided in about my relationship with Adam. Her text came through like a lifeline: Are you okay? I saw the news. Let me come over. I hesitated, but the urge to talk, to voice my confusion and hurt, outweighed my instinct to hide. I typed a quick response, inviting her over, and then sank back onto the couch, feeling both grateful and anxious for the impending confrontation with my own feelings.

Mia arrived just as the sky turned a bruised shade of gray, her presence a burst of energy that filled the room. She swept in with a vibrant scarf draped around her shoulders, her eyes wide with concern as she took in the mess of emotions spilling from my heart. "You look like you've seen a ghost," she remarked, her voice both soothing and unnerving.

"I feel like I've been haunted," I replied, pouring out the details, my words tumbling over each other in a frantic rush. I spoke of Adam, of how we'd met and the moments that felt so magical—dancing under the stars, sharing secrets as we walked hand in hand through the city streets. But those memories were tainted now, overshadowed by the revelations that felt like a wrecking ball swinging through my carefully constructed life. "He lied to me, Mia. All this time, he must have known it would come out. How could he?"

Mia settled beside me, her hand resting comfortingly on my back. "People hide things for all sorts of reasons. Fear, shame. But that doesn't make it right. You deserve honesty, especially from someone you've let into your heart."

A hollow ache filled my chest at her words. "How can I trust him now? What if this is just the tip of the iceberg?" The fear I'd tried to shove deep inside was clawing its way out, its claws sharp and relentless.

"You don't have to figure it all out right now," she said, her voice soft yet firm. "Just take a breath and try to process. When he gets here—"

"Gets here?" My heart raced at the thought of facing Adam again. "What if he comes here and tries to explain? What if he doesn't have any answers?"

Mia's eyes sparkled with determination. "Then you'll confront him. You deserve to know what's really going on. Don't let him wiggle out of this. You have every right to demand the truth."

Before I could respond, the sound of a key in the lock sent a jolt of anxiety through me. Adam was home, and the storm of emotions surged within me, a tumultuous tide threatening to pull me under. I shared a glance with Mia, who nodded, a fierce ally in the face of my chaos.

With a shaky breath, I prepared to confront the man I had thought I knew, bracing myself for the truth that awaited me beyond the door.

The door swung open, revealing Adam with a sheepish grin plastered across his face, as if he was blissfully unaware of the storm brewing in the room. His hair tousled just so, his shirt casually unbuttoned at the collar, he looked like a man who had just stepped out of a dream—my dream, in fact, the one I thought was shared. But the moment his eyes landed on me, the smile faltered, replaced by a flicker of apprehension that sent a chill down my spine.

"Hey, I was just—" he began, his voice trailing off as he noticed Mia perched on the edge of the couch, her arms crossed and an unwavering gaze fixed on him. The tension in the air thickened, palpable and electrifying, like the atmosphere before a summer storm.

"Were you just checking your phone for the latest headlines?" Mia quipped, a playful yet pointed glint in her eye.

"Uh, no. I was—" Adam stammered, fumbling for words as he stepped further inside. His casual demeanor shattered like glass, revealing the cracks beneath the surface. I remained silent, absorbing the scene, wondering how the man I thought I knew could so easily turn into a stranger standing in my living room.

"Mia's here for moral support," I finally interjected, the words slipping out with an unexpected sharpness. "I thought you might need an audience for your grand confession."

The playful banter hung between us like a taut string, ready to snap at any moment. Adam shifted his weight, an uncomfortable fidget that only added to my growing impatience. "I can explain everything, Rachel," he said, his voice steadying as he took a step closer. "I know this looks bad—"

"Looks bad?" I echoed, incredulous. "This is beyond bad. It's a full-blown disaster!" My heart raced, a wild drumbeat echoing in my ears. "You didn't think I'd notice that you've been dodging my questions? You've been more secretive than a cat burglar in the night!"

"Rachel, please—" he pleaded, and I could see genuine concern etched in the lines of his face. He looked at me as if I were a fragile glass ornament, and I wondered how long he had spent perfecting that expression, the one that could coax me back into his arms. "I was going to tell you, I swear. Just... not yet."

"Not yet?" I laughed, a bitter sound that seemed foreign even to my ears. "What were you waiting for? A press release?" The irony hung heavy in the air, my sarcasm sharp enough to cut through the tension that enveloped us. "You should have seen this coming. You've been playing with fire, and now it's burned us both."

Mia shot me a look, her eyes narrowing slightly, as if to say, Let him explain. I swallowed my retort, glancing at her for a brief moment, and then back to Adam, whose hands were raised in surrender.

"I didn't think it would come out this way," he said, his tone shifting from defensive to earnest. "I've made mistakes, yes, but I was trying to protect you."

"Protect me?" I felt the heat rising in my cheeks, a rush of indignation mingling with hurt. "By hiding the truth? By pretending your life was something it wasn't? You've turned me into a fool!"

"Rachel," he said, stepping closer, his voice dropping to a conspiratorial whisper, "you have to understand. It's complicated. There are reasons I didn't want to involve you."

"Complicated?" I scoffed. "I've been to enough therapy sessions to know that 'complicated' usually means you're trying to dodge accountability."

Mia snorted softly, her eyes twinkling as she shifted in her seat. "She's not wrong, you know."

Adam ran a hand through his hair, a gesture of exasperation, his expression morphing from frustration to desperation. "What if I told you that the past isn't what it seems? What if I told you that I've been trying to change, to be better?"

"Then I'd want to know what you were hiding, Adam. Because whatever it is, it's been big enough to keep you from being honest with me," I shot back, the tremor in my voice betraying my resolve.

He paused, the weight of my words settling heavily in the room. The air crackled with unspoken truths, each one waiting for the right moment to break free. I could see the gears turning in his mind as he wrestled with the truth, and I wondered if it was worth it—if uncovering his hidden past would only deepen the chasm between us.

"I... I was in a partnership," he finally admitted, his voice barely above a whisper. "It went bad—really bad. I lost everything: my reputation, my savings. It wasn't just about me anymore. I didn't want you to have to deal with the fallout."

His honesty caught me off guard, the raw vulnerability in his gaze striking a chord deep within me. "What kind of partnership?" I pressed, the question hanging in the air like an unfinished song.

"A business partnership," he said, his jaw tightening. "We were supposed to be starting a tech company together. But he... he betrayed me. Embezzled funds, took everything I had worked for. And when I tried to fight back, it turned into a public scandal."

"Why didn't you just tell me?" I asked, my heart shifting slightly as empathy began to unfurl within me, battling against the waves of anger.

"Because I was ashamed," he replied, his gaze dropping to the floor. "I thought I could fix it before it all came crashing down. I didn't want you to see me as a failure."

"Now look where we are," I said, my voice barely above a whisper. "This is a different kind of failure."

"I know," he replied, stepping closer. "And I'm so sorry. I never wanted to hurt you. You mean everything to me."

His words hung in the air, heavy with the weight of unsaid promises. The sincerity in his voice ignited a flicker of hope inside me, but it was quickly doused by the stark reality of what had just unfolded. "Do you really mean that?" I asked, my heart racing with the fear of being let down again.

"Yes, Rachel. You have to believe me," he urged, reaching for my hand. I hesitated, my pulse quickening as I felt his warmth enveloping me.

"Believing you feels like walking a tightrope over a pit of snakes," I admitted, my voice barely above a whisper.

"Then let me show you. I'll do whatever it takes to make this right."

And just like that, amidst the confusion and heartache, the possibility of rebuilding shimmered in the distance, a fragile light guiding us through the storm. But I knew better than to trust too easily; it would take more than words to mend what had been shattered. The pieces lay scattered around us, and I had to decide if picking them up was worth the risk.

The air between us crackled with the weight of unspoken words, the heaviness of revelation mingling with the fragile hope that perhaps, just perhaps, we could navigate the wreckage together. Adam's fingers brushed against mine, a tentative connection that felt like an unsteady bridge spanning the chasm of our trust. My heart wavered, caught in a storm of conflicting emotions. I longed to believe him, to lean into the warmth of his promise, but the scars of betrayal still throbbed painfully beneath the surface.

"Show me then," I challenged, trying to sound resolute even as uncertainty coiled tight in my gut. "Show me that this isn't just another pretty line, that you really mean what you say."

He drew a deep breath, his gaze locking onto mine with an intensity that sent shivers down my spine. "I'll prove it. Just give me a chance to make this right. Let me take you somewhere—somewhere we can talk without the noise of the world interrupting us."

"Somewhere?" I raised an eyebrow, skepticism threading through my tone. "You think a change of scenery will fix this?"

"It's a start," he replied earnestly. "I just need you to trust me, even if it's just a little."

"Trust you?" I repeated, the word tasting bitter on my tongue. "You've already shattered my trust into a million pieces. What's left for you to build on?"

Mia cleared her throat, her presence a steady anchor amidst the emotional turmoil swirling around us. "Maybe you should at least hear him out, Rachel. It's easy to dismiss him now, but if he's genuine, wouldn't it be worth knowing for sure?"

I shot her a look, caught between gratitude and frustration. She was right; this wasn't just about my feelings anymore. But still, I hesitated. "What if this is just a way for you to buy time? A distraction until things settle down?"

Adam stepped back slightly, running a hand through his hair, frustration etched across his features. "I get it. I do. But I can't just stand here and let you assume the worst without a chance to explain. This mess, it's more complicated than you think."

"Complicated seems to be your specialty," I muttered under my breath, crossing my arms defensively.

"Then let me simplify it for you," he said, desperation creeping into his voice. "I'm willing to lay everything out on the table—my past, my mistakes, everything. No more secrets."

There was something in his eyes, a flicker of vulnerability that tugged at my heart. It was like watching a man standing on the edge of a cliff, pleading with the universe not to fall. I could feel the turmoil within him, the weight of his own choices pressing down, and for a brief moment, I wanted to leap with him into the unknown. But doubt still gnawed at me, whispering that trust could be a dangerous game.

"Fine," I finally relented, the word escaping my lips before I could think better of it. "But don't think I'm going to make this easy for you. You want my trust back? You're going to have to earn it."

"Deal," Adam replied, relief flooding his features. "Let's go to the park—there's a spot I know where we can be alone."

Mia gave me a knowing look, her lips pressed together in a tight line, and I realized I was stepping into a territory fraught with peril. "I'll be right here if you need me," she said, standing up and giving me a gentle squeeze on the shoulder before heading for the door.

Adam and I made our way out into the cool evening air, the sun dipping below the horizon, casting a kaleidoscope of colors across the sky. Each step felt heavier than the last as the reality of what lay ahead settled in. A part of me wanted to turn back, to seek comfort in the familiar chaos of my apartment, but another part urged me forward, drawn to the man who had pulled me into this whirlwind of emotions.

As we arrived at the park, the atmosphere shifted, the buzz of city life fading into the background, replaced by the rustle of leaves and the distant laughter of children. The shadows lengthened around us, creating a cocoon of privacy where we could unravel the tangled threads of our lives.

"Here," Adam said, gesturing to a secluded bench beneath an old oak tree, its branches stretching protectively overhead. "This is where I used to come when I needed to think."

I took a seat, the wood cool against the backs of my thighs. Adam sat beside me, the space between us charged with anticipation. "So," I said, trying to inject some levity into the gravity of the moment, "is this the part where you confess your undying love and beg for forgiveness?"

He chuckled, but it was strained, a hint of tension in the way his shoulders squared. "I think we've established that I'm not great at love confessions."

"Let's hear your best shot," I urged, crossing my arms and leaning slightly forward, trying to mask the nervous energy coursing through me.

"Okay," he began, his voice steadying as he took a deep breath. "I don't want to make excuses for my mistakes. The truth is, I was scared—scared of losing you before we even had a chance to really start. I thought I could handle everything on my own."

"But you didn't handle it, did you?" I challenged, my tone sharp but with an undercurrent of curiosity.

"No," he admitted, the honesty hanging in the air like a fragile glass ornament. "I messed up. I thought I could clean up my mess before it affected you, but it's clear that I only made it worse."

"And what exactly are you planning to do now?" I asked, my voice softer but still edged with caution.

"I'm going to fight for us. For you. I don't want to hide anymore," he said, his gaze unwavering. "This may not be an easy road, but I promise to be here, to be honest. I'll do everything I can to make it right."

I studied his face, the lines of worry etched deeply across his brow. It was tempting to see the sincerity in his eyes, to lean into that desire for connection, but the shadows of doubt still loomed large. "And what if this is just the beginning of another lie?"

Adam reached out, his hand hovering near mine, hesitant yet hopeful. "I won't let it be. I'll show you."

Just as I was about to respond, a rustle nearby broke the moment, the sound cutting through the quiet of our conversation like a knife. We both turned, the instinctive reaction of two people suddenly on guard. There, hidden in the shadows, stood a figure—watching us. The fading light glinted off something metallic in the figure's hand, and my heart dropped as a rush of adrenaline surged through my veins.

"Who's there?" I called out, my voice ringing with a mix of fear and anger. The figure stepped closer, and recognition hit me like a slap to the face, leaving me breathless.

"Surprise," the voice said, low and dripping with menace. "Thought you could run away from me, Adam? You've got a lot of explaining to do."

The tension in the air thickened, wrapping around us like a tightening noose. I glanced at Adam, his expression shifting from hope to alarm, and I knew in that instant that whatever revelations lay ahead, they were about to take a sharp turn into darkness.

Chapter 10: "Running from the Truth"

The clang of the office door behind me echoed like a final note in a symphony, and I blinked against the harsh light of the overhead fluorescents, each flickering bulb a reminder of how stark my reality had become. I was ensconced in a sea of paperwork, endless spreadsheets sprawled across my desk like an unruly crowd at a concert, each demanding my attention yet offering no comfort. I forced my mind to focus on the minutiae of my job, drowning out thoughts of Adam with the rhythm of typing and the soft rustle of files. Each keystroke became a tiny rebellion against the turmoil simmering just below the surface.

Sipping my lukewarm coffee, the bitter taste curled my lips into a grimace, and I pushed the cup aside. It was a feeble attempt to keep the warmth within me, to stave off the chill of uncertainty that had seeped into my bones since the scandal broke. I glanced up at the clock on the wall, its ticking sound an unwelcome reminder of the minutes slipping by, each one tainted with memories of Adam—his laughter, the warmth of his hand on my back, the way he made me feel seen in a world that often left me feeling invisible.

The truth hung over me like a storm cloud, heavy and oppressive. I had thought I was strong, resilient, but that belief crumbled the moment I learned about his past. It was as if someone had flipped a switch in my mind, illuminating all the corners where I had tucked away my vulnerability. I had been so naive, believing in his honesty when all along he had been living a lie that had finally caught up with him. I couldn't shake the anger boiling within me, a cauldron of betrayal that bubbled over whenever I allowed myself to remember the conversations we'd shared, the dreams we'd spun together. It all felt like a cruel joke now.

"Hey, Mia, you good?" My colleague, Jenna, poked her head around my cubicle, concern etched into her features. Her blonde hair fell in soft waves around her shoulders, and her bright blue eyes, always so full of life, seemed dimmed by the gravity of my silence.

"Yeah, just swamped with work," I replied, forcing a smile that felt more like a grimace. "You know how it is."

She stepped closer, arms crossed as if to shield herself from my invisible wall. "You've been swamped for weeks. This isn't like you. Want to talk about it?"

Talk? About what? About how I'd given my heart to someone who didn't deserve it? About the way I had bared my soul to him, hoping for a connection that had turned out to be nothing more than a mirage? I shook my head, though I could feel the tightness in my chest loosening slightly at the prospect of sharing my burden.

"No, really. I'm fine," I insisted, perhaps a bit too forcefully. "Just a rough patch. I'll bounce back."

Jenna's eyes narrowed, the way they always did when she sensed something was off. "Bouncing back isn't usually your style. You're more of a face-it-and-deal-with-it person."

Her words hung in the air, and for a moment, I considered pulling back the curtain on my feelings. Maybe if I spoke them aloud, they wouldn't feel so insurmountable. But the fear of the vulnerability that would follow paralyzed me. Instead, I leaned into the pretense of normalcy. "Really, I just need to focus on my clients right now. They're what matters."

"Okay, but don't forget to take care of yourself too," she said, her voice softer now, like she was walking on eggshells. "You're important, Mia. Don't lose sight of that."

Her words struck a chord deep within me, and I nodded, hoping to dismiss her lingering concern. As she retreated, I sank back into my work, but the echo of her advice reverberated in my mind, a reminder of the self I was losing amidst my emotional retreat. I pulled up the client list, my fingers dancing across the keyboard, but my thoughts drifted. I wondered how Adam was handling everything. Had he been bombarded with questions? Did he regret his choices? Did he think of me at all?

Each question felt like a stab to the heart, and I grimaced as the office around me blurred into a haze of monotony. I wanted to forget him, to expel him from my life like a bad habit. Yet here I was, staring at my screen, as if I could summon him back into my world simply by wishing for it. A deep breath filled my lungs, but the air felt heavy with unshed tears, a tide threatening to wash over me at any moment.

The afternoon wore on, each hour dragging like the weight of a thousand pounds. I could almost feel the walls of my cubicle closing in, suffocating under the oppressive weight of unresolved feelings. My phone buzzed against the desk, jolting me from my reverie. I glanced down to see a message flashing on the screen—Adam's name illuminated in bright letters. My heart raced, an unwelcome thrill coursing through me.

"Can we talk?" it read, simple yet laced with desperation.

A part of me wanted to ignore it, to silence the ringing in my ears that his name always seemed to produce. But another part—the part that ached for closure—nudged me toward the inevitable. I hesitated, fingers hovering over the screen, battling the pull of curiosity against the wall of anger I had painstakingly built. The truth was, I wanted to know. I wanted to hear his side, even if it meant confronting the demons I'd been trying to outrun.

The phone buzzed again, this time a simple follow-up: "Please, Mia."

I swallowed hard, grappling with the mix of emotions flooding my senses. Here I was, caught in the web of my own making, tangled in feelings I had tried so hard to escape. With a deep breath, I typed back, "Where?" The decision was made. Whether it would lead to healing or further heartbreak, I was willing to find out.

As I pressed send, the walls around me shifted, and for the first time in weeks, the air felt charged with possibility.

The café on the corner had always been my refuge, a cozy nook filled with the aroma of roasted coffee beans and freshly baked pastries that whispered comfort into the depths of my soul. I arrived there with a mixture of trepidation and determination, the hum of chatter enveloping me like a warm blanket. It felt surreal to be sitting across from Adam, a man who had once felt so familiar but now seemed like a stranger draped in shadows of my disappointment.

As I settled into a worn leather chair, the plushness hugging me like an old friend, I watched him approach. He was dressed casually, a charcoal gray sweater hugging his form, the sleeves slightly pushed up to reveal strong forearms. A disheveled charm clung to him, like he'd just rolled out of bed, which made my heart clench in a confusing twist of longing and irritation. He looked up, those striking green eyes searching for something in mine. I steeled myself against the vulnerability that threatened to bubble over.

"Hey," he said, a hint of a smile breaking through the tension. It was the kind of smile that could have melted glaciers, but today, it felt like ice.

"Hey," I replied, keeping my tone light, even as my heart thudded heavily in my chest. "You look... different."

"Different good or different bad?" He chuckled, though it was more nervous than playful.

"More like 'I haven't showered in two days' different," I shot back, my voice dripping with sarcasm. The jab made me feel a little better, a flicker of control in this chaotic emotional landscape.

He winced, running a hand through his tousled hair. "Guilty as charged. It's been a week."

I nodded, the tension between us palpable. I wanted to ask how he could let things spiral so out of control, but I bit my tongue. Instead, I gestured to the menu board overhead, hoping to shift the focus. "You still like that horrible pumpkin spice latte, right?"

He smirked, the spark of mischief returning to his eyes. "I thought we agreed it was a guilty pleasure, not horrible."

"Guilty as charged again," I said, crossing my arms. "You're making it hard for me to hate you."

He laughed, and for a moment, the world faded away, leaving just the two of us suspended in that fleeting moment of lightness. But the laughter was brief, the heavy silence returning like an unwelcome guest.

"So," I began, my voice trembling slightly. "You wanted to talk."

His expression shifted, becoming serious, as if he were preparing to dismantle the wall I'd carefully constructed. "Yeah. I just wanted to say... I'm sorry. About everything."

I could feel the walls I had built crack under the weight of his sincerity. "Sorry doesn't really cut it, Adam."

"I know it doesn't," he admitted, his eyes searching mine for understanding. "But I need you to know that it wasn't what you think. I was trying to protect you."

"Protect me?" I scoffed, shaking my head in disbelief. "You think lying to me is protecting me?"

He leaned forward, his voice low, each word a delicate thread weaving through the air between us. "I didn't want you to see the side of me that I'm not proud of. I thought if I kept it from you, I could spare you the pain."

"Spare me the pain?" I repeated, incredulous. "You should have trusted me enough to let me decide what I could handle."

His frustration flickered like a candle in the wind. "You're right. But when you get caught up in something you regret, it's hard to be honest. I thought if I just buried it, maybe it would all go away."

"Buried it like a body?" I quipped, half-joking, though my heart was racing. The notion of secrets, of hidden pasts, wrapped around us like a thick fog.

He laughed softly, the tension easing just a fraction. "Yeah, like that. Except less murdery."

We shared a moment of levity, but it quickly dissolved, leaving a stark void in its wake. I pressed on, forcing myself to peel back the layers of our conversation. "But it didn't go away, did it? It blew up in your face and took me with it."

"I know," he said, his voice heavy with regret. "And I can't change that. But I want to try. I want to make it right."

"Make it right? How?" I challenged, arching an eyebrow. "By lying to me again? Because it seems like you're really good at that."

"I'm not asking for forgiveness," he replied, sincerity etched in every line of his face. "I'm asking for a chance to prove that I can be better. That I can be honest."

I sighed, the weight of his plea settling like lead in my stomach. "And how do I know you won't just—"

"Fall back into old habits?" he interjected, his voice steady. "You don't. But I want to show you I'm capable of change. I'm not the man you think I am."

"Then who are you?" I asked, my voice a whisper. "Because I don't know anymore."

He leaned back, as if the question had knocked the wind from him. "I'm a guy who made mistakes. A guy who thought he could keep his past buried and that it wouldn't come back to haunt him."

"What happens when it does? When it surfaces again? Am I supposed to just act like none of this ever happened?"

His gaze intensified, a fire igniting behind those emerald eyes. "No. You're supposed to tell me when I'm being an idiot. That's part of being in a relationship, right?"

I blinked, caught off guard by the straightforwardness of his statement. "A relationship? Is that what you think we have?"

He opened his mouth to respond, but the words faltered. The reality of the situation hung between us, heavy and foreboding. I could see the uncertainty pooling in his eyes, a reflection of my own hesitation.

"Look, I don't know if we can go back to what we had," I said, struggling to find the right words. "But I also can't pretend this isn't affecting me."

"Then let's take it one step at a time," he suggested, his voice a soothing balm against my anxiety. "No pressure. Just... let's be honest with each other. Starting now."

His offer lingered in the air, an enticing promise woven with threads of hope and fear. My heart pounded, the prospect of opening up again both thrilling and terrifying. Would I be strong enough to face whatever lay ahead, or would the shadows of the past swallow me whole?

In that moment, I realized that our paths had intertwined again, but the journey was far from over. The possibility of rebuilding was fraught with peril, yet it shimmered with the potential for something beautiful—a fragile hope hanging like a single dew drop on a spider's web, waiting for the sun to rise.

The air in the café had grown thick with an unspoken tension, the chatter of patrons a distant hum as Adam and I navigated the complex labyrinth of our emotions. I could feel the heat radiating off him, his presence both intoxicating and infuriating, like a rich dessert that promised delight but left a sickly aftertaste. With each moment, I weighed the precarious balance of trust and betrayal, wondering how it had all unraveled so quickly.

"So, one step at a time," he suggested, leaning forward with an earnestness that made my heart skip a beat. "Let's start fresh. I'll share the truth about my past, the whole ugly truth, and you can decide if it's worth salvaging."

I swallowed hard, my throat dry. "And if I find it's too ugly?"

"Then you walk away," he replied simply, as if that were the most straightforward thing in the world. "But I need you to know me. The real me."

His sincerity tugged at the remnants of my resolve, and I grappled with the idea of inviting his truth back into my life. "Fine. Go ahead. Lay it all out there."

Adam took a deep breath, and for a moment, I feared he might collapse under the weight of what he was about to reveal. "It's not just about the scandal, Mia. There's more." His voice was a low rumble, the kind that commanded attention.

"More?" I echoed, the word tasting bitter on my tongue.

"Before I met you, I was involved in a world I'm not proud of. A world of bad choices and worse consequences. I thought I could outrun it." He paused, the flicker of vulnerability in his eyes cutting through my defenses. "I got caught up in something dangerous. The kind of thing you only hear about in movies. I thought I'd left it behind, but it never really goes away, does it?"

"Dangerous?" My pulse quickened. "Are we talking about criminal activities, or are we taking this to the realm of comic book villains?"

He laughed softly, but the humor didn't reach his eyes. "More the latter. A group I got involved with was into some shady deals. I thought I was just making quick cash, you know? But I got in over my head. When I tried to back out, they didn't take it kindly."

"Adam, are you telling me you were a criminal?" My incredulity mixed with a strange sense of betrayal. "You could have been arrested! Why didn't you tell me?"

"Because I wanted to protect you! If you knew about my past, you would've run the other way." He leaned back, his hands running through his hair in frustration. "And I was just starting to feel like a decent guy. I didn't want to scare you off."

"Scare me off?" I shot back, the anger boiling up. "You thought lying to me would keep me safe? How is that supposed to work? You think I'm so delicate that I'd shatter into pieces if I heard the truth?"

"I know you're strong," he said, his voice dropping to a whisper. "But I've seen the other side, and it's ugly. I didn't want to expose you to that. You deserved better."

"Deserved better? That's rich coming from you," I retorted, the hurt spilling over. "You didn't even give me a chance to make that decision for myself!"

His gaze dropped to the table, and I could see the conflict etched across his face. "You're right. I messed up. But I'm trying to fix it. I've got my life back on track now. I swear it."

"Then what changed?" I asked, narrowing my eyes, sensing a deeper twist in his story. "If you're truly out, why are you here? Why didn't you just leave it all behind?"

A shadow passed over his expression, and I felt a chill race down my spine. "Because they won't let me. The people I thought I could trust? They're watching me. They know I'm trying to get away."

The café's noise faded into the background, and I leaned closer, my heart racing. "What do you mean they're watching you?"

"I've received threats," he admitted, the weight of his words sinking in like a stone in still water. "And now they know about you. I couldn't keep you away from this forever."

"Threats?" I whispered, my voice barely above a breath. "What are you saying? Are you in danger?"

He nodded slowly, the gravity of the situation settling like fog around us. "And now that you know... I need you to be careful. They don't play fair, and I won't let you get caught in the crossfire."

My mind raced, piecing together the fragments of his life that had once seemed so simple. "So, what are you going to do? Run again? Hide?"

"I don't know," he admitted, frustration etching lines across his forehead. "But I want to protect you. That's all that matters right now."

"Protect me?" I scoffed, disbelief mingling with anger. "Or protect yourself? You're good at that. Just like you were good at hiding everything else."

He looked up, the hurt flashing across his features. "Mia, please. I'm not asking for pity. I'm asking for your understanding. I can't change what I've done, but I can change who I am now."

"Understanding?" I spat. "What do you want me to do? Cheer for you as you attempt to outrun your past? This isn't some action movie, Adam. This is real life, and you're dragging me into your mess."

The noise around us resumed, people laughing and sipping their drinks, blissfully unaware of the storm brewing at our table. Adam reached for my hand, his grip firm yet tender, grounding me amid the chaos. "I know it's unfair. But I need you to believe I'm trying to make things right."

"By involving me?" I challenged, my voice wavering. "I don't want to be part of this."

"I can't lose you. Not now." The desperation in his voice sent a shiver down my spine, as if he were confessing a truth that reached far beyond the surface.

"I don't know if I can stay," I said, pulling my hand away, my heart racing. "You have to realize what you're asking of me."

"Just give me a chance," he pleaded, his green eyes searching mine. "I'll do whatever it takes to prove that I'm worth it."

Before I could respond, the café door swung open with a crash, and the chime of the bell was swallowed by a sudden hush. A tall figure stepped inside, silhouetted against the bright sunlight streaming through the door. My heart dropped as recognition washed over me—one of Adam's past associates, a ghost from his shadowy world.

The man scanned the room, his gaze settling on our table, and I felt a rush of fear pulse through my veins. "We need to go," I whispered urgently, my heart pounding in my ears.

Adam's expression shifted from desperation to alarm. "No, stay calm," he murmured, but the tension in his voice belied his words.

The man took a step forward, and I could feel the weight of his stare like a noose tightening around my throat. "Adam," he called out, his voice smooth yet menacing. "I think we need to have a little chat."

The café buzzed back to life around us, but all I could hear was the thunder of my own heartbeat as I gripped the edge of the table, the air thickening with uncertainty. Whatever Adam had been trying to shield me from was here now, and I had never felt more trapped.

Chapter 11: "A Broken Man"

The coffee shop buzzed with the soft murmur of conversations and the comforting scent of freshly ground beans, an aroma that typically ignited a spark of nostalgia within me. As I stepped inside, the bell above the door tinkled, its cheerful sound a stark contrast to the weight settling in my stomach. I had come to see Adam, a man who had made my heart race and my thoughts tumble like autumn leaves in a gust of wind. But today, he was a shadow of the man I remembered, and that shadow cast a long, unsettling presence over the warm café.

I spotted him in a corner, hunched over a small table, his fingers drumming an anxious rhythm against the wood. He looked up as I approached, and the intensity in his blue eyes held a vulnerability that took me by surprise. The confident veneer that usually accompanied him was stripped away, leaving behind a man who seemed almost fragile. The dim light caught the shadows under his eyes, and for a moment, I hesitated. This wasn't the Adam I had known; this was a man who bore the weight of unspoken burdens, and I felt a surge of empathy mingled with a deep-rooted instinct to protect.

"Thanks for coming," he said, his voice low and rough around the edges, as if it had been dragged across gravel. He gestured to the empty chair across from him, and I slid into it, acutely aware of the space between us, a chasm filled with everything we had lost and everything we had yet to say.

"Are you okay?" I ventured, the question hanging in the air, pregnant with unvoiced concerns. I knew the answer would be complex, layered like the intricate designs on the café's wallpaper, but I had to ask.

Adam leaned back, running a hand through his tousled hair, a gesture of frustration. "I don't know," he replied, letting the words fall between us like a brick. "I thought I had everything figured out. I had my career, my plans, and then..." His voice trailed off, and he stared at his coffee, dark and bitter, mirroring the turmoil within him. "Then I crashed. Hard."

I wanted to reach across the table, to bridge that distance, but something held me back—perhaps fear of what I might feel if I crossed that threshold, or maybe the understanding that some things were meant to be kept at arm's length. "You don't have to explain anything to me," I said softly, though the urge to know his truth gnawed at me. "But if you want to talk about it..."

He looked up then, and for a fleeting moment, a flicker of the old Adam shone through, one who could charm a crowd with his wit and warmth. "You always did know how to put me at ease," he said, attempting a smile that never reached his eyes. "I guess that's why I'm here. I need to face this, to stop running."

"Running from what?" I pressed, my curiosity igniting. It felt dangerous, uncharted territory, but part of me longed to dive into the depths of his despair, to uncover the roots of his suffering.

He hesitated, the silence stretching, heavy with implications. "From the truth," he finally admitted, his gaze dropping back to his coffee. "About who I really am. I've built my life on this facade—successful businessman, the charming guy everyone loves. But inside? It's a mess."

A mess. The word echoed in my mind, like a siren calling me closer. I had often wondered what lay beneath his polished exterior, the way he could walk into a room and light it up, yet leave without ever revealing the true man behind the mask. "What do you mean?" I asked, pushing gently, coaxing him to peel back the layers he so carefully guarded.

"I've been running from my past," he confessed, and in that moment, the air thickened with tension. "From mistakes I've made, people I've hurt. It's like trying to outrun shadows—they always catch up with you in the end."

His admission hung in the air like a storm cloud, dark and ominous. I leaned forward, drawn into his vulnerability, sensing the weight he carried. "Everyone has a past, Adam. It doesn't define you," I said, though uncertainty gnawed at my heart. Did I believe that? I wanted to, but the idea that the shadows could swallow us whole was a fear I recognized all too well.

He sighed, a deep, weary sound that resonated with something deep within me. "Maybe, but mine is a little darker than most. I had this... this idea that I could fix everything, that I could be perfect. And then I realized that I was just a broken man, trying to fit pieces together that didn't belong."

His admission felt like a confession, and I sensed a shift in the atmosphere around us. The café buzzed on, oblivious to our conversation, yet I was acutely aware of the world narrowing down to just the two of us, our shared space filled with unspoken truths.

"What happened?" I asked, my voice barely above a whisper.

"I thought I could control it," he said, his tone heavy with regret. "The business, my life... Even my feelings for you." He paused, and the weight of his words landed between us, palpable and raw. "I didn't want to care, to feel anything, because I was scared. Scared of losing it all."

I could feel the air crackle with tension, a charged atmosphere woven from the threads of our history, both beautiful and painful. "But you do care," I countered gently, urging him to embrace the truth that lay beneath his self-imposed armor.

He looked at me then, and for the first time, the flicker of hope ignited in those blue depths. "I do. But admitting it means facing everything I've tried to escape. It means letting you see me—really see me—and I'm not sure I'm ready for that."

The silence that followed his confession was almost deafening, a heavy blanket wrapping around us in the dim light of the café. I searched his face for something—an invitation, a hint of hope, perhaps even a glimpse of that charming smirk I had once found irresistible. But all I saw was a man laid bare, his defenses crumbling like the cookie crumbs left on the plate beside his untouched coffee.

"I want to help you," I said, my voice steady despite the turmoil inside me. It was a bold statement, perhaps even reckless, but the truth was that I was already invested. The idea of walking away was an easy one to conjure but a hard one to execute. The broken man in front of me was tethered to my heart in a way I hadn't fully acknowledged until this moment.

He sighed, a sound heavy with resignation, like the last breath of autumn before winter's chill sets in. "Help is a tricky word. I've spent my life believing I could handle everything on my own. Relying on anyone else... it feels like a betrayal to myself."

"That's the thing about life, Adam," I replied, leaning forward slightly. "You don't have to bear it all alone. Even the strongest people have moments when they need someone else to lean on."

His gaze dropped to the table, where the wood grain swirled like a stormy sea. "But what if I let you down? What if I ruin this, too?" There was a vulnerability in his voice that shook me to my core. It was rare to see a man like him—so used to being the captain of his own ship—admit that he could be unmoored by the very feelings he once dismissed.

"You already have, haven't you?" I shot back, my tone sharper than I intended. "You're ruining everything by not trying. If you let fear dictate your actions, you'll end up in the same place—always running, always hiding."

His eyes met mine, a flicker of defiance igniting in their depths. "You think it's that simple?"

"I think it's worth trying. Just once," I countered, feeling the heat of my own emotions rise. "This is the moment where you can either let the darkness swallow you or step into the light, however painful that might be."

Adam ran a hand through his hair again, the frustration evident in his every movement. "You make it sound like I'm standing on the edge of a cliff, ready to jump. What if I fall? What if I never get back up?"

The challenge in his eyes stirred something within me—a mix of determination and urgency. "Maybe falling isn't the worst thing that could happen. Maybe you'd find out how to soar." I leaned back, allowing my words to settle between us, hoping they would linger like the rich aroma of the coffee swirling in the air.

He opened his mouth to argue but then closed it again, a flicker of doubt crossing his features. The clock on the wall ticked away the moments, each second a reminder that we were still stuck in this tangled web of our own making.

"I want to believe you," he finally admitted, his voice barely above a whisper. "But I've spent so long trying to build a fortress. It feels impossible to dismantle it."

"Fortresses are meant to be taken down, brick by brick," I said, feeling a surge of hope as he considered my words. "It won't happen overnight, and it won't be easy. But you have to let someone in. Let me in."

A small smile flickered at the corners of his mouth, but it was fleeting, as if he was unsure whether he had the right to feel even that much. "What if I'm not worth the trouble?"

The question hung heavy in the air, almost like a dare. I wanted to scoff, to tell him how utterly ridiculous that idea was, but something in my gut twisted at the thought. "Who determines worth? You? Me? The world? We all have our flaws, Adam. What matters is what we do with them."

He shifted in his seat, clearly grappling with my words. The vulnerability in his eyes was unsettling but exhilarating. "And what if I'm just a mess?"

"Then you'd be like the rest of us," I replied, leaning in, our faces mere inches apart. "Perfectly imperfect. Isn't that the beauty of it all?"

He chuckled softly, a sound that sent a flutter through my chest. "You really have a way with words, don't you? You make it sound so romantic."

"Life is romantic if you let it be. Or it can be utterly mundane. Your choice." The challenge in my voice felt electric, sparking a conversation that could shift the very foundations of our relationship.

He leaned back, crossing his arms, a thoughtful look crossing his features. "I guess I've been stuck in the mundane for too long."

"Then let's break free. What do you say we start right now?" The challenge was out there, raw and unfiltered, just like our current moment.

He met my gaze, uncertainty mingling with a hint of resolve. "What do you have in mind?"

"Let's go somewhere. Anywhere but here. Let's shake off these cobwebs and see what life has to offer." The idea burst forth, unexpected and thrilling, my heart racing at the thought of us breaking free from the weight of our pasts.

Adam hesitated, the fear evident in his expression. "You're serious?"

"Completely. We can grab a bite, stroll through the park—something, anything. We need to find that spark again, the one that's been buried under all this heaviness."

He studied me, weighing the offer as if it were a fragile trinket in his hands. "And what if I can't find it? What if I'm just a liability?"

I leaned in closer, lowering my voice conspiratorially. "Then I'll take the risk. Besides, I like a challenge. And you, Mr. Hawthorne, are the most intriguing puzzle I've ever encountered."

He laughed then, a genuine laugh that felt like the first warm sunbeam breaking through a cloudy day. "You really are something else, you know that?"

"Don't change the subject," I teased, nudging him playfully. "So what do you say? Shall we venture out of this fortress you've built?"

He regarded me with a newfound intensity, as if he were weighing the gravity of the moment. "Okay. Let's do it. But only if you promise to keep up with me."

"Deal." The thrill of the unknown unfurled in my chest, and in that moment, as we stood to leave, I realized we were both stepping into uncharted territory—together.

We stepped out into the cool evening air, the café's warmth fading behind us like a memory unwilling to let go. I glanced sideways at Adam, who appeared both exhilarated and terrified, his posture slightly rigid despite the promise of adventure hanging in the air between us. The bustling street was alive with the sounds of laughter and chatter, street vendors calling out to passersby, and the distant thrum of music spilling from nearby bars. It was a world that thrummed with possibilities, and as we moved through the throng, I felt a flicker of hope kindling inside me.

"What do you have in mind?" he asked, his voice a mixture of curiosity and caution. The vulnerability still lingered in his eyes, but there was also a spark—a hint of the man I had once been drawn to so fiercely.

"Let's grab some tacos," I suggested, already scanning the crowd for the little food truck I had discovered last summer. "They have the best street tacos in the city, and trust me, nothing fixes a broken spirit quite like good food."

"Tacos, huh? You sure know how to seduce a man," he said with a wry smile, and for a moment, the tension between us melted, replaced by the easy banter that had once come so naturally.

"Is it working?" I shot back, feigning innocence. "Because I also happen to have a great playlist for our taco dinner. We could blast some tunes and dance right there in the street."

He chuckled, shaking his head. "Now that would be a sight. You dancing in the middle of a taco line while I stand awkwardly in the background."

"I'd be the star of the show," I declared, shrugging off his skepticism with a grin. "You might just get swept up in my brilliance."

With each step toward the food truck, I sensed Adam loosening up, the tension in his shoulders easing just a fraction. When we arrived, the air was thick with the scent of sizzling meat and spices, enticing and warm. I placed our orders, the rhythm of the bustling food truck staff creating a sense of camaraderie that added to the buzz of the evening.

"Two tacos al pastor and one carnitas!" I called out, my excitement bubbling over as I received the steaming paper-wrapped treats. Adam accepted his taco with a grin, and as we stepped aside to enjoy our haul, I couldn't help but feel a swell of triumph.

"This is pretty great," he admitted after taking a bite, his eyes widening in surprise as the flavors exploded on his tongue. "I didn't think I could feel this good again."

"See? The magic of tacos," I said, savoring the moment. "And good company. Let's not forget that."

He chuckled, and for a heartbeat, the weight of his past felt lighter, like the oppressive clouds had parted just enough to let the sun peek through. We wandered down the street, weaving through the crowd, the rhythm of our banter flowing effortlessly as we munched on our tacos.

"Okay, your turn," I said, leaning against a lamppost, the cool metal grounding me. "What's something I don't know about you?"

Adam paused, chewing thoughtfully. "Well, I can juggle."

I raised an eyebrow, intrigued. "You can juggle? Please, show me."

"Not here!" he laughed, glancing around as if he feared a taco-related mob might form. "What if I drop one? I'd never live it down."

"Okay, fine. But I'm still calling you out on this later," I promised, laughing as I took another bite. "Your secret juggling act is going to become a thing."

As we meandered through the crowd, a local musician began strumming a guitar on the corner, filling the air with soft melodies. I felt the music wrap around us like a warm blanket, urging me to let go of the past and live in the moment.

"Let's dance," I suggested impulsively, the music's cadence swirling through me.

Adam's eyes widened, and he held up his hands in mock surrender. "Wait, I'm not ready for that level of spontaneity! What if I step on your toes?"

"You can't dance worse than my ex," I retorted, taking his hand and pulling him toward the small gathering forming around the musician.

With the energy buzzing between us, he finally relented, and as we stepped into the circle, the world around us faded away. We moved to the rhythm, laughter bubbling up as we lost ourselves in the music. Adam's awkward attempts at rhythm soon gave way to a more comfortable ease, and I realized that this moment was something he desperately needed, just as much as I did.

After a few songs, our laughter rang out, mingling with the melodies, our worries dissipating into the cool night air. In that moment, he seemed lighter, freer, as if the fortress he had built around himself was crumbling, brick by brick.

"See?" I said, breathless from the dancing. "This isn't so hard, is it?"

"Okay, maybe you were right," he admitted, a sheepish smile spreading across his face. "But just so you know, I still think juggling is way cooler."

We exchanged playful jabs, each teasing word igniting sparks between us, but beneath the laughter lay an undeniable tension, a current of something deeper that both thrilled and terrified me.

The music wound down, and we stepped back, breathless and a little dizzy from both the dance and the connection that had unfurled between us. It was then that I noticed the figure watching us from a distance, his face partially obscured by the shadows cast from a nearby streetlamp. Something about him felt off, an unsettling presence that shifted the energy in the air.

"Who's that?" I murmured, glancing at Adam, whose expression turned serious, a shadow crossing his features.

"Let's just keep moving," he said, his voice low, an edge of urgency lacing through it.

"Adam, wait—"

But he had already grabbed my hand, tugging me away from the lively street corner, our laughter fading as the weight of his past pressed heavily upon him once again. I stole another glance over my shoulder at the stranger, a chill running down my spine as I tried to shake off the feeling of being watched.

"What's going on?" I asked as we rounded the corner, Adam's grip tightening on my hand.

"Nothing," he replied, though the tension in his voice betrayed him. "Just... it's complicated."

I felt the thrill of our earlier dance slip away, replaced by an unsettling sense of dread. "Complicated how?"

But before he could answer, the stranger stepped into our path, blocking our way. He was tall, with a dark hoodie pulled up over his head, his face obscured. "Adam," he said, his voice a low growl, heavy with menace.

In that moment, the world around us seemed to freeze, the air thick with anticipation as I realized that this encounter would either shatter everything we had just built or ignite a new kind of chaos.

Chapter 12: "Into the Darkness"

The air in Adam's apartment was thick with the scent of old books and something else, something electric that danced along the back of my neck. He stood in the middle of the room, a reluctant host, running his fingers through his tousled hair as if it might help him gather his thoughts. The late afternoon sun streamed through the half-drawn curtains, casting stripes of gold across the wooden floor, and I could see the dust particles swirling lazily in the warm light. It felt intimate yet fraught with tension, as if we were the only two souls left in a world suddenly too vast and empty.

"You don't have to share if you don't want to," I said softly, trying to keep my voice light despite the weight pressing down on us. Adam shifted his weight, leaning against the wall, the faded blue paint chipping under the pressure of his form. The flickering shadows played across his features, emphasizing the angles of his jaw and the shadow under his eyes that spoke of sleepless nights and burdens too heavy for one person to bear.

"I know," he replied, his voice barely above a whisper. "But if I don't talk about it, it'll fester. And I can't keep running from it." There was a vulnerability in his gaze that pierced through my defenses. I had spent so long guarding my heart, convinced that letting anyone in would mean inviting chaos. Yet here I was, wanting to tear down the walls, to let him bleed his truth into the room and make sense of the dark corners that lingered.

"Sometimes," I began, searching for the right words, "sometimes talking about it can be as hard as living it." I knew this truth from my own battles. The nights spent replaying memories like a broken record, each scratch on the vinyl more painful than the last. Adam's eyes held a hint of understanding, a flicker of recognition that told me he had traversed those shadows.

"Do you ever feel like you're drowning, even when you're surrounded by people?" His question hung in the air, a tangible weight that settled between us. I nodded slowly, remembering the moments when laughter felt like a foreign language and smiles became mere masks. "It's suffocating," I replied. "It feels like a fog that closes in, and you can't see the way out."

He inhaled deeply, and I could see the muscles in his shoulders tense, as if the act of breathing was somehow a struggle. "I can't remember when it started," he murmured, his eyes drifting to the window, where the sun dipped lower, casting a warm glow that felt bittersweet. "It's like I woke up one day, and the world was different. It felt... hostile."

The honesty in his words was disarming, and I felt a stirring of empathy that almost took my breath away. My heart raced at the thought of reaching out, of bridging the chasm between us, but I hesitated. What if my comfort only sunk him deeper into despair? Yet, I couldn't remain an observer; the urge to connect was a force I couldn't ignore.

"What happened?" The question slipped from my lips before I could second-guess myself. The weight of his past was heavy, but I sensed that this moment, however precarious, was crucial for both of us.

"I lost my father," he admitted, his voice cracking slightly. "He was my anchor, you know? After that, everything felt unmoored. I didn't know how to keep myself afloat."

His pain hung in the air, thick and palpable, and I wanted to wrap it in warmth, to soothe the sharp edges of his grief. I could feel a fierce protectiveness rising within me, a desire to shield him from the storms that had ravaged his heart.

"I'm sorry," I whispered, the sincerity of my words resonating through the stillness. "You don't have to carry that alone."

He met my gaze, a flicker of hope sparking amidst the darkness. "I don't want to burden you with my history. You deserve light, not shadows."

The irony hung between us, a taut thread of tension. "But light doesn't exist without shadows, does it?" I countered, my voice steady despite the tremor of uncertainty beneath it. "We all have our battles. It's what makes us human."

His expression softened, and I could see the walls he had built around himself begin to crack. "Maybe you're right," he conceded, allowing a small, hesitant smile to bloom. "It just feels easier to hide."

"But hiding doesn't help," I urged, stepping closer, drawn to him like a moth to a flame. "You're not alone anymore, Adam. You have me."

The declaration hung in the air, fragile and yet electrifying. I watched as he absorbed my words, his gaze intensifying. "You don't understand how dangerous that can be," he said, an edge of desperation creeping into his tone. "I could drag you down."

I laughed softly, a sound that seemed to cut through the tension, surprising us both. "Sweetheart, I'm no stranger to darkness. I've danced with it long enough to know the steps."

For a moment, we stood there, two wounded souls seeking refuge in the warmth of shared understanding. It was exhilarating and terrifying, like teetering on the edge of a precipice, wondering whether to leap or retreat. My heart raced at the thought of crossing that threshold into something more—a connection deeper than mere friendship, yet fraught with the potential for heartbreak.

"I don't want to drag you down," he repeated, his voice thick with emotion, but I could see the struggle within him, the desire to reach for something more. The delicate balance of hope and fear hung between us, waiting for someone to tip the scales.

"Maybe we both need to let go," I suggested, my heart pounding in my chest. "Let the darkness show us what we're truly made of."

As the sun sank lower, casting long shadows that danced across the floor, I felt the pull between us strengthen, a magnetic force that promised to unravel our carefully stitched lives. In that moment, I knew we were both standing on the brink, and whatever lay beyond was a leap of faith we would have to take together.

The silence hung between us like an unmade bed, the sheets tangled and the air thick with unsaid words. I could almost hear the heartbeats echoing in the stillness, mine thrumming with a mix of anticipation and anxiety. Adam's expression shifted, the soft flicker of vulnerability now mingling with something more resolute. It was as if he was weighing the gravity of his own emotions, balancing on a tightrope stretched taut between hope and despair.

"I've never talked about this before," he admitted, the admission tumbling out of him like a long-held breath. "It feels... risky." His voice was low, as if he were afraid that saying it out loud might shatter the fragile moment we'd created. "But I think I'm tired of pretending."

"Pretending is exhausting," I replied, my heart quickening. "The mask never really fits, does it?" I took a small step closer, emboldened by his openness. The space between us shrank, and I could see the shadows in his eyes lighten ever so slightly, revealing a hint of trust peeking through.

Adam chuckled softly, the sound mingling with a hint of bitterness. "I feel like I've worn so many masks that I might just be a collection of them at this point. Each one more ridiculous than the last." His lips curled into a wry smile, and for a moment, it was almost disarming. "I could start a museum."

"'The Museum of Emotional Disguises,'" I quipped, gesturing grandly as if unveiling a masterpiece. "I can see the headline now: 'A Cautionary Tale of Avoidance and Anxiety.'"

He laughed more freely this time, the sound genuine and rich, washing away some of the tension that had coiled between us. "Admission fee: your sanity."

"Or your ability to trust," I replied, a smirk dancing on my lips. "No refunds."

Our laughter filled the room, a buoyant sound that sliced through the previous heaviness, and in that moment, I felt a glimmer of something beautiful blooming between us. It was precarious, but undeniably real. The connection we forged was fragile as a soap bubble, shimmering with potential but susceptible to any sudden move that might send it crashing to the ground.

"What if I told you that the mask I wear most often is the one that convinces me I don't need help?" he mused, the smile fading into something contemplative. "It's a comfortable lie."

"Comfortable lies are the coziest," I replied, nodding in agreement. "Like curling up with a warm blanket on a cold night. But at some point, the blanket suffocates."

He glanced at me, surprise flickering in his gaze. "You really get it, don't you?"

"I've spent more time in that suffocating blanket than I'd like to admit," I confessed, my tone softening. "Sometimes, we convince ourselves we're fine, even when we're falling apart inside. It's easier to keep up appearances."

A contemplative silence settled over us, and I could see him wrestling with his thoughts, processing my words. "I've felt lost for so long," he finally said, his voice a mere whisper. "Like I'm wading through a river of murk and can't find the bank."

The image struck me, vivid and raw. "But every river has an end, Adam. And sometimes, we just need someone to help us reach the shore."

His gaze locked onto mine, a flicker of hope igniting in the depths of his eyes. "I want to believe that," he said, almost hesitantly. "But the fear of drowning keeps pulling me back."

"We're not alone in this," I reassured him, my heart aching for him. "We can be each other's life raft." The words felt bold, a promise hanging in the air, and I could sense the delicate weight of it all. We were stepping into the unknown, teetering on the edge of something profound.

His expression shifted, a mix of vulnerability and strength. "You really think we can help each other?"

"Absolutely," I affirmed, a smile tugging at my lips. "I'm a strong swimmer. Just look at how gracefully I dog-paddle through my own mess."

He chuckled, the warmth of the moment wrapping around us like a safety net. "I'd pay good money to see that."

"Careful," I said, raising an eyebrow teasingly. "You might end up on the guest list for my 'Museum of Emotional Disguises.'"

"Only if I get to curate the collection," he shot back, a playful glint sparking in his eyes.

For a heartbeat, we simply stood there, laughter lingering between us, illuminating the space like fireflies in the night. But just as quickly, a shadow flickered across his features, and the gravity of our conversation loomed once more.

"Why do I keep holding back?" he murmured, a hint of frustration in his voice. "It's like there's an invisible barrier I can't break through."

"Maybe it's time to shatter it," I suggested, my voice steady. "You deserve to let it go, Adam. You don't have to carry that weight alone. We can navigate the darkness together."

The determination in my voice surprised even me, but it felt right. He deserved someone who believed in him, someone who would walk beside him through the shadows. "We'll find the way out," I added, my heart racing at the thought.

"I want to believe you," he replied, searching my gaze. "But... what if it's too much?"

"What if it's not?" I countered, my voice unwavering. "What if this is the beginning of something beautiful?"

He paused, the tension hanging thick between us, and I could feel the stir of hope intertwining with fear. It was a dance neither of us had quite mastered yet, but the music was beginning to swell, a melody that promised change and connection.

"Let's find out," he finally said, his resolve firming.

"Together?" I prompted, holding my breath as I awaited his response.

"Together," he affirmed, a spark igniting in his eyes that made my heart skip.

In that moment, everything shifted. We were no longer two lost souls trapped in a cycle of pain; we were explorers venturing into uncharted territory, ready to face whatever awaited us on the other side. The darkness that had loomed so heavily began to dissipate, revealing a path illuminated by the flickering light of our shared vulnerability.

And as the evening deepened outside, wrapping the world in a cocoon of twilight, I knew we had taken the first step toward something that could change everything.

The atmosphere shifted like a sudden gust of wind, and with it, I felt a wild blend of exhilaration and fear. As I stood there, staring into Adam's eyes, I could sense the current of unspoken words bubbling just beneath the surface, ready to spill over. The flickering light from a nearby lamp cast a warm glow, illuminating the sharp contours of his face, but shadows still danced around the edges, reflecting the tumult within.

"Tell me about your dad," I urged gently, eager to keep the door we had opened ajar, to let the light spill in. "What was he like?"

Adam took a deep breath, and for a moment, I feared he would retreat, encasing himself once more in that protective shell. But then he exhaled slowly, a tentative smile ghosting his lips. "He was... larger than life. Like a walking adventure. He could make anything fun, even washing the car. He'd blast music and we'd dance around with soap suds on our hands."

I smiled at the image, picturing a younger Adam, carefree and laughing, caught up in the joy of those moments. "Sounds like he was quite the character."

"He was," he nodded, his gaze drifting into the distance as if he were plucking those memories from the air. "He had this infectious laughter that could light up a room. But when he passed..." His voice broke, and the warmth dissipated. "Everything fell apart. It was like watching a house of cards collapse."

I reached out, resting a hand on his arm, my touch a silent affirmation that he wasn't alone in this. "I can't imagine how hard that was. Losing someone so vital."

His eyes met mine, dark and deep, swirling with the kind of emotions that could either shatter or illuminate. "I was too young to understand. All I felt was this overwhelming emptiness. And now, I keep expecting him to walk through the door and tell me it was all just a nightmare."

There was a rawness in his admission that tugged at my heartstrings. "But it wasn't a nightmare," I whispered. "It was real. And facing it is the bravest thing you can do."

Adam swallowed hard, and I could see the conflict play out on his face. "I feel like I've spent my whole life trying to outrun that emptiness. I've chased after anything that would keep me distracted—work, people, even bad habits."

"Those distractions can feel like the best escape, but they're really just... illusions," I said, searching for the right words. "Like trying to fill a hole with sand. It never truly works."

His expression softened, and I felt the weight of the moment press down on us. "It's funny," he said, a wistful smile creeping back. "You and I, two people who've been hiding, now having a heart-to-heart."

"Maybe we're not hiding anymore," I replied, a surge of hope coursing through me. "Maybe we're finally allowing ourselves to be seen."

The tension between us morphed into something palpable, almost electric, like the air before a storm. He stepped closer, and the heat radiating from him sent my heart racing. "What if we let go of the past? Just for tonight?"

"Letting go is easier said than done," I said, my breath hitching.

"Maybe we don't have to let it all go. Just the parts that weigh us down," he suggested, his gaze unwavering. "Let's just be us. Here. Now."

His proposition hung in the air, rich with possibility, and I could feel my pulse quicken, my mind spinning with what-ifs. "Okay," I finally said, the word tumbling out like a confession. "Let's be us."

As if on cue, a soft melody began to play from the old record player in the corner, an unexpected serenade that filled the space with warmth and nostalgia. Adam's lips curled into a genuine smile, and I found myself matching it, our shared laughter mingling with the music. The weight of our previous conversations faded, replaced by the exhilarating spark of connection.

"See? Not so bad, right?" he said, and the ease of the moment wrapped around us like a comforting blanket.

"Not bad at all," I replied, my heart buoyant. "Just two lost souls sharing a moment."

But then the music shifted, and I noticed a shadow flicker behind him, almost imperceptibly. My heart lurched, and I leaned closer. "Did you see that?"

"What?" he asked, glancing over his shoulder.

"I thought I saw something move."

He frowned, the playfulness fading from his expression. "It's probably just the wind or..."

Another flicker caught my eye, this time more pronounced. I stepped back, my instincts flaring. "No, it wasn't the wind. It felt... intentional."

Adam's face hardened, his previous ease replaced with concern. "You sure?"

"Not sure of anything right now," I admitted, my voice trembling slightly.

Just then, a loud crash erupted from the kitchen, and we both jumped, adrenaline coursing through our veins. "What was that?" he whispered, the tension returning like an unwelcome guest.

"I have no idea," I replied, my heart racing.

He moved toward the door, his body coiled with an anxious energy. "Stay here," he instructed, his tone firm yet cautious. "I'll check it out."

"No way," I shot back, my resolve hardening. "I'm not hiding in here while you go out there."

His eyes met mine, a storm of emotions swirling beneath the surface. "It could be dangerous. I don't want you to get hurt."

"I'm not letting you face whatever that was alone," I insisted, stepping forward, our shoulders brushing together. "We're in this together, remember?"

The moment hung, thick with unsaid words and a rush of adrenaline that left my heart pounding. With a resigned sigh, he nodded, and we moved as one, crossing the threshold into the unknown.

As we tiptoed toward the kitchen, the atmosphere crackled with tension. Shadows danced menacingly in the corners, and I could feel the hairs on my arms standing on end. With each step, the sense of impending danger grew, a palpable force pressing against us.

Suddenly, a figure emerged from the shadows, backlit by the dim light of the kitchen. I gasped, my heart racing as I squinted to make sense of the silhouette. The intruder turned slowly, and as they stepped into the light, a gasp escaped my lips, one that echoed the rising panic in my chest.

Adam's hand tightened around mine, the warmth of his grip suddenly feeling like the only anchor in a storm. The intruder's identity crashed over us like a wave, and in that moment, everything I thought I knew shattered into fragments, leaving us teetering on the edge of something dark and dangerous.

Chapter 13: "Unraveling"

The rain fell in soft sheets, blurring the world outside my window into a watercolor dreamscape, colors bleeding into one another in a melancholic dance. I pressed my forehead against the cool glass, watching droplets race each other down the pane, my heart echoing the rhythm of their descent. Each one seemed to carry away a piece of me, dragging my thoughts deeper into an abyss I was desperate to escape.

Inside, the scent of wet earth mingled with the lingering aroma of the jasmine tea I had made earlier, its warmth offering a false sense of comfort. I closed my eyes, inhaling deeply, but the familiar fragrance only served as a reminder of how things used to be—before I found myself entwined with Adam, before my world tilted off its axis.

Adam. Just saying his name sent a jolt through me, like a double shot of espresso in the morning. His essence wrapped around me, sweet yet bitter, intoxicating and overwhelming. I could almost hear the soft timbre of his voice as he mused about the universe's secrets or the way he'd laugh, a sound like wind chimes in a summer breeze, lifting my spirits yet leaving them suspended in uncertainty. But as his laughter faded, the shadows crept in, and the laughter morphed into silence, echoing through the vast chasm of our shared existence.

I turned from the window, away from the storm that mirrored the tempest inside me. The living room was a mess, scattered with remnants of half-finished projects and forgotten ambitions. Sketchbooks lay open, their pages crammed with designs that had once promised hope and creativity. Now they were a graveyard of aspirations, as lifeless as the wilted flowers that sat in a vase on the table. I glanced at the clock on the wall—its hands moved with a mockingly slow grace, reminding me that time didn't wait for anyone, especially not for those who were lost.

Pulling my sweater tighter around me, I made my way to the kitchen. The clattering of my ceramic mug against the countertop broke the silence, an uninvited sound in the stillness of the afternoon. I absentmindedly fished a spoon from the drawer, stirring the dregs of tea, each swirl mirroring my own chaotic thoughts. What was I doing?

I used to believe that love could be a panacea, that it could mend what was broken and heal wounds that ran deep. I thought that I could fix him, thought that my unwavering support could serve as the balm he needed. But with each passing day, the reality crashed down harder. The more I reached for him, the more I felt myself slipping away. I was unraveling, thread by fragile thread, until I was a tattered remnant of who I once was.

My phone buzzed, a single notification lighting up the dim kitchen. I hesitated, but curiosity got the better of me. I picked it up, fingers trembling slightly as I glanced at the screen. A message from Adam. My heart fluttered—then sank. It was simple: "Can we talk?"

A sigh escaped my lips, heavy with the weight of unspoken words. Every time we talked, it was a dance of delicate footwork, each step calculated, each misstep threatening to lead us into deeper chaos. I knew I should've ignored the message, should've tucked my phone back into my pocket and walked away from the looming storm. But I was drawn to him, like a moth to a flame, despite the burns I had endured before.

I typed back, fingers flying over the keys. "Sure. When?" A fleeting moment of apprehension washed over me as I hit send.

His reply was swift. "Now?"

With a deep breath, I looked around the chaos that was my living space, wondering if it was worth tidying up before he arrived. But deep down, I knew it was futile. The mess reflected the turmoil in my heart; cleaning would only mask the reality. I was a disaster, and he was just as broken.

When he arrived, the air thickened with unspoken tension. The door creaked open, and there he stood, a silhouette framed against the overcast sky, the soft light haloing his tousled hair. He looked as if he had been caught in the rain, droplets clinging to his skin, and for a moment, I forgot all the jagged edges of our relationship.

"Hey," he said, his voice low, a mixture of warmth and vulnerability that shot straight through my defenses. I wanted to reach out, to pull him into an embrace, but instead, I stood rooted to the spot, the ache of longing battling with the need for self-preservation.

"Hey," I managed, forcing a smile that felt more like a mask than a greeting. "You look... wet."

He chuckled softly, the sound like a soft melody cutting through the heaviness in the room. "Guess the weather had other plans."

We settled into the living room, the unkempt state of my life hanging between us like a fragile thread. I poured him a cup of tea, the steam curling upwards like whispers of the past, each swirl beckoning memories both sweet and bitter. "So, what's up?" I asked, hoping to steer the conversation away from the inevitable darkness that always seemed to creep in.

Adam ran a hand through his hair, a nervous habit that tugged at my heartstrings. "I've been thinking a lot... about us."

There it was, the proverbial elephant in the room, waiting to be addressed. I swallowed hard, my heart racing as I waited for the words to tumble out of his mouth like stones from a crumbling wall. The air felt electric, thick with the anticipation of change, and for the first time in a long while, I was afraid of what came next.

The silence stretched between us, thick with anticipation, a delicate thread teetering on the edge of fraying. Adam shifted on the couch, his gaze flickering to the window, where the rain continued its relentless assault. The soft patter seemed to echo the rhythm of my heart, thudding against my ribs like a drummer urging me to take action, to respond. I could see the words simmering just below the surface, a storm brewing in his chest that mirrored the tempest outside.

"Okay, let's not beat around the bush," I said, my voice lighter than I felt, as if I could banish the tension with a simple gesture. "What about us?"

His eyes met mine, a gaze heavy with emotion, and I could almost feel the weight of his thoughts crashing against the fragile barriers we'd built. "I think..." he began, then hesitated, running a hand through his hair again, the gesture both charming and maddening. "I think we've been avoiding the real conversation for a while now."

"Real conversation?" I echoed, trying to keep my tone playful, but the words dripped with an edge of anxiety. "Are we talking about the weather, or the state of my plant collection? Because let me tell you, I've got some serious horticultural issues going on in that corner over there."

A reluctant smile broke through the tension, his lips curling up just enough to remind me why I was still here. But it faded quickly, replaced by that familiar seriousness that had taken up residence in his demeanor. "I mean us, Charlie. What we are. What we've become. I can't keep pretending everything's okay when it's not."

My stomach flipped, an unwelcome feeling creeping up from the depths of uncertainty. I had been playing the game, trying to convince myself that we could hold onto something solid, that if we worked hard enough, we could piece together the shattered remains of what we once had. "Are you saying we're broken?"

He ran a hand over his face, frustration etched in the lines of his forehead. "No, not broken. Just... bent, maybe? A little crooked? I don't want to drag you down with me, and I fear that's exactly what I'm doing."

The honesty in his words hit me like a slap, invigorating yet painful. I couldn't deny that his struggles weighed heavily on me, like a stone in my pocket that I insisted on carrying around despite the toll it took on my spirit. "You know I'm not going anywhere, right? I'm stubborn that way."

"I know," he said softly, and for a brief moment, vulnerability flickered in his eyes. "But it's not fair to you. You're working so hard to hold everything together while I—" He broke off, his voice trailing into a whisper. "I'm falling apart."

I felt a pang of empathy twist inside me, but I pushed it down, determined not to let despair take root. "We all have our moments, Adam. I can't pretend to be perfect either. I'm just as lost as you are." The admission hung in the air, vulnerable yet liberating, and I held my breath, waiting for him to process my truth.

"What if we just—" he started, then paused again, contemplating the delicate nature of what he was about to say. "What if we took a break? A little time apart to figure ourselves out?"

A pause so thick I could almost choke on it. "A break?" The word tasted foreign on my tongue, an unwelcome guest at our already strained gathering. "You mean like a trial separation? Is that what you're suggesting?"

He nodded, his gaze unwavering. "It's not what I want, but it might be what we need. I don't want to drag you down with me, Charlie, and I can't bear the thought of suffocating your light."

I sat back, the weight of his words pressing down on me. "So, you think stepping away will magically fix everything?" I tried to keep the bitterness from seeping into my voice, but it slipped through the cracks, sharp and unsettling. "Isn't that running away? From me? From us?"

"I'm not running. I just think we're at a crossroads." The resolute tone in his voice made it clear he had thought this through. I hated that he was right, that I could see the sense in what he was saying, even as it twisted my insides into knots.

"I thought love was about standing together through the storms, not retreating to different shelters," I countered, my words a thin veil over the rising tide of emotion. "What happens when the storm ends? Do we just come back together like nothing happened?"

"I don't want it to end," he said fiercely, leaning forward as if the intensity of his desire could bridge the gap between us. "But maybe the only way we can truly find ourselves again is by being apart for a while. It doesn't have to be forever."

The honesty of his proposal gnawed at my heart, a cruel twist of fate. I hated the idea but couldn't shake the sense that there was a flicker of truth in his logic. "And what if we find out we're better off without each other?"

"Then at least we'll know," he said, his voice almost a whisper, the weight of his confession settling like dust in the air around us. "We need to be honest with ourselves, and that might mean painful decisions."

I closed my eyes, letting the tears I had held at bay slip free, each drop a tiny relief that mingled with the rain outside. "This hurts, you know. More than I expected."

"I know," he replied, his voice thick with emotion. "But staying in something that feels broken just to avoid the pain might hurt more in the long run."

As the rain drummed against the window, I felt a bitter taste in my mouth. The idea of separation was a jagged pill to swallow, a cocktail of confusion and longing. I didn't want to let go, but deep down, I sensed the truth he spoke—it resonated with a haunting clarity.

"Okay," I whispered finally, as if the word itself was an incantation, sealing our fate with the softest of sounds. "If this is what we need... then I guess we take that step."

His expression softened, and I could see the relief wash over him, but it was tinged with sorrow. "I'll always care about you, Charlie. No matter what happens."

"And I you," I replied, but even as the words left my lips, I felt the gnawing fear of what might come next, the uncertainty wrapping around us like the rain, relentless and cold.

The echo of my admission hung in the air like the remnants of a storm, palpable and heavy. Adam's gaze was locked on mine, a tempest of emotions swirling within those hazel depths. I wished I could look away, but there was a magnetic pull that held me in place, even as uncertainty gnawed at my insides. The corners of his mouth twitched, a shadow of a smile, but it only deepened the chasm between us.

"So... we're really doing this?" he finally said, a lopsided grin breaking through the tension, though his eyes betrayed a deeper apprehension. "We're officially putting ourselves on a shelf?"

I scoffed lightly, trying to hide the tremor in my voice. "More like putting ourselves in storage. You know, that back corner of the attic where you shove old boxes and hope to forget about them for a while."

"Ah, yes, the dusty corner of forgotten dreams." He leaned back, crossing his arms as if contemplating a universe of possibilities. "Maybe we can leave a note for future us. 'Hey, if you ever decide to open this box, things got messy but you were better for it!'"

I couldn't help but laugh, a sound that felt foreign in the weighty atmosphere. "And what if future us just laughs and tosses it back into the abyss?"

"Then we'll know we were fools. But hey, fools with a great story, right?" His attempt to lighten the mood sent a flicker of warmth through me, a reminder of the humor that had once knitted us together.

A moment passed, thick with memories that danced at the edges of my mind—late-night coffee runs, stolen kisses under the stars, and laughter that filled every crevice of my life with joy. Yet, the shadows lurked, the reminders of the hurt that had seeped in like ink stains on a favorite shirt. "What if I miss you?" The question slipped out before I could hold it back, vulnerable and raw.

"Then you can always call me," he replied, a hint of seriousness creeping back into his voice. "I'll be around. Just... not here. Not in this space."

I nodded, my heart twisting. I wanted to be strong, to stand tall amidst the uncertainty, but the thought of distance felt like a dark cloud settling overhead. "Okay. I guess we should just... live our lives, then?"

"Sounds like a plan." His smile was bright but fleeting, a flicker of the light we had always shared, and I couldn't shake the feeling that something essential was slipping away.

The rain had tapered off outside, leaving a lingering dampness in the air, and I watched as the clouds reluctantly parted, revealing the soft glow of the evening sky. The moment felt surreal, as if the world was holding its breath, waiting for the outcome of our decision. "I just wish things were easier," I murmured, staring out into the fading light.

"Don't we all?" he replied, his voice low, the weight of unspoken emotions hanging heavily in the air. "But sometimes, taking a step back is the only way to find clarity."

"I hope clarity comes with a side of happiness," I said, attempting to keep the mood light, even as the gravity of our situation bore down on me.

He stood, hands shoved into his pockets, an uncertain smile dancing on his lips. "Well, if it doesn't, we'll just have to throw a grand reunion party to celebrate our enlightenment."

"Just make sure there's cake. A lot of cake," I shot back, desperate for levity.

"Cake and questionable dance moves," he promised, and in that moment, I could see a glimpse of the old Adam—the carefree spirit who danced through life like it was a never-ending party. But beneath that was the darker truth, the fear of the unknown looming like a shadow at the edges of his smile.

"I'll hold you to that," I replied, a bittersweet smile tugging at my lips.

As the evening deepened, we shifted into a comfortable silence, the kind that envelops you in a cocoon of familiarity. Yet beneath it lurked the unspoken heaviness of what lay ahead. I could sense the clock ticking down the minutes until we would have to confront the inevitable.

"Do you want to talk about anything else?" he finally asked, breaking the quiet, a softness returning to his voice.

"Like what? How I'm definitely going to burn my toast for breakfast tomorrow? Or how my plants are staging a coup in the corner because I've neglected them?"

"Let's go with the toast. It's not a good breakfast if it doesn't come with a side of disaster," he joked, a spark of mischief lighting his features.

"Exactly! I can picture it now: 'Burnt toast and existential crisis, the breakfast of champions!'"

"Now that's a breakfast I'd love to be a part of," he laughed, his eyes lighting up with a playful glimmer that made my heart ache.

But then, a knock at the door shattered our lighthearted moment, a sudden intrusion that sent a ripple of tension through the air. We both turned toward the sound, the laughter evaporating like mist.

"Who could that be?" I asked, feeling a sense of foreboding creep into my chest.

Adam shrugged, but there was a hint of concern in his expression. "Should we check?"

"Do we have a choice?" I replied, standing up and moving toward the door, my heart racing with an instinctive sense of dread.

As I reached for the handle, the weight of uncertainty pressed heavily on my shoulders, the room pulsating with an electric tension that felt almost palpable. With a deep breath, I swung the door open, and the world outside collided with my senses.

Standing before me was a woman, her hair wild and damp from the lingering rain, eyes wide with urgency. "Charlie! I need your help!"

The moment hung suspended in time, and I glanced back at Adam, confusion etched across his face. The storm outside seemed to pale in comparison to the tempest of emotions brewing in that instant. I opened my mouth to ask what was happening, but the words vanished, leaving me unmoored and bewildered.

And then, just as quickly as the moment arrived, the realization crashed down like thunder: everything I had been trying to untangle, everything I thought I understood, was about to shift yet again.

Chapter 14: "The Breaking Point"

The penthouse was as stunning as ever, its panoramic windows revealing a twinkling cityscape beneath a star-studded sky. Yet, within those lavish walls, the air felt heavy, almost electric, charged with an energy that could ignite at any moment. Adam stood across the room, his silhouette outlined by the soft glow of the city lights, and even in his tailored suit, he seemed more like a caged animal than the charismatic man I had fallen for. I could feel the weight of his gaze, a palpable heat that bore down on me, yet I couldn't meet it. I was lost in my own turmoil, wrestling with a whirlwind of emotions that had been swirling inside me for weeks, perhaps even longer.

"Do you even hear yourself?" he asked, his voice low, almost a growl. The frustration dripped from his words like honey gone sour. "You're so quick to blame me for everything. It's exhausting."

Exhausting. It was an innocuous word, yet it hung in the air like an uninvited guest. I took a deep breath, the scent of cedar and something floral mingling around me, a stark contrast to the storm brewing inside. "I blame you?" I shot back, each word sharp, slicing through the tension. "You have no idea what I'm feeling! You're too busy building your empire, leaving me behind like yesterday's news."

His expression shifted, hurt flickering in his eyes before he masked it with a cool indifference. "I'm working for us, Olivia. Everything I do is for us."

The term "us" felt like a phantom—haunting and elusive. It was supposed to represent a partnership, a shared dream, but lately, it had started to feel like a gilded cage, beautiful on the outside but suffocating on the inside. I pressed my palms against the sleek granite countertop, steadying myself, as if the coolness could dampen the heat of our argument.

"You don't get it. You're so wrapped up in your success, in your world, that you've forgotten I exist. It's like I'm just... there, a prop in your perfect life." Each word was a stone, heavy and deliberate, as I fought to keep the tremor from my voice.

"Is that really what you think?" He took a step closer, the distance between us fraught with unsaid words and a chasm of miscommunication. "You're my whole world, Olivia. I love you."

The admission fell between us like a flash of lightning—stunning, bright, and ultimately destructive. I felt the air leave my lungs, and for a moment, I was paralyzed, the weight of his words pulling me under. Love. It should have been a comfort, a balm for the raw edges of our conflict, but instead, it left me feeling adrift, suspended in a reality that felt increasingly surreal.

"Do you?" I whispered, more to myself than to him. "Do you really love me, or is it just another thing to check off your list? 'Be in a relationship, make partner by thirty, love the girlfriend'?" The sarcasm dripped from my tone, bitter and sharp, but I couldn't help it. It was easier to lash out than to admit that I craved his love, that it was the one thing I yearned for more than anything else.

He flinched at my words, a crack in the armor he wore so well. "You think I would treat you like that? You think I would use you as a means to an end?" The hurt in his voice echoed in the vastness of the room, reverberating against the walls that seemed to close in around us.

"I don't know what to think anymore!" The words burst from me, a dam breaking under pressure. "I feel like I'm losing myself in your shadow. You have everything figured out, and I'm just... floundering." The tears came then, unbidden, a rush of saltwater that stung as it fell. I wiped at them angrily, as if I could erase the moment, the admission, the sheer vulnerability of it all.

And then, as if the world had tilted on its axis, Adam did something I never expected. He stood there, his expression shifting from anger to something softer, a confusion that mirrored my own. He didn't reach for me, didn't try to pull me back from the precipice of my despair. Instead, he just watched, his eyes wide and uncertain, as I fell apart.

"I can't keep pretending everything is fine when it's not," I sobbed, my voice breaking. "You can't expect me to just sit back and smile while you climb the ladder of success. I have dreams too, Adam!"

Silence enveloped us, thick and suffocating. I could hear the city outside, the distant honk of cars, the faint sound of laughter wafting in from a nearby bar. Life continued, oblivious to our struggles, to the tempest raging between us.

And when the storm finally subsided, when I was left gasping for breath, he stepped forward. "Olivia," he began, his voice low and steady, cutting through the remnants of my anger. "I love you. And I want you to tell me what you really want, because I can't do this without you."

His words were like a lifeline thrown into turbulent waters, but I hesitated. What did I want? The answer felt elusive, dancing just beyond my reach. Instead of clarity, I felt only a gnawing fear that clawed at my insides. I opened my mouth, but the truth was tangled, a jumbled mess of hopes and fears.

I wanted him to hold me, to assure me that I mattered, that my dreams weren't lost in his ambitions. I wanted to scream that I was scared, terrified of losing myself completely. But instead, I remained silent, caught between the weight of his love and the gravity of my insecurities.

And then, when I thought my heart couldn't take any more, he stepped closer, the distance shrinking until his warmth enveloped me. "Tell me, please," he urged, his breath brushing against my cheek, and in that moment, I could feel the tether that bound us both.

Yet, even in that intimacy, I felt the fraying of our connection, the unsettling realization that our love, once vibrant and unwavering, was now walking a tightrope, teetering dangerously above the abyss.

The air felt electric as I stood there, a jumble of raw emotions swirling within me. Adam's eyes searched mine, reflecting confusion mingled with an earnestness that both soothed and unsettled me. I wanted to reach for him, to melt into the familiarity of his arms, but a part of me was terrified of what that embrace might mean. Would it be a simple reconciliation, or would it be an admission that I was willing to bury my own needs once more beneath his ambitions?

"Olivia, I know things have been tough," he said, his voice now steady and laced with a calmness that contrasted with the chaos in my heart. "But I promise I'll make time for you. We can figure this out together."

I bit my lip, uncertainty coiling tighter around my chest. "Together," I echoed, tasting the word on my tongue like a sweet but unfamiliar treat. "Is that how it feels to you? Because it hasn't felt that way for a long time."

The flicker of hurt in his eyes made my heart twist. I hated causing him pain, yet it was hard to ignore my own wounds, the scars that had formed from feeling invisible next to his towering ambition. It was as if I were standing in the shadow of a magnificent skyscraper, beautiful but cold, while I languished in its darkness.

"Just... talk to me," he urged, stepping closer, the warmth radiating from him like a beacon. "I can't fix it if I don't know what's broken."

I hesitated, every instinct telling me to just spill it all out, to lay bare my fears and frustrations. But vulnerability was a tricky beast, one I had rarely tamed. Instead, I turned away, pacing the sleek marble floor, my mind racing. "You don't get it," I said, my voice rising again as I struggled to find the words. "I feel like I'm suffocating in your world, Adam. I need to breathe. I need to know that I'm more than just a part of your life's decor."

"Life's decor?" he repeated, incredulous. "Is that really how you see yourself? As just... an accessory?" The disbelief in his tone made me flinch, but I pressed on, my pulse quickening.

"Yes! No! I don't know! It just feels like I'm in this constant dance, following your lead while my own music plays quietly in the background." I ran a hand through my hair, frustration bubbling to the surface. "I want to be a part of your world, but I also want to carve out my own space. Is that too much to ask?"

His brow furrowed as he absorbed my words. "I thought we were doing this together. I thought you were happy with how things were."

"Happy?" I laughed, the sound bitter and sharp. "Happy is a light that flickers, Adam. One gust of wind, and it's gone. I need something solid, something that doesn't vanish when the wind picks up." I turned to face him, determination filling my chest. "You've built a life—an amazing one, no doubt—but I can't be the only one making sacrifices. I need to see that you're willing to meet me halfway."

As the silence hung between us, I watched the conflict play out on his face. "So what do you want?" he asked finally, his tone cautious, as if he were testing the waters of a deep and uncertain sea.

"I want to feel valued," I said, my voice dropping to a near whisper. "I want to chase my dreams without feeling like I'm holding you back. I want to know that I matter just as much as your next business deal."

"Then let's make that happen," he replied, his sincerity almost palpable. "What if we scheduled regular 'us' time? I'll block it out on my calendar if I have to. No phones, no work—just us. We can go on adventures, try new things. I'll meet you in the middle."

I felt a flicker of hope ignite, a warmth that was long overdue. "You really mean that?"

"Of course," he replied, a faint smile breaking across his face, and the tension between us began to thaw, replaced by a cautious optimism. "And I can't imagine my life without you in it. So tell me what your adventure looks like."

I paused, the weight of his question settling over me like a gentle fog. "I've always wanted to see the Northern Lights," I confessed, my voice barely above a whisper. "It's been on my bucket list forever, but I've never had the courage to chase it. Maybe it sounds silly, but I want to stand beneath the sky and just... be. Feel small and magnificent all at once."

"Then let's go," he said without hesitation, the spontaneity of his words shocking me. "I'll take you wherever you want to go. I'll make it happen."

The rush of excitement mingled with disbelief. "You're serious? Just like that?"

"Just like that," he affirmed, his grin widening as he stepped forward again, closing the gap between us. "I want to be the person who makes your dreams come true, just like you've made mine."

"Wow, you're really laying it on thick," I teased, half-laughing, half-reeling from the unexpected promise. "What's next? Are you going to serenade me under the stars?"

"Only if you promise to sing along," he replied, his eyes glinting with mischief.

The lightness that settled around us felt like a soft blanket, warming the edges of our earlier confrontation. I couldn't help but smile, the tension slowly unfurling into something more manageable.

As our laughter danced through the air, the gravity of the past lingered, but it began to feel less like a burden and more like a stepping stone. We were standing at the edge of a precipice, and I could sense the potential for change.

Then, as if summoned by the magic of the moment, his phone buzzed on the counter, a jarring reminder of the world outside our intimate cocoon. He glanced at the screen, the humor in his expression vanishing. "It's work," he said, frustration etching his features. "I should probably—"

"No," I interrupted, my heart racing. "Let it wait. Just for a moment. We can't let everything intrude on this."

He hesitated, his hand hovering over the device, torn between duty and the fragile intimacy we were rebuilding. I held his gaze, imploring him to choose us, if only for a moment longer.

"I want to hear you promise that you'll prioritize this, that you won't let your world push us apart again," I urged, the vulnerability in my voice surprising even me.

"Okay," he said finally, his fingers hovering just above the screen. "I promise. No more distractions. Just us."

With a nod, he silenced the phone, and I felt a small victory ripple through me. It was a step—a small one, perhaps—but one that pointed toward the future we could build together. As he returned to my side, I reveled in the warmth of his presence, the uncharted path ahead shimmering like the lights of the city below, a promise waiting to be fulfilled.

The quiet that followed Adam's promise settled like a soft blanket over the chaos that had erupted just moments before. My heart thudded in my chest, caught between the urgency of his words and the weight of everything left unsaid. He reached out, hesitating just a moment before brushing his fingers against mine, a tender gesture that felt both like a lifeline and a silent agreement.

"Can we take this one day at a time?" I asked, my voice a mere whisper, unsure of what tomorrow would bring. "I don't want to overpromise and underdeliver. Let's just... be present, together."

"Absolutely," he replied, his eyes warm and serious. "No more distractions, I swear. We'll start right now."

With that, he turned away from the world outside, leading me toward the living area, the soft glow of the city casting shadows that danced across the walls. I could feel the tension loosening its grip on my shoulders, the weight of the world beginning to lift just a little.

He pulled out a small box from a nearby cabinet, his grin reappearing like the sun breaking through clouds. "You remember our first date? You ordered that fancy cheese platter, and I tried to impress you with my knowledge of wine. Spoiler alert: I still don't know anything about wine."

I chuckled, a warmth spreading through me as memories of that night flooded back. "You paired it with a Pinot Grigio when it should have been a Merlot. I knew nothing about wine either, but it didn't matter."

He laughed, and the sound was like music, a refreshing note in a symphony of uncertainty. "Right? But that cheese? It was a travesty. I'm still not sure how I survived it."

I leaned into his playful banter, feeling lighter than I had in days. "And yet you still asked me out again. How brave of you."

"Or foolish," he shot back, his eyes twinkling with mischief. "But the truth is, I was captivated. I wanted to learn everything about you."

He opened the box, revealing a collection of gourmet cheeses, carefully arranged like a beautiful tableau. "So tonight, we're recreating that first date, but this time, I did a bit of research."

My heart warmed at the effort he'd put into this moment. "Is that your way of saying I get to pick the wine this time?"

"Only if you promise not to roll your eyes at my choices," he said, feigning a dramatic pout.

"Oh, no promises there. I'm a wine snob now." I grinned, pretending to inspect the cheeses like a connoisseur. "But it all looks amazing, Adam. Thank you for this."

As we shared laughter over our makeshift picnic on the sleek, modern coffee table, I could feel the bond between us mending, stitch by stitch. The worries about the future, the doubts about our relationship, began to fade in the warmth of shared memories and culinary exploration. Yet, even amidst the lightness, a persistent flutter of anxiety remained in the back of my mind, whispering warnings that I couldn't fully ignore.

"Okay, I'm going to pour us some wine," he said, standing and heading toward the kitchen. I watched him go, admiring the way he moved with purpose, the confidence that surrounded him. Yet beneath that surface, I felt the familiar stirrings of doubt. Did I really have the strength to face the challenges ahead?

While he rummaged through his cabinets, I took a moment to gather my thoughts. The conversation from earlier loomed in the corners of my mind—could we really navigate this new terrain? My heart longed for stability, yet a part of me remained skeptical.

"Here we go!" he announced, reentering the living space, two glasses of wine in hand, a proud smile on his face. "I went with a Syrah. A little bold, a little spicy—just like us."

"Bold and spicy? That's quite the compliment," I teased, raising an eyebrow.

"Only the best for you," he replied, handing me a glass and settling onto the couch beside me. As we clinked our glasses together, I felt a surge of warmth rush through me, grounding me in the present, if only for a moment.

"Okay, let's see if you're right about this cheese," I said, taking a bite. The rich, creamy flavor exploded in my mouth, and I couldn't help but let out a satisfied sigh. "You've definitely redeemed yourself. This is fantastic!"

"See? I told you I could learn," he said, smugness creeping into his tone.

"Don't let it go to your head," I replied, rolling my eyes playfully. "Next thing I know, you'll be making reservations at the finest French bistro in town, and I'll have to compete with a Michelin-star chef."

"Or I could just let you handle the reservations," he shot back, and we both laughed, the sound echoing off the walls, filling the empty spaces that had once felt so heavy.

But as we continued to enjoy our evening, a sudden chime from his phone shattered the moment, cutting through the laughter like a knife. I watched as his expression shifted, the lightness in his eyes replaced by something darker, more serious.

"Just a second," he murmured, glancing at the screen, his brow furrowing.

My stomach sank, the sudden change in his demeanor chilling the warm glow that had enveloped us moments before. "Is everything okay?"

He hesitated, his thumb hovering over the screen. "It's work. I should—"

"Adam, we just said no distractions," I interrupted, a tinge of frustration creeping into my voice. "You promised."

"I know," he said, biting his lip. "But this could be important. I have to at least check."

I sat back, feeling the warmth between us dissipate like steam on a cold morning. "Fine, check. But if it's something that can wait, I hope you'll choose us instead."

He nodded, still focused on the phone, a flicker of uncertainty crossing his face. "Just a minute."

As I watched him, a knot tightened in my stomach. This was a pivotal moment, one that could tip the scales of our evening. I wanted to believe that he would choose me, choose us, but the doubt gnawed at the edges of my newfound hope.

The seconds stretched into minutes, each tick of the clock echoing the silent tension in the room. "You're not going to believe this," he said finally, looking up, his expression a mix of surprise and something else—fear, maybe?

"What is it?" I leaned forward, a chill creeping into my bones.

"There's been a development in the merger," he said, his voice dropping to a hushed tone. "They want me in a meeting tomorrow morning—last-minute strategy session."

My heart raced, not just from the news but from the realization that this could change everything. "And they didn't think to give you more notice? What kind of company operates like this?"

"Apparently, a cutthroat one," he replied, running a hand through his hair. "But it gets worse. They want me to present, and I might have to fly out."

"Fly out? When?" I demanded, feeling my pulse quicken as my fears resurfaced.

"Tonight. I'm sorry, Liv. I have to go."

As he stood, the finality of his words hung heavy in the air, drowning out the laughter and warmth we'd just shared. The fragile bridge we'd been building felt like it was collapsing beneath us, and in that moment, I realized I was standing at the edge of a precipice, uncertain if I would fall or find my footing again.

"Adam," I started, desperation creeping into my voice. "We just—"

"I know! But this is my job, and I can't just walk away from it," he interrupted, frustration mingling with sadness in his eyes.

"Neither can I!" I shot back, rising to my feet, my heart pounding. "I can't stand by and watch you sacrifice everything for this. Not again."

The words hung in the air, a challenge and an accusation. I searched his face for any sign of understanding, any hint that he would choose me over his career, but all I saw was the storm brewing within him.

"I have to make this work, Olivia. It's not just my future—it's ours."

"Is it?" I felt the ground shifting beneath me, the reality of our situation settling in. "Because right now, it feels like you're choosing your job over me."

He opened his mouth, but before he could respond, his phone buzzed again, and I felt the familiar weight of uncertainty crashing down around us.

"Answer it, Adam," I said, my voice trembling. "Just go. Go do what you have to do."

His expression faltered, torn between duty and desire. "Liv, please—"

"Just go!" I yelled, the emotion spilling over as I turned away, my heart shattering with the finality of it all.

He paused, uncertainty flickering in his gaze, and for a split second, I thought he might stay. But then, he nodded, his phone pressed to his ear, and the door clicked shut behind him, sealing away the warmth of the evening, leaving me standing alone in a silence that echoed with the weight of a thousand unsaid words.

And in that moment, as the darkness closed in around me, I realized that the distance between us was wider than I ever could have imagined—a chasm that would take more than promises and cheese platters to bridge

Chapter 15: "The Space Between Us"

The morning sun crept through the slats of my blinds, casting stripes of golden light across my bedroom floor. I lay there, tangled in my sheets, staring at the ceiling. Each flicker of light reminded me of the warmth we once shared, but today it felt like a foreign language I no longer understood. I could still hear Adam's laughter echoing in my mind, a melody that used to wrap around my heart like a favorite song. Now, it felt distant, muffled, as if the universe had placed a barrier between us. The sweet scent of freshly brewed coffee wafted through the air, teasing me with the promise of comfort, yet I found myself reluctant to leave the cocoon of my bed.

The distance was palpable, a silent intruder lingering in every conversation, every glance. I could see the way Adam would check his phone, the flicker of irritation in his eyes when I reached for his hand, as if I were grasping at smoke. It was as if I was drowning in a sea of unanswered questions, and every attempt to swim back to the surface left me gasping for air. "Is everything okay?" I had asked him countless times, my voice dripping with concern. Each time, he would offer a nonchalant shrug, masking whatever turmoil churned beneath the surface.

Pulling myself from the warmth of my bed, I padded into the kitchen, the coolness of the tile awakening my senses. I poured a cup of coffee, the steam curling up like tendrils of hope. My mind wandered back to that night, the moment that had shifted our world. Underneath the stars, we had shared dreams and fears, a moment of reckless abandon where words flowed as freely as the wine. But when the dawn broke, so too did the magic of the night, leaving us with the sobering realization that some things are too fragile to hold on to.

I took a sip, letting the warmth spread through me, but it did little to ease the chill in my heart. The clock ticked loudly in the silence of my apartment, a reminder of time slipping away. Shouldn't love feel lighter? Shouldn't it be a source of joy rather than this tight knot of confusion? I sighed, staring out the window at the bustling street below, life moving on without me. That was the problem, wasn't it? Adam was still moving forward, while I felt rooted to the spot, waiting for a sign, a clue to navigate this labyrinth of emotions.

Deciding I couldn't spend another moment trapped in my thoughts, I dressed quickly, throwing on a faded sundress that had always made me feel alive. The fabric fluttered around my legs, and for a moment, I allowed myself to indulge in the illusion that I was still the carefree girl who danced under the stars with Adam. But the reality was that I felt more like a ghost haunting the remnants of our happiness, drifting aimlessly from room to room in search of something I could no longer grasp.

The café on the corner was a comforting refuge, filled with the aroma of freshly baked pastries and the soft chatter of familiar voices. I made my way to the counter, exchanging pleasantries with the barista, a cheerful woman with a warmth that felt like a hug. I ordered my usual—an almond croissant and a latte—and settled into my favorite corner seat by the window. The sunlight poured in, illuminating the dust motes swirling lazily in the air, a perfect distraction from the turmoil brewing within.

As I took my first bite of the croissant, the flaky layers crumbled delightfully on my tongue, a brief moment of bliss amid the chaos. Just then, the door swung open, and my heart did a little flip. Adam stepped in, his familiar presence radiating warmth, yet the distance that separated us felt as sharp as a knife. He caught sight of me, a flicker of something passing over his face—was it relief? Guilt? I couldn't tell anymore.

"Hey," he said, his voice laced with the kind of casual charm that used to make my heart race. But today, it fell flat against the weight of our silence. I gestured for him to join me, my stomach fluttering with a mix of hope and apprehension. He slid into the chair across from me, his gaze darting away as if he were trying to avoid the tension that hummed between us.

"Been busy?" I asked, attempting to sound lighthearted, but the tremor in my voice betrayed me. He nodded, running a hand through his hair, a gesture that usually made me weak in the knees but felt oddly mechanical today.

"Yeah, just work stuff," he replied, the edge in his tone sending a chill down my spine. I wanted to reach out, to break the ice encasing us, but the words stuck in my throat like candy floss, too sweet and sticky to spit out.

"Do you want to talk about it?" I ventured, my heart racing. The unspoken words between us felt like a bridge, ready to either collapse or take us somewhere new. He hesitated, his eyes flickering to the window, watching the world pass by as if he were searching for answers among strangers.

"It's nothing," he said, but the weariness in his voice told a different story. I knew it wasn't nothing. It was something—a chasm growing wider with each passing day.

"Adam, we can't keep doing this," I finally blurted out, the words spilling out like a dam breaking. "You're pulling away, and I—"

His gaze snapped back to mine, sharp and challenging. "And what? You want me to just pour out my heart and soul? That's not how I operate."

I blinked, taken aback by his defensiveness. "No, I just want you to let me in."

"Let you in?" He leaned back, crossing his arms, his expression a mixture of annoyance and vulnerability. "What do you think I'm doing? I'm just trying to figure things out."

The silence stretched between us, thick and suffocating. I could feel the walls closing in, the café fading into the background. What was once a sanctuary now felt like a battleground, and I was ready to lay down my arms.

"Adam, I can't be in this limbo anymore," I said, my voice barely a whisper. "I want to love you, but I can't do it alone."

His expression softened, and for a fleeting moment, I saw a flicker of the man I fell in love with, the one who danced under the stars and made me laugh until my sides hurt. But then it faded, replaced by uncertainty. He looked away again, as if he could find clarity in the chaos outside.

"Maybe we need to take a step back," he suggested, the words striking me like a thunderbolt.

I felt the world shift beneath me, the ground unstable and threatening to swallow me whole. "Are you serious?"

He nodded slowly, and the finality of his gaze pierced through me. It was like watching a beautiful painting slowly fade, colors running together until there was nothing left but gray. The distance I had feared was no longer just an echo; it was real, and it was here to stay.

The café felt like a stage, the hum of conversation swirling around us as I tried to make sense of Adam's words. "Maybe we need to take a step back." It was like he'd dropped a boulder in the middle of our fragile landscape, and I stood there, grappling with the shockwaves rippling through me. I could hardly breathe, the air thick with unspoken confessions and the weight of possibility.

"Step back?" I echoed, incredulity lacing my tone. "What does that even mean? A step back to where? The beginning? The ending? Because from where I stand, it feels like we're already halfway off the cliff." I waved my arms, feeling absurdly dramatic, but the heat of frustration surged through me, a fire I hadn't known I still possessed.

Adam leaned forward, his elbows resting on the table, fingers intertwined, his brows knitted in thought. "I just... I don't know if I can give you what you want. Maybe we need to reassess this, figure out if it's worth it."

"Figure out if it's worth it?" I laughed, a short, bitter sound that drew curious glances from the nearby patrons. "You're saying we need to measure the value of our relationship like it's some clearance sale at the grocery store? Just slap a price tag on it and walk away?"

His eyes flared with annoyance, and for a moment, the distance between us felt more like a chasm. "I'm not trying to dismiss what we have," he said, his voice steady but strained. "It's just complicated right now."

"Complicated? That's putting it mildly. I feel like we're stuck in some kind of twisted romantic limbo, and every day that passes, I'm more certain I'm the only one trying to bridge this gap." I could feel the tension in my shoulders, a knot tightening with every syllable. "You act like you're doing me a favor by letting me in your life, but it's exhausting. I'm not asking you to solve world hunger, Adam. I just want to be with you—fully, completely."

He flinched at my words, and I immediately regretted my tone. My heart twisted, recognizing the truth of what I'd said. Maybe this wasn't just about him. Maybe I was holding on to something that had already slipped through my fingers. The realization hit me like ice water in the veins.

"I don't want to lose you," Adam admitted, his voice softening, but it didn't quite reach the vulnerability I longed to see. "But I also can't keep pretending everything is fine when it isn't."

"Then let's not pretend!" I implored, leaning in, desperate for connection. "Let's lay it all out on the table. You're scared, and I get it, but that doesn't mean we have to throw in the towel."

Silence enveloped us, heavy and awkward, like a thick fog rolling in off the sea. I could see the inner battle playing out on his face—conflict, fear, and that damned stubbornness that had drawn me to him in the first place. But I had to push; I had to break through.

"Tell me what you're afraid of," I urged, my voice a gentle nudge instead of a shove. "Maybe if we talk it out, it'll lose its power over you."

He looked at me, his expression a mix of appreciation and reluctance, and for a moment, I thought he might just let me in. But then he exhaled deeply, the fight leaving his body. "I don't know if I'm ready for what comes next. We've been through so much already. What if we get hurt again?"

"Isn't that what love is? A risk worth taking?" I countered, my pulse racing. "The chance of getting hurt doesn't erase the joy of being with someone you care about. I'd rather risk it all than live in this in-between world we've created."

He frowned, his gaze falling to the table as if seeking answers in the grain of the wood. "I just... need time."

"Time?" I repeated, frustration bubbling beneath the surface. "Time is what got us here. If we keep waiting for the perfect moment, we'll miss out on everything that's happening right now."

As the words left my lips, I could feel the energy shifting around us. The once vibrant café now felt stifling, the laughter of friends and lovers mingling with my growing anxiety. My heart raced, not just from fear of losing him but from the unsettling thought that I had become a mere shadow of the person I used to be—chasing after his approval while letting my own needs slip away.

"Maybe you're right," he said finally, his voice a low murmur. "But what if we're better off apart?"

"Is that what you really want?" My voice trembled, and I hated that I felt the sting of tears threatening to spill over. "To give up without even trying?"

He hesitated, and in that moment, a crack appeared in the armor he had built around himself. "I don't know what I want anymore."

The vulnerability in his admission felt like a weight lifted, but I also knew it was a double-edged sword. "Then let's figure it out together," I said, my voice steadier now. "Let's stop avoiding the mess and lean into it. Let's be a little reckless."

Adam's eyes met mine, and for a brief instant, I saw the flicker of hope that had long been absent. "Reckless? You mean like a romantic comedy?"

"Exactly! A witty banter-filled romantic comedy with more plot twists than a soap opera. Who doesn't love a good dramatic arc?"

He chuckled softly, the sound a balm to my frazzled nerves. "You know, that actually sounds appealing. If only life came with a script."

"Who needs a script?" I leaned forward, a conspiratorial grin spreading across my face. "Let's improvise. We can take turns being the hero and the sidekick—though I call dibs on being the lead."

"Deal," he replied, the ghost of a smile forming on his lips. But even as the warmth returned, I felt the lingering caution in his posture. There was still a distance, still a gap to bridge, but now it felt less like a chasm and more like a hurdle waiting to be overcome.

As we resumed our conversation, I could feel the air shifting, our words carving pathways through the fog of uncertainty. We spoke in tentative tones, exploring each other's fears and hopes like children weaving through a maze. The more we shared, the more I sensed the potential for something real—a deeper connection that could withstand the tremors of our doubts.

But as we settled into a comfortable rhythm, I couldn't shake the feeling that this was merely the calm before the storm. Just as laughter began to bubble up between us, a sudden commotion at the entrance drew our attention. A tall figure burst through the door, breathless and wide-eyed, and I recognized her immediately—Maya, my best friend and confidante, looking like she'd just run a marathon.

"Sorry, sorry!" she gasped, scanning the café until her gaze landed on us. "You'll never believe what I just found out!"

The playful mood dissipated as curiosity took its place. I exchanged a look with Adam, and though a part of me was relieved for the distraction, another part felt a rush of dread. What could Maya possibly say that would change everything?

Maya's presence, like a burst of sunlight breaking through the clouds, shattered the tension that had hung over the café. Her wild hair, usually tamed into a bun, danced in chaotic curls, and her cheeks flushed from her hasty entrance. "Sorry, but you won't believe what I just found out!" She was practically vibrating with energy, her eyes wide with excitement, as if she held the key to the universe tucked away in her pocket.

"Is it that Adam's a secret agent?" I teased, leaning back in my chair, grateful for the distraction. "Because I'm ready for that plot twist. I could really use some excitement in my life."

"Better! Way better!" she exclaimed, waving her arms like a conductor summoning an orchestra. "I just heard that—" She paused dramatically, glancing around as if the walls themselves might be listening, before lowering her voice conspiratorially. "The old Hawthorne estate is up for grabs. And get this—it's being sold at auction."

The mention of the Hawthorne estate sent a ripple of nostalgia through me. The crumbling mansion on the outskirts of town had always been a local legend, its creaky floorboards and ghost stories adding to the allure of my childhood adventures. "The haunted one? The place that's been sitting empty for decades?"

"Exactly! And you know what that means?" Maya was practically bouncing in her seat, and I could feel my curiosity piquing.

"Um, a chance to finally prove the ghosts are real?" I joked, but she wasn't laughing. Her eyes sparkled with a seriousness that quelled my sarcasm.

"No, silly! It means that anyone can buy it. We could turn it into something incredible—a bed and breakfast, a retreat for artists, or even a haunted Airbnb! Just think of the possibilities!"

As she spoke, my mind began to swirl with images of vintage furniture, painted walls, and the scent of fresh coffee wafting through sunlit rooms filled with laughter. The thought of transforming that forgotten place into a haven was intoxicating. "That could be amazing," I admitted, picturing myself flitting around the estate, my worries fading into the background.

Adam remained silent, his expression unreadable. I glanced at him, hoping to share in my excitement, but he sat back in his chair, arms crossed, a shadow flickering across his face.

"What do you think?" I asked him, trying to draw him into the vision Maya had painted. "It could be a fresh start for all of us, something fun and adventurous. Right?"

He shrugged, the familiar tension returning to his shoulders. "I mean, it sounds interesting, but it's just an old house. It's not going to fix anything."

"Maya's right," I pressed, my frustration bubbling back to the surface. "It's not just a house; it's an opportunity. We've been talking about needing change. This could be it. We could be the ones to breathe new life into that place."

Maya's enthusiasm was contagious, and I could see the flicker of interest in her eyes as she leaned forward, her enthusiasm sharpening. "Imagine the parties we could throw! The ghost tours! We could make it a local legend."

"Or a local disaster," Adam interjected, his skepticism heavy in the air.

"Come on, Adam," I said, fighting the urge to roll my eyes. "When was the last time you let loose and did something spontaneous? This could be your chance to escape whatever it is that's been dragging you down."

"I'm not trying to rain on your parade," he replied, but there was an edge in his voice, a hint of irritation that made me question if he was truly against the idea or just against stepping outside his comfort zone.

Maya, ever the mediator, jumped in. "Why don't we go see the estate together? We could check it out and see if it has any potential. You might change your mind once you see it!"

"Fine," Adam said, and I could hear the reluctant concession in his tone. "But if it's a dump, don't say I didn't warn you."

I felt a rush of victory, a flicker of hope igniting as the tension began to melt away. "That's the spirit! We'll make a day of it." I turned to Maya, my excitement bubbling over. "Let's plan for this weekend. We can take a picnic, explore, and who knows? Maybe we'll uncover some hidden treasures."

But as we plotted our grand adventure, I couldn't shake the feeling that Adam's reluctance was rooted in something deeper. There was a storm brewing beneath his calm exterior, and I was beginning to wonder if he would ever let me in on what really haunted him.

Later that evening, as we sat in my living room with leftover takeout, I attempted to probe deeper. "What do you really think about the estate?" I asked, my fork hovering over my plate. "You seem skeptical."

"It's just an old house," he said, avoiding my gaze as he pushed his food around. "I don't see the point in getting excited over something that could end up being a huge disappointment."

"Or it could be the best thing that ever happened to us," I countered, my voice steady. "It's about the adventure, Adam. We've been playing it safe for too long. Isn't that what you want? To feel something?"

He finally looked at me, the intensity in his eyes making my breath hitch. "I want to feel something real, not some fairy tale."

Before I could respond, the doorbell rang, shattering the moment. I jumped up, surprised at the interruption. "Who could that be?"

When I opened the door, my heart dropped. There, standing on my doorstep, was a figure I hadn't seen in years. It was Jenna, my college roommate and the one person I had thought I'd never see again. Her hair was longer, cascading in waves down her back, and her smile was both warm and anxious.

"Hey, is this a bad time?" she asked, biting her lip, as if unsure whether to step into my world or not.

"Jenna!" I exclaimed, pulling her into a hug that felt both familiar and strange. "What are you doing here?"

"I just got back to town, and I thought I'd drop by. It's been too long." She stepped back, and her eyes flickered to Adam, recognition flashing across her face. "Oh, I see you brought company."

"Uh, yeah, this is Adam," I said, gesturing between them. "We were just—"

"Planning our next big adventure," Adam interjected, his tone surprisingly smooth, but I could sense the tension. "We're going to check out the Hawthorne estate this weekend."

"The old mansion?" Jenna's eyes lit up with intrigue. "I've always wanted to see that place. You have to take me with you!"

Just as I was about to agree, a strange sense of foreboding washed over me. There was something about her sudden reappearance, the way her smile didn't quite reach her eyes, that made me hesitate. Before I could voice my concerns, she leaned closer, her voice dropping to a whisper.

"Listen, there's something you need to know about the estate," she said, glancing back over her shoulder as if checking for eavesdroppers. "Something I didn't tell anyone before I left."

I exchanged a quick glance with Adam, my heart racing. The air was thick with unspoken secrets, and as Jenna prepared to reveal whatever it was that had brought her back, I felt the ground shift beneath my feet once more. The tension, the uncertainty—it all swirled around us like a brewing storm, and I couldn't help but wonder what kind of chaos was about to unfold.

Chapter 16: "A Choice to Make"

The air was thick with the scent of blooming jasmine as I stood on my balcony, the soft light of dusk wrapping around me like a familiar blanket. Each inhalation was an echo of summer nights spent dreaming under star-specked skies, moments that felt endless yet fleeting. Below, the cobblestone street shimmered, reflecting the golden hues of the setting sun. My heart raced, not from the beauty surrounding me, but from the storm of emotions swirling within. The decision that awaited me felt monumental, like a ship teetering on the edge of a great abyss.

I glanced down at my phone, the screen illuminated with Adam's name—always a beacon of warmth and chaos in my life. It had been weeks since he'd let me in, weeks since he'd shared more than the surface-level banter that had once flowed so easily between us. I craved depth, the kind of connection that made the world outside fade into a distant hum, and yet here I was, tethered to a man whose demons danced just out of reach. He had a way of pulling me close, his laughter spilling into the quiet spaces of my life, only to leave me cold when the moment passed. I loved him fiercely, but love alone couldn't bridge the chasm of his fears.

"Hey there, overthinking again?" a voice chimed from behind me, pulling me from my reverie. It was Jenna, my best friend and reluctant confidante, with her wild curls bouncing like sunshine and her smile disarming. She leaned against the doorframe, arms crossed, the embodiment of supportive mischief.

"Just contemplating the universe," I replied, my voice tinged with a playful sarcasm that masked my inner turmoil.

"The universe? More like the Adam situation, right?" she teased, stepping onto the balcony. She settled beside me, her eyes dancing over my expression. "You know, it's almost comical how you're trying to solve his problems while ignoring your own."

I sighed, running a hand through my hair, feeling the weight of it all. "It's not like that, Jen. He's just... complicated. It's hard not to want to fix things for him."

"Fix things? Or fix him?" she shot back, her tone light but her gaze sharp. "You can't be the one to save him, you know. He's got to want it for himself."

The truth of her words hit me like a splash of cold water, leaving me breathless and raw. I turned my gaze back to the horizon, where the last rays of sunlight dipped beneath the world, casting a pinkish glow across the sky. "I know," I murmured, more to myself than to her. "But I don't want to lose him."

"And you won't, if you choose yourself first," Jenna replied, her voice steady and soothing. "You have to put yourself at the top of your priority list for once. If he can't meet you there, it's time to rethink things."

Her words lingered in the air between us, wrapping around my thoughts like tendrils of ivy. I thought of Adam, his laughter that always danced just above the surface, and the way his eyes turned stormy when he retreated into his thoughts. What I wanted was not just to be his girlfriend but to be his anchor, to navigate the turbulent waters of his mind together. But every time I reached out, he stepped back, leaving me grasping at shadows.

Just then, the phone buzzed in my hand, breaking the silence. I glanced down to see a message from him: "Can we talk? I need to see you." My heart skipped, a mix of anticipation and dread flooding through me. Was this the moment he would finally open up, or was it just another moment of him pulling me deeper into his confusion?

"Answer him," Jenna encouraged, nudging my shoulder lightly. "What's the worst that can happen?"

I hesitated, fingers hovering over the screen, the weight of the moment pressing down on me. "What if he's just going to shut me out again?"

"Then at least you'll know. Better to find out now than keep wondering," she replied, her voice unwavering. "You can't keep living in limbo, and you deserve more than half-hearted affection."

With a deep breath, I typed a quick response, my pulse racing. "Sure, when and where?"

"Your place, 8?" he replied almost instantly.

"See? Easy," Jenna said, clapping her hands together. "Now, let's give you a glow-up. You need to feel like a million bucks when he gets here."

I couldn't help but chuckle at her enthusiasm. "A glow-up for a conversation? What am I, a contestant on a dating show?"

"Hey, confidence is key! Plus, if he sees you looking fabulous, it might help him realize what he's risking," she quipped, her eyes gleaming with mischief.

As we moved through my apartment, Jenna rummaged through my closet, pulling out outfits, offering playful critiques on each choice. With her help, I transformed from a bundle of nerves into someone who felt more like herself, but still, doubt lurked at the edges of my mind.

Finally, as the clock inched closer to eight, I stood in front of the mirror, examining my reflection. My heart thrummed in my chest, a rhythm of hope mixed with uncertainty. I caught Jenna's eye in the mirror, and she flashed me a thumbs-up, but my stomach knotted with the weight of impending decisions. The doorbell rang, and I felt my breath hitch, each inhale a testament to the storm brewing inside me. It was time. Time to confront my feelings, time to face the man who both ignited my soul and left it in shadow.

"Go get him, superstar," Jenna whispered, her voice a soft encouragement as I made my way to the door, each step echoing the choice that loomed before me.

The door swung open, revealing Adam standing there, silhouetted against the golden light spilling from the hallway. His tousled hair caught the glow, creating an almost ethereal halo around him that sent a jolt of familiarity through me, a rush of warmth tempered with trepidation. I could see the hint of a smile creeping onto his lips, but his eyes held a vulnerability that made my heart ache.

"Hey," he said, his voice low, laced with an uncertainty that mirrored my own.

"Hey," I replied, trying to match his casual tone while feeling anything but. The air crackled between us, electric and thick, as if it bore the weight of unspoken words. I stepped aside, letting him in, and closed the door behind us.

Inside, the soft glow of the lamps cast a warm light across the room, wrapping us in an intimate cocoon. I could see him absorbing the surroundings—my carefully curated collection of mismatched furniture, the array of books lining the shelves, the hint of lavender wafting from a candle on the coffee table. His gaze lingered for a moment too long on a framed photograph of us from a happier time, one where the future felt as vibrant as the colors in the image.

"Nice place," he said, an attempt at lightness in his tone that felt both comforting and painfully out of sync with the gravity of the moment.

"Thanks," I replied, watching him as he sank into the plush couch. He ran a hand through his hair, a gesture I had come to recognize as a sign of his restlessness. It made my heart twist. "So, what did you want to talk about?"

His gaze darted away, focusing instead on the abstract painting hanging on the wall. It was a swirl of blues and greens, evocative of the ocean, and I suddenly wondered if he found the turbulent waves reflective of his own inner chaos. "I've been thinking... about us," he started, the words hanging in the air like an unanswered question.

"Us," I echoed, the weight of it hanging between us. "What about us?"

He shifted, visibly uncomfortable, and I could almost see the gears turning in his mind. "I've been a mess lately, and I know I haven't exactly been... available. I don't want to keep you in the dark, but it's hard for me to talk about what's going on." His voice dropped to a whisper, and he seemed to shrink into himself, like a turtle retreating into its shell.

I took a deep breath, the moment stretching out like a rubber band ready to snap. "You don't have to explain yourself, Adam. I just wish you'd let me in, even just a little." My heart raced as I let the words tumble out, honesty spilling into the space between us. "I can't keep living like this, feeling like I'm on the outside looking in."

His eyes finally met mine, and the flicker of vulnerability in them sent a jolt through me. "I know. But every time I try, it's like I'm standing at the edge of a cliff, afraid to jump. I don't want to hurt you."

"By not letting me in, you're already hurting me," I countered, my voice steady but my heart racing. "You keep pushing me away, and I don't know how much longer I can pretend it doesn't bother me."

Adam sighed, running a hand through his hair again, his frustration palpable. "I get that. I really do. But what if I can't give you what you want? What if I'm not capable of being the guy you deserve?"

"Then let me decide that for myself," I said, the firmness in my tone surprising even me. "You don't get to dictate what I can or can't handle."

The silence that followed was heavy, thick with the weight of the unspoken. I could see the flicker of indecision in his eyes, the struggle within him palpable. "I don't want you to get hurt, especially not by me," he finally said, his voice barely above a whisper.

"What's hurting me is this uncertainty," I shot back, frustration bubbling beneath the surface. "Every day that goes by without you opening up feels like a step further away from what we could be. I can't be the only one fighting for this."

He leaned back into the couch, running his hands over his face in exasperation. "You're right. I just... I don't know how to let you in without dragging you into my mess. I've got things in my past that still haunt me. It's not fair to put that on you."

"Life isn't fair, Adam. But that doesn't mean we have to face it alone," I countered, my heart pounding in my chest. "We can figure this out together. But you have to meet me halfway."

His gaze was intense, searching mine for something—perhaps a glimmer of hope, or maybe a sign of retreat. "And what if I can't?" he asked, his voice low and raw.

"Then I'll have to make a choice," I replied, feeling the gravity of my own words. "But I won't let you push me away without knowing what we could be. I deserve that chance, and so do you."

The tension between us shifted, and I could see him wrestling with his thoughts, battling the demons that kept him from being fully present. For a moment, it felt like time suspended, the world outside fading into a blur as we stood on the precipice of something monumental. "I don't want to lose you," he admitted finally, his voice cracking slightly, revealing the depth of his struggle.

"You won't lose me if you let me in," I said softly, the air thick with the weight of our unspoken promises. "But you have to be honest with me. I can't build anything real on half-truths."

He took a deep breath, his chest rising and falling as he weighed his options. "I've never been good at sharing. It terrifies me."

"Then let's take it slow," I suggested, the warmth in my voice cutting through the tension. "Tell me one thing—something simple. Just one piece of your truth."

He stared at me, his eyes searching, and for a moment, I thought he might back away, retreating into the comfort of silence. But then, as if he had crossed an invisible threshold, he leaned forward, his voice barely above a whisper. "Okay. I'm scared. Scared of letting anyone in, scared of what they'll find."

And in that moment, a crack formed in the wall he'd built around himself, letting a sliver of light seep through. I could feel the gravity of his confession wash over me, pulling me closer to him, a whisper of hope flickering in the darkness. We were standing on the edge, teetering between fear and vulnerability, and for the first time, it felt like we might just find a way to bridge the chasm between us.

Adam's confession hung between us like a fragile thread, a newfound clarity illuminating the shadowed corners of his heart. I could see him wrestling with his vulnerability, the admission drawing him closer to the precipice of something he had long feared. It was a moment teetering on the edge of possibility, and I felt a heady mix of hope and trepidation bubble within me. "Being scared doesn't mean you're weak," I said softly, my voice breaking the silence that threatened to suffocate us. "It just means you're human."

He looked at me, the stormy depths of his eyes searching mine for something—understanding, perhaps, or the promise that I wouldn't flinch. "I don't want to hurt you, but I don't want to lie to you either. It's been easier to pretend everything's fine."

"Pretending is exhausting," I replied, leaning forward, wanting to bridge the gap between our two worlds. "And it's not working for either of us. I need to know who you really are, Adam—the good and the bad. You don't have to carry this alone."

He took a deep breath, his vulnerability flickering like a candle in the wind. "Okay, then. I guess it's time I start sharing more than just my jokes and casual flirts. The truth is, I've been through things that still haunt me. It's like I'm living in a shadow, always trying to outrun my past."

"What kind of things?" I asked, my heart pounding with each beat, aware that he was opening a door that could either lead us into light or plunge us deeper into darkness.

He hesitated, a flicker of pain passing over his features. "After my parents divorced, everything changed. I was stuck in the middle, always trying to please both sides while feeling like I was being torn apart. And when I was finally starting to find my footing, I lost my brother in an accident. It shattered everything. I've been so terrified of losing anyone else that I built walls instead of bridges."

My breath caught in my throat, the weight of his confession settling heavily in the air between us. "I'm so sorry, Adam. That's so much to carry. I can't even begin to imagine how hard that must have been."

His eyes softened, and for a fleeting moment, the facade cracked just a little more. "It's not your fault, and I don't want pity. I just don't know how to navigate these feelings. When I'm with you, I feel something real, but I'm terrified it won't last. So I pull away, thinking it's for your own good."

"Adam, you're not just some fragile thing I can break," I said firmly, feeling a rush of emotion. "I'm here because I want to be. You don't have to carry the weight of your past alone anymore. Let me in. Let us figure this out together."

A silence fell, thick with tension, as he processed my words. I held my breath, wishing I could physically weave a thread between our hearts, binding us together in understanding. His expression shifted, a mixture of yearning and fear washing over his features, and I felt a flicker of hope ignite within me.

"I want that," he admitted, voice raw. "But I don't want to hurt you. The idea of losing you... it terrifies me more than anything."

"We can't live in fear," I replied, my heart racing at the possibilities. "What if we let go of what we're afraid of? What if we choose to take a leap together?"

He was silent for a moment, contemplating the gravity of my words. Then, in an unexpected twist, he stood up abruptly, pacing the small space of my living room. "It's not that easy, you know? I can't just flip a switch and be the guy you need. I feel like I'm in a dark tunnel, and I can't see the light at the end."

"Then let's walk through it together," I suggested, my heart pounding. "One step at a time."

As the words left my lips, the doorbell rang, slicing through the tension like a knife. We both froze, and I glanced at the clock. It was too late for anyone else to be visiting, and a shiver of unease ran down my spine.

"Who could that be?" Adam's voice held a hint of anxiety, his earlier bravado evaporating in the face of the unexpected interruption.

"Maybe it's just a neighbor," I said, trying to sound nonchalant as I moved toward the door. But as I approached, a gut feeling told me it was more than just an ordinary visit.

When I opened the door, my heart dropped at the sight before me. There stood Melanie, Adam's ex-girlfriend, her presence as unsettling as a storm cloud on a clear day. Her auburn hair cascaded around her shoulders, and the smirk on her face was unsettling, a calculated veneer that felt all too familiar.

"Surprise! I thought I'd drop by," she said, feigning cheerfulness, but her eyes glinted with something darker, something predatory.

I turned back to Adam, whose expression was a mix of disbelief and something I couldn't quite place—guilt, perhaps? It twisted my stomach into knots.

"Melanie," he said, his voice flat, clearly caught off guard. "What are you doing here?"

Her gaze darted between us, and I could almost see the cogs turning in her mind as she processed the scene. "I thought you might want to talk," she said sweetly, the tone belied by the glint in her eye. "It's been a while since we've had a proper chat, don't you think?"

"Now?" Adam's disbelief was palpable, his tension radiating off him.

"Why not?" she replied, stepping inside without invitation, as if she owned the space. The air thickened with the unsaid, her presence an unwelcome shadow that threatened to unravel everything we had just begun to build.

I felt my heart racing, the ground shifting beneath me. The moment I had envisioned—one of hope, vulnerability, and openness—had been derailed in an instant. I glanced at Adam, whose face had drained of color, caught between his past and the uncertainty of our future.

"Adam, I—" I began, but the words stuck in my throat as Melanie turned her full attention to me, her smile dripping with false sweetness.

"Don't worry, sweetie. I just need to talk to Adam about a few things. You know how it is," she said, her voice a syrupy blend of condescension and mock concern.

As she leaned closer to Adam, the space between us felt impossibly vast. I could see the confusion swirling in his eyes, and in that moment, I realized that the choices I thought were mine to make were now tangled in the complexity of his past. The weight of uncertainty pressed down harder than ever as I stood on the precipice of something monumental, unsure if we could survive this new storm together or if I was about to lose him forever.

Chapter 17: "A Heart Divided"

The air was thick with the scent of earth after a day of unexpected rain, the kind that left the grass glistening like a thousand tiny diamonds beneath the fading sunlight. I leaned against the wrought iron railing of the bridge, the steady cadence of the water beneath creating a melody that played in perfect harmony with my tangled thoughts. The vibrant autumn leaves rustled gently overhead, their colors a riot of orange, gold, and crimson, a reminder of the beauty that still thrived even as change loomed around me. I let out a slow breath, letting the crispness fill my lungs and chase away the weight pressing down on my chest.

Adam's laugh echoed in my memory, a rich sound that could light up the darkest corners of my mind. I could picture him now, his unruly hair tousled by the wind, that mischievous glint in his eyes when he talked about his dreams. Dreams of adventure, of traveling to places where the sky kissed the ocean, of a life that felt as boundless as the horizon. He had this wild spirit that both captivated and terrified me. Every moment spent with him was a delightful whirlwind, yet each laugh and shared glance pulled me deeper into a chaos I could scarcely comprehend.

"Why do you look like you just watched a puppy get kicked?" A voice cut through the reverie, snapping me back to reality. It was Jessa, my best friend, and partner in crime, her trademark smirk in place. She approached with her usual flair, the vibrant fabric of her flowy sundress swirling around her as she walked, the colors a cheerful contrast to my heavy heart.

"I'm just pondering the meaning of life," I replied dryly, crossing my arms as I turned to face her. "Or maybe just whether I'll ever be able to choose between my heart and my head."

"Ah, the classic dilemma." Jessa leaned against the railing beside me, her gaze drifting to the shimmering surface of the lake. "You know, when I was dating that guy from the coffee shop, I spent hours debating whether I wanted a venti latte or a cappuccino. In the end, I chose the cappuccino and ended up with a caffeine buzz and a broken heart."

Her attempt to lighten the mood was endearing, and I couldn't help but chuckle despite myself. "It's not quite the same, Jess. You weren't choosing between two men—one of whom has a penchant for wandering off to save the world every few weeks."

"That's fair. But really, what's the worst that could happen?" She nudged me playfully. "You could end up heartbroken. Or you could end up happily in love and living your best life. I mean, look at me! I went from a caffeine crisis to a whole new dating scene. Sometimes you just have to leap."

"But what if I leap and land on a rock instead of a soft patch of grass?" I sighed, the image of me plummeting into uncertainty felt all too real. "Adam's life is filled with risks, and I can't help but feel like I'm standing at the edge of that cliff with him. One misstep, and it could all come crashing down."

Jessa's expression softened, and I could see the wheels turning in her mind, contemplating how to navigate this emotional labyrinth I found myself in. "You've always been the sensible one, the one who keeps everyone grounded. But love isn't about safety; it's about the thrill of the unknown. Maybe you need to embrace the chaos instead of fearing it."

Her words hung in the air between us, mingling with the scent of rain-soaked earth and the distant hum of city life. The park was starting to fill with the golden glow of streetlights, their warm illumination reflecting off the tranquil water. I could feel the tension in my shoulders begin to ease as I turned to Jessa, her presence a reassuring anchor amidst my turbulent thoughts.

"I guess I'm just scared of losing everything. Adam's everything I didn't know I needed. But what if he's just a fleeting moment?" The honesty of my vulnerability spilled out, and I felt lighter, as if each word were a stone removed from the weight I'd been carrying.

"Maybe it's time to redefine what everything means." Jessa shrugged, her tone casual, yet the glint in her eyes suggested she had hit on something deeper. "It doesn't have to mean forever right now. You could enjoy what you have without the pressure of what it might become. Just take it one day at a time."

I pondered her words, watching as a couple strolled by, fingers entwined, laughter dancing through the air like music. Their joy was palpable, a reminder that life was meant to be experienced in all its messy glory. Maybe Jessa was onto something. Perhaps I could embrace this moment, allowing it to shape my future without the need to control every aspect of it.

"Okay, but how do I go from scared rabbit to daring adventurer?" I asked, a hint of humor creeping into my voice, a spark igniting in the pit of my stomach.

"Start by being honest with Adam. You're not the only one feeling the pressure, you know." She flashed a knowing smile, the kind that spoke volumes. "Talk to him. Find out where he stands. You might discover you're both more in sync than you think."

As I stood there, feeling the lightness of hope settle within me, I realized that the decision I faced didn't have to be the end of something beautiful. It could be the beginning of a new adventure, one where love was the compass guiding me through the chaos.

The moment I left Jessa behind on the bridge, the shimmering cityscape seemed to pulse with life, each glowing window a reminder of the myriad stories unfolding in parallel to my own. I walked along the winding paths of Central Park, where the cool evening breeze danced through the trees, carrying with it the faint sounds of laughter and music from nearby gatherings. Each step felt heavier than the last, my mind spinning with Jessa's words and the swirling uncertainty about my relationship with Adam.

I found a secluded bench beneath a sprawling oak, its branches weaving a natural canopy that shielded me from the world. Sitting down, I closed my eyes, letting the sounds of the park envelop me—the distant strum of a guitar, the chirping of crickets, and the soft rustle of leaves. In that moment of solitude, I felt the weight of my choices pressing down on me, like the heavy clouds that sometimes blanketed the sky before a storm.

Just as I began to find some clarity, the familiar rumble of a motorcycle engine pierced the evening air, drawing my attention. My heart skipped a beat as Adam's figure materialized, silhouetted against the fading light. He parked his bike a few feet away, the sleek machine glinting under the glow of a nearby lamp. He was just as I remembered, clad in a leather jacket that hugged his broad shoulders, and an easy grin that could melt the toughest exterior.

"Fancy meeting you here," he called out, striding over with an energy that matched the vibrancy of the sunset. "I thought you were afraid of the dark."

"I'm not afraid of the dark, just the decisions that come with it," I shot back, attempting to mask the nervous flutter in my stomach with a playful tone. His presence had a way of making the world tilt slightly off-kilter, like a rollercoaster ready to plunge into the unknown.

"Sounds ominous," he said, dropping onto the bench beside me. He leaned back, his arm resting casually along the back of the seat. "What's going on in that beautiful head of yours?"

"Just contemplating the mysteries of the universe," I replied, allowing a teasing smile to break through my facade. "You know, the usual."

Adam chuckled, the sound rich and warm. "You always did have a flair for the dramatic. But really, what's eating at you? You've got that look." He turned to me, his expression serious now, those piercing blue eyes searching mine for answers.

"Do I?" I feigned innocence, though I could feel the weight of his gaze, the way it drew out the truth from deep within me. "Maybe I'm just trying to decide what to order for dinner. You know, the real dilemmas in life."

"Dinner? Seriously?" He raised an eyebrow, a playful smirk tugging at the corner of his lips. "You can't fool me. There's a storm brewing beneath that calm exterior, and it's not the kind you can fix with takeout."

His insight cut through my defenses, and I found myself leaning closer, the air thick with unspoken tension. "You're right," I admitted softly, my voice barely above a whisper. "I've been trying to figure out how to navigate this... us. It's like trying to dance on a tightrope without a safety net."

Adam sighed, running a hand through his tousled hair, a gesture I had come to associate with his moments of contemplation. "I get it. My life is chaotic, and I don't want to pull you into that storm if you're not ready. But you have to know that you're not just a passing fancy for me."

The sincerity in his voice washed over me, warm and genuine, and I felt my heart thump loudly in response. "But what does that mean for us?" I asked, my voice tinged with a vulnerability I couldn't quite suppress. "I'm not sure I can be the calm in your storm when I'm still trying to figure out my own direction."

He turned to face me fully, his gaze steady and unwavering. "What if we don't have to have it all figured out right now? What if we just take it one day at a time? I'm not asking you to leap into the abyss with me. I'm asking you to stand by my side as we navigate the uncertainty together."

His words hung in the air, the weight of their promise swirling around us like the cool breeze that swept through the park. I could feel the pull of something genuine, something worth exploring, yet the specter of fear clung to me like a shadow. "What if that leads us both to heartbreak?" I countered, my heart racing at the thought.

"Heartbreak is a part of life, isn't it?" he replied, a flicker of mischief in his eyes. "You're a therapist; you know that better than anyone. But you also know that love—real love—can be worth the risk. And sometimes, the best stories come from the messiest beginnings."

A shiver ran down my spine at the thought, but before I could respond, he reached out, his fingers brushing against mine—a tentative gesture that sent sparks dancing through my veins. "Just think about it," he murmured, his voice low and sincere. "I want you to be a part of this, whatever this may be. And I'm willing to wait until you're ready to take that step."

I sat in silence, feeling the warmth of his hand against mine, the connection between us as palpable as the crisp night air. The uncertainty that had loomed over me now felt like a challenge, a puzzle waiting to be solved. In that moment, I realized that perhaps the fear of heartbreak didn't have to dictate my choices.

"Okay," I said finally, my heart pounding with a mix of hope and apprehension. "Let's take it one day at a time. But you have to promise me something."

"Anything," Adam said, his gaze unwavering, filled with an intensity that made my stomach flutter.

"Promise me we'll be honest with each other. No games, no hiding. Just... the truth."

A slow smile spread across his face, lighting up the dimming evening. "I promise. The truth it is."

As we sat there, hands entwined beneath the canopy of stars that began to dot the night sky, I felt a warmth bloom within me. A fragile thread of connection was forming, one that intertwined our fates, and I knew that whatever lay ahead, I was willing to face it together with Adam, heart divided but hopeful.

The night air was thick with unspoken words and the heady scent of impending rain. Adam and I sat side by side, our fingers intertwined, feeling the warmth radiate between us like a lifeline amidst the swirling uncertainties. The world around us felt both vibrant and distant, the laughter of couples and the distant strumming of a guitar blending into a gentle hum that enveloped our moment.

"Do you remember the first time we met?" Adam broke the silence, a playful grin spreading across his face. "You were practically arguing with the barista about the merits of oat milk."

"Oh, please." I rolled my eyes, though the memory made me chuckle. "I was merely expressing a valid opinion. Oat milk is superior."

"Right, because nothing says 'I have my life together' like a caffeine-induced debate about milk alternatives." His laughter echoed softly, and I felt a rush of warmth spread through me. It was moments like this that reminded me why I was drawn to him. Beneath the charm and charisma lay a deeper understanding that felt intoxicating.

"I can't help it if I take my coffee seriously," I said, pretending to be offended. "A good cup of coffee is an art form."

"Art, huh?" He leaned closer, his shoulder brushing against mine, the intimacy of the gesture sending a jolt through me. "Well, I appreciate the passion, but I'm still not convinced oat milk can compete with the richness of whole milk."

"Careful now, that sounds dangerously close to a challenge," I quipped, a spark of mischief igniting within me. "Are you prepared for a coffee-off? I'll bring my best beans, and you can just show up with your... questionable taste."

His eyes danced with amusement. "You're on. Just don't cry when I win, okay?"

I couldn't help but laugh, the tension that had shadowed our conversation beginning to dissipate like the clouds drifting across the night sky. But beneath the playful banter, I sensed something deeper simmering between us—an undeniable connection that seemed to pulse with each shared glance and teasing remark.

As the evening wore on, we talked about everything and nothing, weaving a tapestry of shared dreams and fleeting fears. I found myself opening up in ways I hadn't anticipated, recounting stories from my childhood, the moments that shaped who I was, and the longing that drove me to help others.

"I always wanted to make a difference," I said, my voice softer now. "It's why I became a therapist. But sometimes, I feel like I'm trying to fix everyone while neglecting my own heart."

Adam studied me for a moment, his expression serious as if he could see straight through the carefully constructed facade I presented to the world. "You don't have to fix anyone but yourself. And maybe that's the most important thing of all."

His words settled over me, both a comfort and a challenge. I had been so focused on helping others navigate their lives that I had nearly forgotten to examine my own. But how could I balance my instinct to guide with the desire to follow my own heart—especially when that heart was inexplicably tied to him?

"Maybe that's why I'm terrified of this," I admitted, my voice barely above a whisper. "I don't know how to be vulnerable without feeling like I'm losing control."

"Vulnerability isn't losing control; it's gaining strength," he replied, his tone steady and reassuring. "It's about trusting someone enough to let them see you for who you truly are. And I promise, I'm here for all of it—the messiness and the beauty."

As I looked into his eyes, I saw the sincerity reflected back at me, and I felt a surge of hope. But just as the words began to settle, a sharp voice cut through the tranquility of the park, yanking us from our cocoon of intimacy.

"Adam! There you are!" A woman's voice rang out, brimming with urgency.

I turned, my heart sinking as a striking figure emerged from the shadows, her long, dark hair cascading over her shoulders like a waterfall. She was radiant, exuding confidence as she approached us, and the moment she laid eyes on Adam, I felt a pang of unease grip my stomach.

"Where have you been? I've been looking everywhere for you!" she exclaimed, her expression shifting from concern to irritation.

I glanced at Adam, whose expression was one of confusion, quickly morphing into something unreadable. "Jessie? What are you doing here?"

"I came to see you, obviously," she replied, her tone clipped. "I thought we had plans tonight."

Plans? My mind raced, the warmth that had blossomed between Adam and me suddenly turning cold. I had no idea who this woman was, but her presence felt like a storm cloud rolling in, threatening to overshadow the fragile connection we had been building.

"I thought we agreed to give each other some space," Adam said, a hint of defensiveness creeping into his voice.

"Space? Seriously? This isn't about you and your need for time alone. I'm not letting you run away from this," she retorted, her voice rising slightly.

I shifted in my seat, my heart pounding as the tension in the air thickened. The energy between Adam and this woman crackled, and I could feel my own insecurities bubbling to the surface. What did this mean for us? What was their history?

"I think you should go," Adam said firmly, though his gaze darted toward me, seeking reassurance.

The intensity of the moment sent a rush of adrenaline through my veins. I wanted to scream, to demand clarity, but instead, I sat frozen, caught in a whirlwind of emotions. Jessie looked from Adam to me, her expression softening just a fraction before her eyes narrowed again.

"Fine. But don't think this is over. We need to talk." With that, she turned on her heel, walking away with a confidence that felt almost predatory.

I glanced at Adam, who appeared equally bewildered and frustrated, his brows furrowed in thought. "I didn't know she would be here," he said, running a hand through his hair in exasperation. "I thought I was clear about needing some space."

"Clearly, she didn't get the memo," I replied, trying to mask the tremor in my voice with humor, but it fell flat. "So what does this mean for us?"

Adam's expression shifted, uncertainty creeping into his eyes. "I don't know," he said, and in that moment, the fragile bubble we had built began to crack under the weight of reality.

As the echoes of laughter faded and the park around us transformed from a haven into a battleground of emotions, I realized that love was not just about the beautiful moments; it was also about facing the storms together. But with Jessie's return, the future felt more uncertain than ever, leaving me wondering if we could weather this tumultuous wave or if it would sweep us apart for good.

Chapter 18: "The Last Goodbye"

The air was thick with the scent of impending rain, a damp promise that clung to the city streets like an uninvited guest. I walked through the bustling throngs of people, each face a blur in the soft glow of the streetlights, my heart drumming a rapid, anxious beat. Adam's penthouse loomed ahead, a glass fortress that glimmered under the weight of the gathering clouds, and with every step I took, the distance between us felt as vast as the ocean. Inside, I imagined the scent of his cologne mingling with the faint aroma of whatever dinner he might have prepared. I forced myself not to dwell on that image, on how he'd slip his arms around my waist and pull me close, wrapping me in a cocoon of warmth.

As I approached the entrance, the doorman offered me a polite nod, his expression unreadable, but I could see curiosity flicker in his eyes. I was the girl who often turned to Adam's penthouse for solace, laughter, and love—though it felt like a distant memory now. Steeling myself, I entered the elevator, its polished walls reflecting my apprehensive expression. I took a deep breath, and the scent of his place—freshly brewed coffee and the faintest hint of something floral—welcomed me as the doors opened.

Adam was standing by the floor-to-ceiling windows, the city sprawling beneath him like a shimmering sea of lights. His silhouette was striking, accentuated by the glow of the metropolis, and for a moment, my breath caught in my throat. There he was, the man I had given so much of myself to, and yet, the chasm that had opened between us felt insurmountable. I took a step forward, the plush carpet absorbing the sound of my footsteps, and his head turned slightly, just enough for me to catch a glimpse of his expression. It was pensive, shadows dancing across his features as he processed the weight of my presence.

"Hey," he said softly, the single word holding a multitude of meanings that hung heavy in the air. I could feel the unspoken words—the ones that begged to be articulated—swirling around us like the autumn leaves that danced outside. I swallowed hard, the lump in my throat feeling like a stone.

"Hey," I managed to reply, my voice a mere whisper. There was a gravity in the room, an invisible force pulling us together and yet pushing us apart. I knew what I had to say, yet it felt as if the words were caught in a web of emotions, tangled and resistant.

He stepped closer, and I could see the storm brewing in his eyes. "You look beautiful," he said, his tone a mix of admiration and a hint of sadness. The sincerity of his compliment tugged at my heartstrings, and for a fleeting moment, I almost forgot why I was there.

"Thanks," I replied, forcing a smile that felt more like a mask than genuine happiness. I had always loved how he saw me, how he noticed the smallest details—a new dress, the way my hair fell just right. But tonight, that warmth was replaced by a chill that ran deeper than the brisk air outside.

"Is everything okay?" he asked, his brow furrowing with concern. I could see the flicker of hope in his eyes, that perhaps this was just a visit to reconnect, to reaffirm the bond we once shared. But I was a thief of hope, and I couldn't allow myself to indulge in illusions.

"I... I need to talk to you about something important," I said, trying to keep my voice steady, to inject a sense of control into the whirlwind of feelings churning within me.

He nodded, a hint of worry crossing his face, and gestured for me to sit on the plush couch. The fabric felt soft against my skin, a stark contrast to the jagged edges of my heart. I glanced at him, his fingers intertwined, betraying a tension that mirrored my own.

"Look, I know things have been complicated between us," I started, searching for the right words. "And I've been doing a lot of thinking." The familiar warmth of his presence made it hard to remain resolute, but I forced myself to push through the haze of my emotions. "I just don't think I can keep pretending that everything is okay."

His gaze sharpened, the vulnerability in his eyes turning to something steely. "What do you mean? Is this about me not being there for you?"

"No," I replied quickly, not wanting him to think it was solely about him. "It's not just you. It's me too. I've been feeling... lost. Like we're dancing around something we're both afraid to face."

A flicker of confusion passed over his features, and I took a deep breath, summoning the courage to lay it all bare. "I need more than what you can give, Adam. I need to be able to trust that I can count on you, but it feels like you're always one step away."

He opened his mouth to respond, but the words caught in his throat. The silence stretched between us, palpable and suffocating, as he processed my confession. "So, what are you saying?" His voice was low, almost a rumble, and I could see the hurt in his eyes.

"I'm saying that I can't do this anymore. I need to walk away before I lose myself entirely."

His expression hardened, a storm brewing behind his dark eyes. "So, you're just going to give up?"

The intensity of his words shocked me. "I'm trying to protect myself, Adam! I can't keep waiting for you to make a decision."

The tension in the room was electric, crackling like static before a thunderstorm. I could feel the air thickening, the walls closing in, and I braced myself for the onslaught of emotions I could see brewing in him. But deep down, I knew I had to be strong, even as I felt the pieces of my heart shatter behind me.

The silence in the room was suffocating, thick enough to slice through with a knife. Adam's gaze bore into me, and I felt the heat of his stare as he wrestled with my words. "Protect yourself? Is that really how you see this?" His voice was low, edged with disbelief. "You think running away will fix anything?"

I opened my mouth, searching for the right rebuttal, but it was as if the words had turned to ashes on my tongue. Instead, I stood there, caught in the grip of the moment. The city outside pulsed with life—the distant sound of laughter and the honk of horns barely filtered through the glass. It was a world in motion, while we were ensnared in this suspended animation, teetering on the precipice of an unthinkable goodbye.

"Running away?" I finally managed, my voice trembling, betraying the strength I desperately tried to maintain. "It's not running if I've already been trying to find my way back for so long. I've been here, Adam, hoping you'd meet me halfway."

He ran a hand through his hair, a gesture I knew well, a telltale sign of his mounting frustration. "And what if I'm not the person you want me to be? What if I can't give you what you need?" His eyes darkened, a mix of sorrow and anger swirling within them, creating a tempest I feared might engulf us both.

"Then I can't keep hoping," I said, my heart racing, each pulse echoing the gravity of the moment. "You say you care, but your actions say otherwise. I need someone who can show up, who can be here in every sense of the word. It's not about me wanting you to change; it's about you wanting to be that person."

The tension was palpable, almost like a living entity between us, pushing and pulling, testing our limits. I watched as his expression shifted, the frustration giving way to something softer—an understanding that perhaps he had known all along, deep down, what I was trying to say. "You're right," he admitted quietly, his voice barely above a whisper. "But does that mean we just... stop?"

The vulnerability in his question struck me hard, like a raw nerve exposed to the air. I could feel my own heart breaking at the thought of "stopping," of ending something that had been so beautiful and chaotic, filled with laughter and whispered dreams. "I don't want to stop," I said, my voice cracking under the weight of my emotions. "But I don't want to keep pretending, either. That's a different kind of heartbreak."

"Maybe we can figure it out together," he suggested, stepping closer, and for a fleeting second, I dared to entertain the thought of what that might look like. I could see a glimmer of hope in his eyes, a reflection of the affection that had always simmered beneath the surface of our relationship. But then the image of us fractured, splintered by the reality of our differences.

"Can we?" I countered, unable to hide the skepticism in my voice. "You're so consumed with work, and I feel like I'm chasing a ghost half the time. I'm tired, Adam. I'm tired of being the one left waiting for you to arrive."

The silence returned, heavier this time. I could see him grappling with my words, the weight of truth pressing down on him. I could almost hear the gears turning in his mind, the conflict between his desire to hold on and the acknowledgment that perhaps we were two ships passing in the night.

"Maybe you're right," he finally said, the resolve in his voice faltering. "But I can't just let you go without knowing we've tried everything."

The sincerity in his words struck a chord within me, and for a moment, I considered the possibility of trying again, of what it might mean to give him another chance. But the voice of reason whispered fiercely in my ear, reminding me of all the moments I'd spent hoping for change that never came. "And what does that trying look like, Adam? More late nights and half-hearted conversations? I need something tangible."

He stepped back, running a hand along the back of his neck, the gesture a mixture of frustration and helplessness. "What do you want me to say? That I'll quit my job? That I'll give you everything, no questions asked?"

"Maybe not everything," I said, trying to lighten the mood even as my heart felt like it was being crushed. "But I need more than this vague promise of 'I'll try.' I need commitment, connection. I need you to be present, not just in body but in spirit."

"God, you make it sound so easy," he muttered, a mix of admiration and exasperation coloring his tone. "But you know it's not that simple. Life doesn't just stop because we're in a rut."

"Maybe life doesn't stop, but relationships do," I countered, my heart racing as I challenged him, "if we're not willing to put in the effort. I can't keep pouring myself into something that feels so one-sided."

His eyes narrowed, a flash of anger mixed with desperation. "So what, we just call it quits? Throw away everything we've built?"

"I don't want to throw anything away!" I replied, frustration bubbling to the surface. "But I'm tired of feeling like I'm not enough for you. I want to feel valued, cherished. If that means we have to end this, then I need to face that truth, no matter how much it hurts."

The silence that fell between us felt monumental, like the slow collapse of a bridge that had taken years to build. I could see the battle waging in his eyes—part of him desperate to cling to what we had, and another part that recognized the inevitable truth of my words.

"Maybe... maybe I need time," he said finally, the admission tasting bitter on his tongue. "Time to figure out who I want to be, who I want us to be. But I can't do that if you're not here."

His words hung in the air, heavy and fraught with unspoken implications. The weight of our choices pressed down on me, and I found myself teetering on the edge of a decision I'd long dreaded.

"I can't keep waiting," I murmured, feeling the tremor in my voice. "If we're meant to be, then we'll find our way back to each other someday. But for now, I have to let you go."

The look in his eyes shifted from desperation to something more profound, a mixture of understanding and sorrow, and it shattered me to see it. But as I took a step back, creating the space between us, I felt a flicker of hope. Sometimes, in the act of letting go, we give ourselves the chance to truly find ourselves.

The air around us hung heavy with unsaid words, a delicate tension weaving through the space as I took in Adam's troubled expression. He was standing at the edge of that precarious chasm we had created, and I could see the struggle in his eyes—between the instinct to reach for me and the cold reality that maybe we were simply not meant to bridge this divide.

"Are you really okay with this?" he asked, the weight of his question pressing down like a leaden blanket. I could sense the desperation underlying his words, a plea for reassurance that this wasn't the end of everything we'd built. But as I looked at him, all I could feel was the rush of emotions swirling within me, a cacophony of hope and fear and the bitter taste of loss.

"I don't think I can be okay with it," I admitted, my voice barely rising above a whisper, thick with sorrow. "But staying would be even worse. I can't keep waiting for something to change. I've been doing that for far too long."

His silence was loud, echoing in the space where our laughter used to fill the air. It was as if time itself had slowed down, and in that moment, I could see everything I had wanted with him reflected in his eyes: laughter, companionship, warmth. But it felt like watching a movie that was playing out of sync, the scenes flashing before me, but the sound was just static.

"Maybe we can start over," he suggested suddenly, the earnestness in his voice pulling at my heartstrings. "What if we take a break, you know? Just a moment to breathe and think without all this pressure? We could—"

"A break?" I interrupted, incredulous. "A break is just a fancy word for prolonging the inevitable. If we're being honest with each other, we've been on a break since the day you started putting your job ahead of everything else."

His expression hardened, and I could see the defensive walls rise, a protective barrier against the onslaught of my words. "That's not fair. You know I'm doing this for us, for our future."

"Is that what you call it?" I shot back, feeling the heat of anger bubble beneath my skin. "How am I supposed to see a future with someone who's always absent? Your job is important, I get it, but it shouldn't eclipse everything else. It shouldn't eclipse us."

He took a step back, his hands sliding into the pockets of his tailored pants, a gesture I had come to associate with him feeling cornered. "What do you want me to say? I can't just walk away from my career. It's a part of who I am."

"Then you need to decide what you want more—your career or this relationship. I can't be a secondary character in your life, Adam," I said, my heart racing as I realized the gravity of what I was suggesting. "I deserve to be a priority."

His eyes narrowed, and for a moment, I feared I'd pushed him too far. "You make it sound so simple. Like it's just a matter of choice," he said, his voice dripping with sarcasm. "But you know life isn't that black and white."

"Life is a series of choices, Adam! We choose what we want to fight for. Right now, I'm choosing to fight for my own happiness." The words hung in the air, bold and trembling with raw honesty. I had never been the kind to lay my heart bare, but desperation had pushed me to the edge, and now I felt exhilarated and terrified all at once.

The flicker of defiance in his eyes dimmed, replaced by a dawning realization. "So you're really saying this is it? That you want to walk away from everything?"

"I'm saying I need to walk away for now, maybe forever," I replied, my voice steady even as my heart crumbled. "I can't keep hoping for something that isn't coming. I won't be the girl who waits for a prince to realize she's worth the effort."

For a moment, he just stared at me, a mixture of disbelief and something softer—regret? Anger? It was hard to tell. "I wish you would have told me this sooner," he said finally, his tone flat, devoid of the spark I once adored.

"I did tell you, Adam. You just didn't listen."

His jaw tightened, and I could see the storm brewing behind his eyes. "So, that's it? You're walking away, just like that?"

"It's not just 'like that,'" I shot back, feeling the sting of my own tears. "It's everything. It's the nights spent alone while you're at work, the missed calls, the promises that never materialize. I need to know that I matter."

He turned away from me, staring out at the city lights that twinkled like distant stars, each one a reminder of everything we could have been. "I never meant to make you feel like you didn't matter," he said softly, almost to himself.

"I know you didn't," I replied, my voice trembling. "But intentions don't change reality. And reality is that I feel invisible."

In that moment, something shifted between us, a palpable change in the air. The tension morphed into a thick silence, filled with a gravity that made it hard to breathe. I could feel the heat of his gaze on me, a mixture of longing and despair.

"You're really going to leave, aren't you?" he asked, his voice cracking ever so slightly.

"I have to," I said, each word heavier than the last. "I can't keep waiting for you to choose me. It's time for me to choose myself."

He looked at me, and for a fleeting moment, I saw the flicker of pain reflected in his eyes—a pain that mirrored my own. "You don't have to do this alone," he offered, his voice barely above a whisper.

"I don't want to do it alone," I admitted, the truth hitting me with a rush. "But I can't keep tethering myself to someone who might never anchor me."

Adam's expression shifted, the shadows deepening as he took a step toward me, and I felt the air thrum with tension. "If you walk out that door, you may not come back. I can't promise I'll be here if you change your mind."

His words hung in the air, a challenge and a plea all at once. I could feel the warmth of his presence, the ache of his need to hold on to what we had, but I was terrified of falling back into old patterns.

"I have to take that risk," I said, my heart pounding in my chest. "And so do you."

The space between us felt charged, electric, and I took a deep breath, steeling myself for what I had to do. "Goodbye, Adam," I said, turning to face the door.

But just as I reached for the handle, the phone on the table buzzed, cutting through the tension like a knife. I paused, glancing back at Adam, whose expression had shifted from anguish to something more urgent.

"Wait," he said, his voice filled with sudden alarm. "Don't leave yet. You need to hear this."

Curiosity piqued, I hesitated, torn between my instinct to flee and the nagging pull of what could be unfolding. "What are you talking about?"

His eyes were wide, and I could see the storm of emotions raging within him. "It's about the project I've been working on—the one I told you about. There's been a development."

"What kind of development?" I asked, apprehension flooding my veins.

"Just... just listen." His voice was urgent, and I found myself drawn back toward him, caught between the precipice of goodbye and the unknown.

As he reached for the phone, the gravity of the moment pressed down on us. I could sense that whatever was about to happen could change everything. And then, before he could say another word, the doorbell rang, a sharp, jarring sound that echoed through the silence, sending a shiver down my spine.

I froze, the reality of the moment crashing down around me. "Who could that be?"

Adam's expression shifted again, something dark and foreboding crossing his features. "I don't know," he said slowly, his eyes narrowing. "But it's not good."

I felt a rush of adrenaline, the sense that the world around us was about to unravel in ways we couldn't have anticipated. "What do you mean?"

He opened his mouth to respond, but the door swung open before he could speak, revealing a figure standing in the dim light, shrouded in mystery.

"Adam," the figure said, their voice low and steady. "We need to talk. It's about the project."

The weight of the world hung in the air, and I could feel the tension snap like a taut string, the promise of chaos just waiting to be unleashed. My heart raced as I realized that this unexpected visitor was about to upend everything we had just fought for, leaving me teetering on the edge of an unknown future.

Chapter 19: "Finding Me Again"

The sun slanted through the tall windows of my studio, casting long shadows that danced across the floor like playful spirits. I'd hung my latest creation on the wall—a vibrant canvas splashed with bursts of color that seemed to pulse with energy. I stood back, hands on my hips, studying it with a mix of pride and uncertainty. It was a reflection of the chaotic whirlwind inside me, a cacophony of emotions that I was slowly learning to express through paint. Each stroke was a little piece of my heart, and in that moment, I felt a rush of exhilaration. Art had always been my refuge, a sanctuary where I could hide my vulnerabilities. Yet now, it was also a stage where I could showcase my revival.

Just as I was lost in thought, my phone buzzed, a sharp reminder of the world outside my artistic cocoon. A message from Lily popped up, her playful banter lighting up the screen like fireworks. "Coffee? Or are you still in your cave, Miss Van Gogh?" The jibe was familiar, comforting. It felt good to know that someone was waiting for me on the other side of my solitude, ready to pull me back into the fold of laughter and companionship.

I quickly typed a response, feeling the corners of my mouth lift into a smile. "I'll meet you at our spot. Just let me grab my keys!" I tossed the phone onto my cluttered work desk, a small island of chaos surrounded by tubes of paint, brushes, and half-finished canvases. As I slipped into my favorite leather jacket—a relic from my past adventures—I caught my reflection in the glass pane of the window. The woman staring back at me had a new light in her eyes, a resilience that hadn't been there before. I realized I was shedding the remnants of my heartbreak, layer by layer, much like the paint on my canvases.

The café was buzzing when I arrived, a comforting hum that wrapped around me like a warm embrace. The rich aroma of roasted coffee beans mingled with the sweet scent of pastries, enticing and familiar. Lily waved enthusiastically from her usual corner table, her curls bouncing as she called out to me. "Finally! I thought you might have joined a monastery or something!"

I rolled my eyes but couldn't suppress a chuckle as I slid into the chair across from her. "You know I could never give up caffeine and art. They're practically my lifeblood."

Lily leaned in, her expression a mix of mischief and concern. "So, tell me, how's the rebranding of Sarah? You know, the new and improved version who doesn't pine for lost loves?"

I paused, the smile faltering for just a moment. The truth was, I felt caught between two worlds: the vibrant present filled with potential and the lingering shadows of the past. "It's...getting there. I'm just trying to keep busy, you know?"

"Busy is good, but you have to live a little too," she teased, her eyes twinkling. "When was the last time you actually went out, like, for fun? Not just to grab a coffee or see the latest exhibition?"

I drummed my fingers against the table, my mind flitting back to the nights when laughter and music filled the air, when spontaneous decisions led to wild adventures. "Okay, okay, I'll admit it. I haven't been out in a while. But I've got work to do, and you know how it is. I need to rebuild."

"Rebuild? Or distract?" She leaned back, arms crossed, clearly not buying my defense. "You can't paint over your feelings, Sarah. Eventually, they'll just seep through the cracks."

Her words hung in the air between us, challenging yet gentle. I sighed, the weight of her insight pressing against me. "I know. It's just...Adam and I had something special. It's hard not to think about what could have been."

Lily softened, her tone shifting to one of understanding. "But it's also hard to find you in the 'what could have been,' right? You deserve to explore what's ahead, not just what's behind you."

"Maybe I need to start saying yes more often," I mused aloud, feeling the flicker of possibility ignite within me. "Yes to spontaneity, yes to new experiences."

"Exactly! Why not shake things up? Let's make a pact. This weekend, we'll go to that new art exhibit downtown, followed by dinner at that Italian place you love. It'll be fun, I promise!"

Her enthusiasm was contagious. I couldn't help but smile, a genuine grin spreading across my face. "Alright, I'm in. But you know I'll be the one insisting we order a ridiculous number of desserts afterward."

"Deal!" she laughed, her energy infectious. We spent the next hour chatting, sharing stories and laughter that lifted the lingering heaviness in my chest. With every shared anecdote, every burst of laughter, I could feel the pieces of me that had shattered begin to realign.

But as I walked back to my studio later, the shadows returned to tease the edges of my thoughts. The city was alive around me—cars honked, pedestrians hustled, and the distant sound of music floated through the air, a reminder that life continued to move forward. Yet, in the quiet moments, I felt the echo of Adam's laughter, the warmth of his smile, and the way he had made the world seem more vibrant.

As I reached for the door to my studio, I paused, allowing myself to linger in that bittersweet remembrance. The past was a part of me, undeniably woven into the fabric of who I was, but it didn't have to define my future. With a deep breath, I pushed the door open, stepping into the realm where I could create and reclaim myself. Today was just one step, but it was mine.

The weekend arrived with a crispness in the air that felt electric, a harbinger of the adventures I had promised myself. I had spent the morning pouring over my sketches, but as noon approached, the thrill of anticipation nudged me to set aside my paintbrushes. I slipped into a pair of sleek boots and a flowing scarf that danced around my neck like a playful breeze. With a quick check in the mirror—yes, the glimmer of excitement was unmistakable—I grabbed my bag and headed out the door.

The streets buzzed with life, the autumn leaves swirling at my feet as if welcoming me back into the world. I found myself smiling at strangers, absorbing the vibrant tapestry of life around me. Coffee shops spilled laughter and conversations onto the sidewalk, while artists displayed their wares at pop-up stands, each piece a story waiting to be told. I felt lighter, buoyed by the prospect of the afternoon ahead.

Lily was already at the gallery when I arrived, bouncing on her heels as she scanned the entrance for me. She was a whirlwind of color and energy, her outfit a riotous mix of patterns that somehow harmonized like a well-composed symphony. "You made it! I was beginning to think you'd forgotten how to have fun," she teased, pulling me into a quick hug that felt like an electric jolt of warmth.

"Forgotten? Please, I was just in a very intense relationship with my art," I replied, rolling my eyes playfully. "But I'm here now, and I promise to soak up all the fun like a sponge."

The exhibit was a celebration of contemporary artists, and as we entered the gallery, my senses were overwhelmed. The walls glowed with the brilliance of color, and the air was thick with the scent of fresh paint and creativity. Each piece seemed to pulse with life, telling stories of heartache, joy, and everything in between. I felt my heartbeat quicken with excitement; art had a way of weaving connections, and today felt like a tapestry unfurling before me.

"Look at this!" Lily exclaimed, leading me toward a sprawling mural that depicted a cityscape under a swirling night sky. The stars seemed to shimmer, beckoning viewers into the depths of the artist's imagination. "Can you even believe the colors? It's like he's inviting us to step into another world."

"It's breathtaking," I replied, my fingers itching to grab a brush and replicate that emotion. "It makes me want to create something completely new."

As we wandered through the exhibit, our laughter mingling with the soft murmur of art enthusiasts, I could feel the shadows of my past receding further into the background. Lily's infectious energy was a balm to my soul, and I allowed myself to relish in the present, indulging in the beauty of creativity that surrounded me.

When we finally settled into a small café nearby for dinner, I felt as though the universe had conspired to uplift my spirit. Over plates of pasta and glasses of red wine, we shared stories, our words weaving a tapestry of friendship that felt unbreakable. "You know," Lily said, her brow furrowing playfully, "I was thinking we should make our next adventure even more outrageous. Maybe a spontaneous weekend trip?"

I chuckled, envisioning the chaotic packing that would ensue. "And where exactly do you propose we go? Las Vegas? Because I'm not ready to gamble my love life again just yet."

"Very funny! No, I was thinking more like a cozy cabin in the woods. Just us, some wine, and endless starry nights. What do you think?"

The idea sparked a flutter of excitement deep within me. I could almost hear the crackling of a fire, feel the cool night air against my skin as we sat beneath a blanket of stars, far away from the noise of the city. "A cabin sounds delightful, actually. Just us and nature. Count me in!"

We clinked our glasses together, sealing our pact as if it were a sacred ritual. But the excitement was quickly interrupted by a sudden commotion outside the café. A familiar voice cut through the clatter of dishes and laughter, and my heart sank as I turned to see Adam standing there, framed by the warm light spilling from the café's entrance.

He was engrossed in conversation with a group of friends, his laughter ringing out like music that once filled my own heart. The sight of him sent a cascade of memories rushing back—lazy Sunday mornings, spontaneous road trips, and laughter that felt like sunshine. Just then, he turned his head, and our eyes met for the briefest moment. The world around me faded away, and I felt the pull of our past like a gravitational force.

"Is that...?" Lily began, her eyes darting between Adam and me, her expression a mix of concern and excitement. "Oh, this just got interesting."

I couldn't look away, my heart racing in a way that was both exhilarating and terrifying. "What do I do?" I whispered, my voice barely above a breath.

"Just breathe, Sarah. You're a fierce artist, remember? You can handle this." Her encouraging words barely registered as my thoughts spiraled into chaos. What was he doing here? Was this some kind of cosmic joke? Just as quickly as he had appeared, Adam turned back to his friends, laughter bubbling up once again.

"What's he laughing about?" I mumbled, a knot forming in my stomach. "Why is he here, of all places?"

"Let's just be cool about it," Lily suggested, reaching for my hand as if to tether me to reality. "Just enjoy the moment. If he comes over, you'll handle it. You're strong, remember?"

Just then, fate took an unexpected turn. One of Adam's friends stepped away from the group, glancing over in our direction. With a swift nod of recognition, he made his way toward us, his face lighting up as he approached. "Hey, Sarah! Long time no see!"

I forced a smile, feeling the warmth drain from my cheeks. "Hi, Jake! It's been a while."

He leaned in, oblivious to the storm brewing in my heart. "Yeah, we just wrapped up a project downtown. Adam was telling us about his recent trips. You should join us sometime! The whole group has missed you."

I shot a glance back at Adam, who was now watching us, his expression unreadable. The tension in my chest tightened, and I could hear the laughter from my past, but it felt like a haunting melody now—sweet yet bittersweet, full of memories that felt too raw.

"Thanks, Jake," I managed, my voice steadier than I felt. "It's great to hear from you."

Just then, the moment stretched like an elastic band, and I sensed the eyes of everyone around us turning toward the unspoken history lingering in the air. Adam was still there, and I could feel the magnetic pull of the past competing with my newfound determination to step forward into my future.

As Jake chatted away, his easygoing demeanor a stark contrast to the storm of emotions brewing within me, I felt a curious mixture of comfort and discomfort wash over me. I forced myself to focus on his words, the rhythm of his voice a familiar background noise, but my eyes kept drifting back to Adam. He was surrounded by friends, yet he seemed detached, his laughter echoing in a way that felt far away, almost like a distant memory that tugged at my heartstrings.

"And you know, Adam still insists on being the designated driver for every outing," Jake continued, a smirk dancing on his lips. "He thinks he's the moral compass of our group. It's hilarious. Last week, he actually tried to convince us to walk back from a bar six miles away."

I couldn't help but laugh at that. "I can't believe he'd do something so ridiculous. He never was one to back down from a challenge, was he?"

Jake grinned, and for a moment, it felt as though we were simply old friends catching up, the past sliding away like water under a bridge. But then the air thickened, and I could feel Adam's gaze on me again, a palpable weight that sent my heart racing. It was as if he were an artist scrutinizing a half-finished canvas, trying to understand the layers beneath.

"Are you two going to ignore each other all night?" Jake quipped, arching an eyebrow in that effortlessly charming way of his. "Because if so, I'm afraid that's a crime against art, and we'll have to report you."

I turned to Jake, surprised by the hint of challenge in his voice. "Oh, I'm sure it's just a matter of timing," I said lightly, but even I could hear the tension weaving its way into my words.

"Timing is everything," Jake said, leaning back in his chair, a knowing smile on his face. "But sometimes you just have to jump in, you know? Life is too short for hesitation." He looked back toward Adam, who was now looking right at me, his eyes piercing through the noise of the café.

"Right," I said, my heart racing. "Like jumping off a cliff and hoping the water is deep enough?"

"Exactly! You'll either land on solid ground or get an unforgettable story," Jake said, laughter sparkling in his eyes. "And I bet you're due for a good story, Sarah."

As if summoned by fate, Adam stepped away from his group, his gaze steady as he approached our table. My breath caught in my throat. I felt like a rabbit caught in the headlights of an oncoming car, paralyzed by the mixed emotions flooding through me.

"Hey, Sarah," he said, his voice calm but laced with an undercurrent of something deeper. "Fancy seeing you here."

I forced myself to meet his gaze, searching for the warmth I had once known, but it was like staring into an abstract painting—beautiful, yet chaotic. "Yeah, just indulging in a bit of culture," I replied, my tone slightly sharper than I intended. "What about you?"

He glanced at Jake, who was suddenly engrossed in his coffee, the air thick with unspoken tension. "Just catching up with friends. You know how it is."

The unflinching gaze between us felt like an unspoken challenge, as if we were both testing the waters to see if we could navigate this moment without drowning in the past. "I didn't know you were back in town," he said, his tone neutral, but I could sense the question hanging in the air—why hadn't I reached out?

"Just visiting for the weekend. Thought I'd reacquaint myself with some old haunts." I gestured to the gallery behind me, the art now serving as a backdrop for our personal drama. "The exhibit was too good to miss."

"Looks like you're really throwing yourself into things," he said, a hint of something—admiration or concern—flickering in his eyes. "I'm glad to see that."

"Yeah, well, life goes on," I replied, an edge creeping into my voice that I couldn't quite suppress. I wanted to maintain that buoyant spirit I had felt earlier, but the weight of our shared history pressed heavily on my shoulders.

There was a brief, awkward silence, and I could feel Jake shifting uncomfortably in his seat. I didn't want to revisit old wounds in front of him, but I also couldn't help but notice how the dynamic between Adam and me felt so charged, so unfinished.

"Sarah, can we talk?" Adam asked, his eyes softening slightly, a flicker of vulnerability breaking through the tension.

Before I could respond, Lily emerged from the café's entrance, a bright whirlwind of energy, her presence a much-needed distraction. "There you are! I was looking for you two!" she exclaimed, her eyes darting between us. "What's going on? Is this a reunion I didn't get the memo for?"

I sighed in relief, grateful for the interruption. "We were just catching up, you know. The usual small talk."

"Right, small talk," Adam echoed, but there was a tightness to his smile that betrayed his true feelings. "I'm sure it's just riveting."

"Oh, come on! Let's get out of here," Lily said, her enthusiasm infectious. "We can grab ice cream or something and have a real catch-up! I'm starving."

"Great idea!" Jake chimed in, clearly eager to diffuse the tension.

As we filed out of the café, the night air enveloped us like a blanket, crisp and full of possibilities. But even as we walked down the street, laughter bubbling around us, I felt the unshakable awareness of Adam walking beside me, an invisible thread binding us together.

"Listen, can we talk later?" he said quietly, leaning in just enough for me to hear. "I really want to catch up. Just us."

I nodded, my heart hammering in my chest. "Sure, later sounds good." But as the words left my mouth, a sense of trepidation settled in. The night held promise, but it also carried the weight of unresolved feelings, questions left hanging in the air like an unfinished canvas.

Our laughter echoed through the streets, yet my thoughts remained tangled in a web of uncertainty. Ice cream was soon replaced by unexpected silences and shared glances, but my mind was focused on that impending conversation. Adam's presence was a bittersweet reminder of what had been, and the possibility of what might still be.

Just as we reached the ice cream parlor, the jingle of the doorbell ringing behind us, I felt a tremor of unease course through the atmosphere. A sudden shout erupted from the street, drawing everyone's attention. I turned to see a figure racing toward us, their face obscured by a hood, urgency etched in every movement.

"What the—?" I began, but the world around me shattered into chaos as the figure lunged forward, and everything I had been holding in came rushing to the surface.

"Sarah!" Adam shouted, his voice a mix of fear and determination, but before I could react, the figure was upon us, and my heart plummeted into the depths of uncertainty. The night had just taken a turn I never saw coming.

Chapter 20: "Unfinished Business"

The ballroom sparkled under a sea of twinkling chandeliers, each light casting a golden glow over the glittering gowns and tailored suits that swirled in a kaleidoscope of color. The air was thick with the scent of expensive perfumes mingled with the delicate notes of hors d'oeuvres being passed around by waitstaff in crisp white jackets. I clutched my glass of champagne, the bubbles tickling my nose as I scanned the crowd, hoping to catch a glimpse of anyone I knew.

Manhattan's elite were a peculiar breed, each person more polished than the last, a shimmering façade that concealed the cracks and shadows of their lives. I had come to this charity gala with the intention of networking—because in my world, you were only as valuable as your last successful connection. But all my plans were derailed the moment my gaze landed on him. Adam stood across the room, his broad shoulders silhouetted against the backdrop of laughter and chatter. He wore a tailored navy suit that accentuated his height, but it was his expression that caught me off guard.

Gone was the cocky, charming smile I had once known so well; instead, his features held a certain softness, as if the years had molded him into a more thoughtful version of himself. Our eyes locked, and a shiver raced down my spine. Time had twisted and tangled around us, yet in that instant, it felt as if no time had passed at all. The noise faded into a muffled hum, and I felt the world around us blur into insignificance.

"Can we talk?" His voice cut through the haze, low and tentative, as if afraid of the answer. I could see the tension etched around his mouth, the way he shifted slightly, unsure whether to take a step closer or retreat. My heart drummed a staccato rhythm in my chest, a mix of excitement and trepidation.

"Sure," I said, unable to mask the tremor in my voice. "Let's find somewhere quieter." The words slipped out before I could fully process them, and before I knew it, I was leading him toward a less populated corner of the room, away from the prying eyes and eager ears.

The space was framed by velvet drapes, dimly lit, a stark contrast to the opulence of the gala. A small table stood in the corner, untouched by the bustle, and I motioned for us to sit. He followed, his movements measured, as if he were stepping into an uncertain future.

The moment we were seated, the air crackled with the unspoken weight of our past. I sipped my champagne, the bubbles exploding in my mouth, but they did little to quell the tension. Adam ran a hand through his hair, the gesture familiar and comforting, yet it sent a jolt of memory coursing through me—the late-night conversations, the laughter, the promises made in whispered tones.

"I didn't expect to see you here," he began, his eyes searching mine for a flicker of the affection we once shared. "You look... incredible."

"Thanks," I replied, a smile tugging at my lips, though I fought to keep it subdued. "You look different yourself. Less... intense."

"Intense?" He chuckled, the sound rich and warm. "I'll take that as a compliment."

"Good luck with that. You're not exactly the soft type, Adam." I raised an eyebrow, matching his gaze with a playful challenge.

"People change," he said, leaning in slightly, the earnestness in his voice almost disarming. "I've changed."

The weight of his words hung in the air between us, heavy and thick. I could see the shadows of his past lingering just behind his eyes. "What do you mean?" I probed, my curiosity piqued despite my better judgment.

He hesitated, the playful banter fading as he considered his words carefully. "I've been doing a lot of thinking. About us. About the choices I made."

"Choices? Is that what we're calling it?" My voice was sharper than intended, and I regretted the edge that crept in, but the scars of our history still stung.

He flinched, then straightened, determination flickering across his face. "I was a fool, alright? I was so focused on my career, I didn't see what was right in front of me. I didn't see you."

The admission landed heavily between us, and for a moment, I was lost in the flood of emotions—the warmth of nostalgia battling the bitterness of the past. "You had your reasons," I said, trying to keep my voice steady. "And I had mine."

"Can we just... start over?" he asked, his sincerity striking a chord deep within me. The thought of wiping the slate clean felt both exhilarating and terrifying. I wanted to believe him, to believe that the Adam I once adored could reemerge from the shadows of his past.

"Start over?" I echoed, a mix of hope and skepticism dancing in my chest. "You think it's that easy?"

"Nothing worth having ever is," he replied, a hint of a smile tugging at his lips. "But it's worth a shot, isn't it?"

I wanted to scream at the unfairness of it all—how could he stand there, exuding confidence and charm, while I was still grappling with the aftermath of our shared history? Yet, as I looked into his eyes, I saw a flicker of the man I once loved, the one who had turned my world upside down and left me to piece it back together.

"Maybe," I whispered, my heart caught in a battle between longing and self-preservation. The night felt electric, and the air between us crackled with the possibility of what could be. The chaos of the gala faded into the background, leaving only the two of us and the whispers of our unfinished business.

The soft glow of the dim lighting painted Adam's features in a gentle hue, and as I leaned forward, my curiosity eclipsed the lingering uncertainty. There was something undeniably magnetic about him, something that made the years apart dissolve into mere minutes. I couldn't help but notice the faint lines around his eyes, the kind that hinted at sleepless nights and hard-won wisdom.

"Starting over sounds great in theory," I said, tapping the rim of my glass with a finger, my thoughts swirling with hesitation. "But it's not just a flick of a switch. There's so much history here, Adam."

"I know," he replied, his gaze unwavering. "And I'm not asking you to forget it. Just to... consider the possibility that I'm different now."

"Different how?" I challenged, needing to gauge whether he was genuinely sincere or merely the same charming façade cloaked in a new outfit. "Is this about the new suit? Because I'm not convinced."

He chuckled, a genuine sound that reminded me of simpler times when laughter came easy between us. "You know me too well. It's not the suit, I promise. It's about realizing what I've lost and wanting to find a way back to it."

His words danced in the air, a promise wrapped in vulnerability. The part of me that longed for connection stirred, but another part—a more cautious part—held back. "You had your chance, Adam. You made your choice," I countered, forcing myself to remain grounded.

"I didn't just choose my career," he said, his voice dipping lower, the earnestness in his tone pulling at something deep within me. "I thought I was doing the right thing. But now I see it's the wrong way to live. I sacrificed too much, and for what? A few more zeros on my paycheck?"

"Zeros that could buy you a cozy penthouse and a table at the hottest restaurants."

"Maybe," he admitted, his expression softening. "But those tables are empty without the right company."

A silence stretched between us, thick and loaded with unspoken words. I could see it in his eyes—the regret, the longing. It made my heart twist, as if caught in a vice. I leaned back slightly, trying to regain my composure, but I was no longer sure where I stood in this conversation.

"Do you really think we can just pick up where we left off?" I asked, the doubt lacing my words.

"Maybe not exactly where we left off," he replied, his tone now more thoughtful. "But I think we can find a new path forward together. I want to earn back your trust."

"Trust, huh?" I raised an eyebrow, skeptical. "That's a tall order. It's not just a matter of a handshake and a smile."

"Then let's take it one step at a time," he suggested, leaning in, his voice dropping to a conspiratorial whisper. "What if we start by being honest with each other?"

"Honest?" I echoed, a wry smile forming at the corner of my lips. "Oh, this should be entertaining."

"I'll go first," he said, his demeanor shifting from playful to serious. "I missed you. Not just on a surface level, but in a way that's deep and unsettling. There hasn't been a day that I haven't thought about what could have been."

My heart raced at his admission, the truth of his words resonating like a drumbeat within me. "You really think you can just say that and I'll forget the years of silence?"

"No, but I hope you'll hear me out," he replied, his sincerity cutting through my defenses. "Every time I looked in the mirror, I saw the man who walked away from something precious. I was the fool, and I'm not proud of it."

"Being a fool doesn't usually come with a complimentary 'I'm sorry' card," I said, crossing my arms as if to shield myself from his words.

"Fair enough," he conceded. "But I'm here now, ready to own up to my mistakes."

I stared at him, feeling the tension shift as I weighed his words against the backdrop of memories that played like an old film reel in my mind. "What if I'm not ready for this? What if I've finally moved on?"

"I'm willing to take that risk," he said, his voice steady and earnest. "I want to prove to you that I've changed. Not just for you, but for myself as well."

"Prove it?" I echoed, intrigued yet guarded. "And how do you plan on doing that?"

"Let's start small," he suggested, his eyes gleaming with determination. "How about coffee? No expectations, just two people reconnecting."

I paused, the idea rolling around in my mind like a stone skipping across water. The thought of sharing a simple cup of coffee felt deceptively easy, yet it carried the weight of our past—both daunting and liberating.

"Okay, coffee," I finally replied, the word escaping my lips with a mix of apprehension and anticipation. "But no grand gestures, no heartfelt proclamations. Just coffee."

"Deal," he said, the corners of his mouth lifting into that familiar half-smile that had once made my heart flutter. "I can handle that."

Just as the tension began to lift, a commotion erupted from the other side of the ballroom. A loud crash interrupted our moment, drawing the attention of the elegantly dressed guests who turned to see what had transpired. A waiter, overwhelmed by the crowd, had spilled a tray of champagne flutes onto the polished floor, the sound shattering the bubble of our intimate conversation.

"Perfect timing," I muttered under my breath, my heart racing again—not from the unexpected chaos, but from the reminder that the world was still spinning around us.

Adam chuckled softly, and the warmth of his laughter wrapped around me like a cozy blanket. "Looks like life doesn't want us to have a dull moment."

"Or a quiet one," I replied, my spirits lifting slightly at his humor. "What do you say we salvage this evening and find a quieter corner?"

"Lead the way."

As we stood, the distance between us felt charged, filled with the potential of what lay ahead. I could sense that unfinished business wasn't just a lingering ghost of our past; it was the foundation of something new, something we could build if we dared to tread carefully.

The gala swirled around us, a whirlpool of laughter, music, and sparkling conversation, but in that moment, it was just the two of us, embarking on a journey neither of us could fully predict. The thrill of possibility hung in the air, tinged with the sweet scent of change and the bittersweet taste of what we had once shared.

We navigated through the shifting currents of the gala, weaving past clusters of guests animatedly discussing their charitable contributions and the latest fashion trends. The din of voices faded slightly as we found a quieter alcove draped in rich, deep red fabric. It felt almost like a secret hideaway, cocooned from the glittering chaos outside. I took a breath, trying to center myself amid the storm of emotions swirling within me.

"Coffee sounds innocent enough," I mused, my voice almost swallowed by the plush fabric around us. "But we both know it could lead to something more complicated. You want me to believe you've changed, but what if we tumble back into old habits?"

"I wouldn't expect you to trust me right away," Adam replied, his tone measured and sincere. "But I want to show you that I'm not the same man who left without looking back. This time, I'm here to listen."

"Listen?" I echoed, the word teasing my skepticism. "Or are you here to lecture me on the virtues of forgiveness and the importance of second chances?"

He chuckled softly, the sound brushing against the tension like a balm. "No lectures, I promise. Just a genuine conversation between two people who might have lost their way."

"Two people or just one?" I shot back, unable to suppress the sharpness in my voice. "Because it sure feels like I've been standing alone in this mess for a while."

"I know it must seem that way," he admitted, the sincerity of his gaze holding me captive. "But I'm here now, and I want to hear your story. All of it. Not just the highlights."

I crossed my arms, weighing his words against the tangled web of memories and emotions that tied us together. "Fine. You want honesty? Let's start with why I'm even here tonight."

"Please do," he said, leaning in as if he could siphon the secrets from my lips.

"I was supposed to network, connect with potential clients, and build my brand," I confessed, the words tumbling out. "But instead, I find myself tangled up in the past, with you."

His eyes softened, understanding flickering across his features. "Is that a bad thing?"

"Depends," I replied, feeling a spark of defiance. "If I walk away tonight with nothing but a broken heart and another round of 'what ifs,' then yes, it's a terrible thing."

His expression turned serious. "Let's make sure that doesn't happen. I don't want to be just a 'what if' in your life anymore. I want to be a 'what is.'"

"Bold statement," I said, allowing a flicker of a smile to dance across my lips. "Do you have any idea how much is at stake?"

"Everything," he replied, the intensity of his gaze igniting a flutter of warmth in my chest. "Including your happiness."

The way he spoke made it hard to remain unaffected. I had spent years cultivating a wall around my heart, and now here he was, threatening to dismantle it with mere words. "You're really delving into dangerous territory," I warned, my voice low. "This isn't a game, Adam."

"Trust me, I know the stakes. I've lost before, and I don't want to go through that again—especially if it's with you," he said, a flicker of vulnerability breaking through his confident exterior.

A rush of emotions bubbled within me—desire, fear, a cautious hope that maybe, just maybe, we could rewrite our narrative. "Okay, let's say I entertain this notion of a fresh start. What does that look like for you?"

"Coffee, for starters. I want to hear about your life since I messed things up. I want to know what you've been up to, what makes you laugh, what drives you insane."

"Wow, getting deep for coffee, aren't we?" I quipped, rolling my eyes, but the warmth in my chest expanded at the thought of sharing those details with him.

"Only because I want it to mean something," he said, and I could see the resolve in his eyes. "I don't want to waste any more time."

"Fine. Coffee it is," I replied, unable to suppress a smile. "But you know I'm not just going to spill my life story like it's some evening gossip."

"I wouldn't expect anything less from you," he grinned, and for the first time that evening, the weight of our past began to feel lighter.

Just then, the sound of laughter erupted nearby, and our moment was interrupted by the arrival of a group of familiar faces. Friends from my past—people who had been part of my life when things had been simpler, before Adam had turned it all upside down.

"Hey, look who we have here!" One of them, Claire, exclaimed, her voice carrying over the thrumming music. "What a surprise to see you two together!"

The way she raised her eyebrows and smirked made it clear she had her suspicions. I exchanged a quick glance with Adam, an unspoken understanding passing between us that we weren't ready to share this new chapter with the world just yet.

"Just catching up," I said, forcing a lightness into my tone. "Nothing too scandalous, I promise."

"Sure, just two old flames reigniting, no big deal!" Claire teased, her laughter ringing out like a bell.

"Old flames? Is that what you're calling it?" I shot back, trying to keep the panic from creeping into my voice.

"Just a figure of speech!" Claire winked, unaware of the way my heart raced at the prospect of what that might mean.

Adam chuckled, his gaze still steady on me, but I could see the flicker of tension behind his playful demeanor. "We should probably wrap this up before the rumor mill goes into overdrive," he suggested, shooting me a look that told me he was equally aware of the situation.

"Agreed," I replied, trying to maintain a semblance of composure as the group continued to chatter around us, oblivious to the tension and potential brewing in our little corner of the world.

Just then, another voice cut through the crowd, one that sent a shiver of recognition down my spine. "Adam! There you are!"

I turned, my heart dropping as I spotted a woman striding toward us, her confidence radiating like the sun. Her long, flowing dress swayed around her, and her striking features were impossible to ignore.

"Sarah," Adam greeted her, his voice shifting slightly, a subtle change that didn't escape my notice.

"Oh, I was hoping you'd show up!" Sarah said, her tone breezy yet laced with something I couldn't quite identify. "I've been dying to introduce you to some friends."

As she beamed at Adam, the unspoken invitation lingered in the air, and I felt the weight of uncertainty settle back around me like an unwelcome cloak.

"I, uh—" Adam started, glancing at me with a hint of unease.

"Just let me steal him for a minute," Sarah insisted, her smile broadening as she looped her arm through Adam's. "Come on, I want to show you off!"

The words struck like a bolt of lightning, shattering the fragile moment we'd just begun to build. My heart raced, and I felt a familiar knot tighten in my stomach.

"Wait—" I began, but the laughter of the group drowned out my voice, leaving me standing alone in the alcove, watching as Adam was swept away into the sea of guests, the promise of our conversation fading into the background noise.

What had begun as a tentative step toward rekindling a connection had turned into a precarious cliffhanger, and suddenly, I was left to wonder if I would ever get the chance to finish what we had started.

Chapter 21: "A Second Chance?"

The aroma of freshly brewed coffee mingled with the faint scent of cinnamon wafting from the bakery counter, a comforting embrace in the crisp morning air. I took a seat at the small table tucked in the corner of the café, the sun streaming through the window and casting a warm glow across the polished wooden surface. It was my favorite spot, a little nook where I could watch the world go by, but today, the world felt impossibly heavy. The moment Adam walked in, I felt the tension settle like a dense fog, smothering the usual comfort of my surroundings.

His entrance was punctuated by a quick glance around the café, a searching look that locked onto mine as if he'd been holding his breath, hoping I'd be here. There was a slight hesitance in his step, a familiar swagger tempered by something deeper—a newfound humility, perhaps? I hadn't seen him since the day I'd walked away, the day his words had cut deeper than I ever thought possible. Now, sitting across from him, I noticed the way his eyes flickered, almost nervously, as he pulled out a chair and sank into it. The confident man I once knew seemed replaced by a more introspective version, one who bore the weight of regret like a well-worn coat.

"Thanks for meeting me," he said, his voice steady yet soft, as if every word was carefully measured. "I know this might seem sudden, but I needed to see you."

I took a deep breath, forcing the remnants of bitterness and hurt to the back of my mind. "It's... fine. I needed coffee, anyway." The casualness of my words felt like a flimsy shield against the onslaught of emotions bubbling just beneath the surface. I stirred my coffee absentmindedly, watching the cream swirl into a soft, tan embrace.

He leaned forward, the distance between us suddenly feeling like a chasm I had no idea how to cross. "I've changed," he asserted, the conviction in his voice tinged with vulnerability. "I spent the time apart really thinking about us—about what I did. I've been working on myself." His eyes searched mine for signs of understanding, for a flicker of hope, but all I could feel was the weight of his past mistakes pressing down on my heart.

"Adam," I started, searching for the right words, "change doesn't happen overnight. I've heard all of this before." The memories flooded in, the promises of change he had whispered before, each one more hollow than the last. Yet, as I gazed into his eyes, I saw something raw, something I hadn't recognized before—a depth that suggested he had confronted his demons. But could I trust that?

"I know," he said, the regret heavy in his tone. "But this time, it's different. I'm different. I didn't realize how much I was running from—how much I was pushing you away. I was scared, and instead of facing it, I hid." His admission hung in the air, palpable and raw, a testament to his struggles. "I've spent months working on myself—going to therapy, actually thinking about my actions instead of brushing them off. I've realized what I could lose."

The barista approached, setting down our drinks with a practiced ease, but the words between us remained unspoken. I took a sip of my coffee, the bitterness tinged with a hint of sweetness, much like the conflicted feelings swirling within me. "And what is it you want now?" I asked, my voice steadier than I felt. "What do you want from me?"

"I want a second chance," he replied, his eyes unwavering. "I want to show you that I can be the man you deserve—the man I should have been all along."

My heart raced, a chaotic symphony of hope and doubt. "You don't think it's too late?" I shot back, the sharpness in my tone revealing more than I intended. The thought of rekindling what we once had was intoxicating yet terrifying.

"It's never too late if you're willing to fight for it," he said, a hint of determination flashing in his gaze. "And I'm ready to fight. For you. For us."

His words lingered between us like an uninvited guest. I wanted to believe him; the sincerity in his voice tugged at something deep inside me. I recalled the laughter we once shared, the ease of our connection. Yet, the memories of pain and betrayal loomed like shadows, reminding me of why I had walked away in the first place.

"I don't know, Adam," I whispered, a fragile sigh escaping my lips. "Trust is hard to rebuild. It's like trying to put together a shattered vase."

He reached across the table, his fingers brushing against mine, sending a jolt of electricity up my arm. "I'm willing to take that risk if you are. I know I have to earn your trust back, and I'm here to do just that."

A small part of me yearned to believe him, to lean into this fragile moment and let the walls I had built begin to crumble. But fear gripped my heart, wrapping around it like ivy, threatening to choke out any semblance of hope. "What if it's not enough? What if you fall back into your old habits?"

"I won't," he insisted, his voice low and earnest. "I swear. This isn't just about me anymore; it's about us. I've learned that love isn't something you take for granted."

I pulled my hand away, creating distance where I craved closeness. "Love shouldn't come with conditions, Adam. It should be freely given, not something we have to fight for every day."

He leaned back, his expression shifting from determination to a quiet acceptance. "I get that. But sometimes, love requires effort. It's messy, it's complicated, and it doesn't always look pretty. But I'm willing to work through the mess if you'll let me."

The café buzzed with laughter and clinking cups, but I felt as if we were suspended in our own world, one filled with uncertainty and uncharted territory. I looked into his eyes, searching for the truth hidden within the shadows. And for the first time, I saw a glimmer of the man I had fallen for so long ago, battling to emerge from the wreckage of his own mistakes.

The café was alive with murmurs and laughter, yet my world had narrowed down to just Adam and me, each of us ensnared in our own thoughts and memories. As he spoke, a familiar tension twisted within me, a battle between the cautious remnants of my heart and the tentative hope threatening to unfurl like spring blossoms against the stubborn chill of winter. I watched him carefully, noticing the way his brow furrowed slightly when he was deep in thought, the way his fingers drummed nervously against the table.

"I mean it," he continued, his tone softening. "I've spent so long hiding behind excuses. I let fear dictate my choices, and I don't want that for us anymore." The sincerity in his voice was like a balm against my doubts, yet it was also a reminder of the wounds that had yet to heal.

"Fear, huh?" I leaned back, crossing my arms as a shield against the vulnerability swirling between us. "That sounds about right. But I've learned that hiding is a lot easier than confronting the mess we leave behind."

His gaze intensified, and I felt the weight of his scrutiny as he processed my words. "You're absolutely right. I'm not asking for a free pass or an instant reboot. I'm just asking for a chance to show you that I can do better. We can be better."

As he spoke, I could see the flicker of a fire igniting in his eyes, a passion fueled by the desire to reclaim what we had lost. The flame warmed me, but it also frightened me. I longed to reach out, to touch that fire, but the ashes of our past were still too hot, too raw. "But what if you don't?" I challenged, the defensive edge to my voice unmistakable. "What if you fall back into your old patterns? You know what that did to us."

"I don't want to hurt you again," he replied, and there was a depth of sincerity in his tone that made me pause. "I know I can't erase the past, but I want to build a future that honors it. Let me prove it to you."

The sincerity in his plea tugged at my heart, and I couldn't help but wonder what it would be like to stand by his side again, to laugh with him without that gnawing worry in the back of my mind. The barista appeared, refilling our cups, and I seized the moment to collect my thoughts, swirling the coffee in my mug as if it held the answers I desperately sought.

"I need time," I said finally, forcing myself to meet his gaze. "Time to think. It's not that simple."

He nodded slowly, a flicker of disappointment crossing his features, but he quickly masked it with an encouraging smile. "I can give you that. Just... don't shut me out completely. I'll be here whenever you're ready."

"Great. Just what I need—more pressure," I shot back, the wry humor escaping my lips before I could catch it. "The last thing I want is a walking reminder of my emotional turmoil."

Adam chuckled, his laughter rich and infectious, momentarily cutting through the tension like sunlight through clouds. "I guess I'll have to work on my stealth skills, then. Go incognito so you can forget about me completely."

"Good luck with that," I replied, a grin breaking through my façade. "You might need a disguise, a fake mustache, or something. 'Hello, I'm not Adam.'"

He feigned surprise, lifting an eyebrow dramatically. "A mustache? Really? That's your solution? You're right; it wouldn't suit me."

As the laughter faded, a comfortable silence settled between us, but the weight of our conversation lingered in the air. I was acutely aware of how quickly this could all unravel. Could I really allow myself to believe in his sincerity? The ache of my heart weighed heavily on my chest, and I could feel my resolve teetering.

"What do you want?" I asked, my voice quiet but steady. "What do you truly want from me?"

He took a deep breath, and for a moment, I thought he would falter, but he leaned forward, his expression earnest. "I want to build something real. I want us to face our fears together. I want to be a part of your life, not just a chapter that fades into a memory."

The vulnerability in his admission sent a shiver through me. I wasn't ready to dismiss his words entirely, but the thought of stepping back into our old rhythm felt like slipping on an old pair of shoes—comfortable yet full of holes. "That's a tall order," I finally said, attempting to temper the whirlwind of emotion churning within me.

"I know it is," he acknowledged, nodding. "But I believe we're worth the risk. We had something beautiful, and I can't shake the feeling that it's still there, waiting for us to uncover it again."

I watched him, the way his passion shone through, illuminating the shadows of uncertainty that clung to my heart. I wanted to let go of the doubt that anchored me, but fear whispered incessantly, reminding me of the pain that lingered like a ghost. "What if we try just being friends first? You know, ease into it?"

His face broke into a wide smile, a mix of surprise and delight lighting up his features. "Friends? I can do that. I mean, I'll miss the thrill of 'us,' but I can adapt."

"Wow, a man of flexibility," I teased, leaning back in my chair, enjoying this banter that felt so familiar. "Just don't start practicing yoga or anything."

He laughed again, the sound warm and inviting, drawing me in. "I'll leave the yoga to you. I don't think my body is quite ready for those poses."

"Good call. I'm not sure the world is ready for a yoga-practicing Adam," I said, shaking my head with mock seriousness. "Imagine the headlines."

"'Local Man Discovers Inner Peace—And Falls Out of Tree While Trying to Meditate,'" he quipped, adopting a mock serious tone that made me burst out laughing.

As the laughter faded, I realized that while I was still hesitant, the cracks in my defenses were beginning to show. The walls I had erected felt less imposing, a possibility of something more looming in the distance. Adam's charm was still intoxicating, and beneath my caution, I sensed a flicker of hope blooming. It was a dangerous feeling, one I had buried deep, but as I gazed across the table into those earnest eyes, I began to wonder if perhaps a new chapter could emerge from the ashes of the old, one that was built on honesty, friendship, and the promise of second chances.

The laughter between us had woven a fragile thread, one that connected the past with the present, bridging the chasm of uncertainty. I found comfort in the playful banter, a safe zone where our old rhythm returned, though the echoes of past heartbreak loomed just behind us like shadows ready to pounce. As the café buzzed around us, I realized this was a dance we both knew well, one I had almost forgotten.

"So, friends it is," I declared, attempting to reclaim the lightness of the moment. "But that means no more intense heart-to-hearts over coffee. We keep it casual."

Adam raised an eyebrow, a mischievous glint in his eye. "Casual? So, like, we can only discuss the weather and avoid eye contact? Sounds riveting."

I laughed, shaking my head. "Okay, maybe not that casual. But let's not dive into the depths of our feelings just yet. It's a bit like diving into a pool without checking if there's water."

He leaned back, crossing his arms with a mock pout. "Fine, but I refuse to be your weather reporter. I have feelings, too, you know."

"Sure, your feelings can go right in the 'mostly cloudy with a chance of drama' section," I teased, enjoying this playful side of him that reminded me of better days.

The warmth between us felt almost electric, but the moment was cut short when the door swung open with a rush of cold air, and a figure entered, disrupting our playful exchange. My heart sank as I recognized her immediately—Lila, the woman I had known as Adam's friend and occasional confidante during our relationship.

Her eyes landed on us, and in that split second, I could see the gears turning in her mind. Adam tensed beside me, and I could feel the shift in the atmosphere, like the calm before a storm.

"Well, well, well," she said, her voice dripping with that sugary sweetness that always masked her sharp tongue. "What a surprise to find you two together."

I forced a smile, the façade a thin veneer over the tension creeping in. "Lila! What a coincidence. We were just—"

"Having a heart-to-heart?" she interrupted, her tone playful yet pointed, eyes flickering between us. "I hope this isn't a repeat of the last time I found you together."

My heart raced, and I shot Adam a glance, searching for reassurance, but he remained stoically neutral, his expression unreadable.

"It's not what you think," Adam said, the steadiness of his voice surprising me. "We're just catching up."

Lila chuckled softly, the kind of laugh that sent a chill down my spine. "Oh, Adam, you do know how to charm a girl. But you know what they say—once burned, twice shy."

"Thanks for the reminder," I replied, my voice sharper than I intended. "I think we're both acutely aware of the past."

"Touché," she said, her eyes gleaming with amusement. "But it's nice to see you've forgiven him. That takes some serious courage."

"It's not about forgiveness; it's about moving forward," I countered, trying to keep my tone light while feeling the heat rising in my cheeks. "And figuring out what that looks like."

"Ah, so you're still in the 'let's see where this goes' phase?" Lila shot back, leaning in as if the words were a tasty morsel. "That's a risky game, isn't it? Especially with someone like Adam."

"Someone like Adam?" I echoed, the challenge hanging in the air. "You make it sound like he's a wild animal."

"He might as well be," she replied, tilting her head in a way that suggested she found the entire situation amusing. "Charming, enticing, but oh-so-dangerous if you're not careful."

"Careful? Is that what you think I am?" I asked, my heart pounding with indignation. "I'm not made of porcelain, Lila."

"Never said you were, but you might want to watch your back," she warned, her eyes narrowing slightly. "Not everyone gets a happy ending, you know."

The tension in the air thickened, and Adam shifted slightly, the warmth between us beginning to dissipate. I felt the ground beneath my feet becoming unstable, and I was acutely aware of how easily this could spiral out of control.

"I appreciate your concern, but I think I can handle myself," I said, attempting to project confidence I wasn't sure I felt.

"Oh, I know you can," Lila replied, a smirk tugging at her lips. "But what about him? Is he really worth the risk?"

Adam's expression darkened at her insinuation, his patience wearing thin. "This isn't a game, Lila. And it's not your place to comment on my choices."

"Isn't it?" she countered, her tone light but her words laced with an edge. "I've been around long enough to know how this plays out. You can't fool me."

I could feel the temperature in the café drop, the lighthearted atmosphere replaced by an electric charge that was anything but comfortable. "I think we're done here, Lila," I said firmly, standing up from my chair, trying to regain control over the situation. "This is my life."

She smirked, clearly enjoying this little standoff. "Sure it is. But remember, I'm just looking out for you. Sometimes the truth hurts."

As she turned to leave, I felt a wave of relief wash over me, only to be swiftly followed by the realization that the moment had shifted irrevocably. Adam and I had been thrust back into the chaos of our past, and I couldn't shake the feeling that Lila's words would linger like a shadow over our renewed connection.

"Are you okay?" Adam asked, concern etched across his face.

"Do I look okay?" I snapped, the tension of the encounter spilling over. "This whole thing just became infinitely more complicated."

"I didn't want her to show up like that," he admitted, his voice low. "I wanted this to be simple."

"Simple? We're talking about us here. Nothing has ever been simple." I rubbed my temples, frustration bubbling up. "Now I'm questioning everything all over again."

Adam leaned forward, urgency creeping into his voice. "I know it's complicated, but I'm here for you. I want to make this work, no matter what Lila thinks."

"And what if it's all just smoke and mirrors?" I shot back, my heart racing. "What if we're just setting ourselves up for another fall?"

He reached for my hand, his warmth grounding me amidst the turmoil. "Then we'll figure it out together. You won't be alone this time."

But before I could respond, a commotion erupted at the entrance. A group of patrons turned their heads, and I instinctively looked over my shoulder. My stomach dropped when I saw the unmistakable figure of Chris, my brother, storming through the door, his expression one of barely contained fury.

"Why the hell are you here?" he shouted, his voice echoing through the café, turning every head in our direction.

The room fell silent, tension coiling tightly as all eyes locked onto us. I froze, shock and disbelief crashing over me like a wave. I hadn't anticipated this, hadn't considered that my past would come barreling into my present like a freight train.

"Chris, wait!" I called, rising from my seat. But he was already advancing, and I could see the storm brewing in his eyes, ready to unleash a tempest I had no idea how to navigate.

"What is going on?" he demanded, his voice loud and unyielding, drawing the attention of everyone in the café. "What are you doing with him?"

Time seemed to stretch, my heart racing as I stood there, caught between the past I had tried so hard to escape and the future that felt more uncertain than ever.

Chapter 22: "Learning to Trust"

The evening air was thick with the scent of jasmine, curling around the soft glow of streetlights like an old friend reluctant to leave. As I strolled through the park, the crunch of gravel beneath my shoes punctuated the stillness, each step echoing with the weight of unspoken words. Shadows danced between the trees, and for a moment, I allowed myself to get lost in the beauty surrounding me. But it was Adam's laughter that pulled me back, a rich, warm sound that fluttered through my thoughts like a bird on the wing.

I had known him long enough to recognize the ache in his smile, the shadows lurking behind his playful banter. Yet here we were, standing together on the cusp of something new, a tentative hope woven between our shared past and uncertain future. I caught sight of him leaning against an old oak, arms crossed, his brow furrowed as if he were wrestling with demons only he could see. The sunlight caught in his hair, illuminating the flecks of gold like stars in a fading twilight.

"Still trying to figure out the meaning of life?" I teased, forcing a smile, my heart quickening as he turned to face me. His expression softened, and for a heartbeat, the world around us blurred into insignificance.

"Something like that," he replied, his voice low and gravelly, laden with unspoken truths. "Or just how to get through the next hour without messing it up."

A playful retort bubbled on my lips, but it faded as I registered the seriousness in his tone. Trust didn't come easy, not for either of us. The scars of our past, both personal and shared, loomed over our tentative connection, demanding acknowledgment. Still, there was a warmth in the air, a flicker of something alive between us that begged for attention.

"I guess we all have our own riddles to solve," I said, leaning against the tree beside him. The bark was rough against my skin, grounding me in a moment that felt both electric and fragile. "What if the answer isn't so complicated?"

He arched an eyebrow, his lips quirking into a half-smile. "What do you suggest? A cosmic joke? A fortune cookie prophecy?"

"More like realizing that we're not meant to have it all figured out. Sometimes, it's enough to just be here." I gestured vaguely, encompassing the park, the golden light filtering through the leaves, and him.

"Here, huh?" He chuckled softly, but I could see the vulnerability flickering in his eyes. "You make it sound so simple."

"Because it is," I insisted, a hint of determination creeping into my voice. "It's the 'how' that's complicated. But trust—trust is about taking that first step, isn't it?"

His gaze shifted to the horizon, where the sun dipped lower, casting a warm glow that danced along the edges of the clouds. I knew the weight of his past was heavy, and yet, here he was, standing before me, a man who had fought against his own darkness. There was a stubborn hope building between us, and despite the ghosts that haunted him, I couldn't help but feel drawn closer.

"I've never been good at trusting," he admitted, his voice barely above a whisper. "Especially not after..."

"After everything," I finished, knowing the shadows that loomed in his past mirrored my own. It was as if we were two broken pieces of glass trying to fit together, sharp edges threatening to cut but yearning for connection.

"I guess I'm just afraid," he said, vulnerability washing over him, leaving his walls momentarily unguarded. "Afraid that if I let you in, you'll find something I can't change."

"What if I'm here because of those things?" I challenged gently, feeling the warmth of his body close to mine, the heartbeat of something that felt dangerously like hope. "What if it's those very flaws that make you who you are?"

He studied me for a long moment, his expression shifting as if he were weighing my words against the silence that enveloped us. "You think you're brave enough to stick around for the messy bits?"

"I think brave is doing it anyway," I said, meeting his gaze with unwavering conviction. "You're not the only one with scars, Adam. We're all a little messy. That's what makes us human."

He shifted closer, a spark of curiosity igniting in his eyes. "You make it sound like I'm worth it."

"And what if you are?" I replied, my heart pounding in my chest. "What if we're both worth it? Worth the risk?"

A moment stretched between us, charged with unspoken possibilities. The air hummed, thick with anticipation as I saw the flicker of uncertainty dissolve in his gaze, replaced by a glimmer of something brighter, something hopeful.

"I want to believe that," he said softly, and for the first time, the barriers between us seemed to falter.

"Then let's believe together," I urged, my voice steady despite the tempest brewing inside me. "We can take this step, just one at a time. Together."

His eyes searched mine, a silent conversation passing between us, full of hesitation and promise. The sun dipped below the horizon, casting us into the cool embrace of twilight, and I felt the first threads of connection weaving through the spaces we had once filled with fear. In that moment, I realized that trust wasn't a destination; it was the journey we embarked upon, one step at a time, finding our way in the darkness together.

The sun dipped lower, drenching the park in shades of peach and lavender, and the evening air took on a coolness that wrapped around us like a gentle embrace. As we lingered in the growing dusk, I felt a warmth blooming inside me, igniting a flicker of courage I hadn't realized I possessed. It was a strange juxtaposition, this feeling of vulnerability entwined with the thrill of possibility. Adam shifted slightly, his shoulder brushing against mine, and the electricity was palpable.

"Okay, let's play a game," I suggested suddenly, unable to resist the urge to lighten the moment. "I'll ask a question, and you have to answer honestly. No dodging, no white lies. You in?"

"Is this a 'two truths and a lie' situation?" he asked, a teasing grin breaking through the heaviness that had settled around us.

"No, something far more dangerous. A 'tell me your deepest secret' situation," I replied, my voice dripping with mock seriousness. "This is your chance to lay it all out. Consider it therapy on the go."

He chuckled, though his expression turned contemplative. "Alright, I'm game. What's your question?"

"Let's start simple. What's your favorite guilty pleasure?" I leaned in, eager to hear what lay behind his bravado.

Adam paused, his brow furrowing as he considered his response. "This is going to sound lame, but I really enjoy baking," he said, a hint of sheepishness creeping into his voice. "I find it calming. But I don't tell anyone—too many jokes about 'real men' and their baking skills."

"Baking?" I laughed, thoroughly entertained. "What do you bake? Cookies? Cakes? Brownies?"

"Mostly cookies," he admitted, a hint of pride creeping into his voice. "Chocolate chip. Classic."

"Who would have thought? The man who looks like he could take on the world also has a soft spot for cookies," I teased, nudging him playfully. "Do you wear an apron while you bake? Please tell me you do."

"Only when I'm feeling fancy," he shot back with a wink, and the playful banter ignited a spark between us.

"Okay, your turn," he said, leaning back against the tree, his expression earnest. "What's your guilty pleasure?"

I hesitated for a moment, weighing my options. "You know those ridiculous reality shows about survival in the wilderness? The ones where people have to build their own shelters and catch fish with their bare hands?"

"Ah, yes. The ones where you question the contestants' life choices."

"Exactly! I'm captivated by the utter chaos and desperation. There's something so mesmerizing about watching people suffer for my entertainment," I replied with a smirk.

"Noted. I'll avoid camping with you," he said with mock seriousness, and I felt the tension ease between us, our laughter mingling in the evening air.

As the sky deepened into a tapestry of stars, the conversation shifted, weaving through lighter topics before taking a more serious turn. "What about your childhood?" I asked, the question slipping out before I could second-guess myself. "What was it like growing up?"

Adam's expression shifted, the playfulness receding like the tide. "It was... complicated. My parents divorced when I was young, and I think that left me a little adrift." His gaze drifted to the horizon, the vulnerability in his tone palpable. "I spent a lot of time trying to navigate that, figuring out where I fit in."

"I can relate to that," I said softly, the words resonating with my own memories. "It's hard to feel anchored when the foundation beneath you keeps shifting."

He met my gaze, his eyes reflecting a deep understanding. "Yeah. I think that's why I struggle with trust. When you feel unmoored as a kid, it's hard to believe in anyone else."

"But you're trying, right? With us?" I urged gently, desperate to keep the conversation flowing, to bridge the chasm that had once separated us.

"I am. It's just... terrifying." His honesty hung in the air, a fragile thread connecting us. "Every time I think I'm making progress, I find myself second-guessing. What if I mess this up again?"

"Then we'll pick up the pieces," I said firmly. "You're not alone in this. I have my own fears too. Trust isn't just about the other person; it's about ourselves, our willingness to take that leap, to believe in something greater than our past."

He nodded slowly, processing my words as the moon began its ascent, casting a silvery glow over everything. "How do you do it?" he asked, his voice barely above a whisper.

"Honestly? I fake it until I make it," I replied with a chuckle, hoping to lighten the moment. "Sometimes, it's just about putting one foot in front of the other, even when your heart is doing backflips."

"Interesting strategy," he said, his lips twitching into a smile. "I might have to adopt that."

We sat in companionable silence, the soft rustle of leaves and the distant sounds of laughter from the park enveloping us like a warm blanket. I could feel the tension easing, like a dam finally cracking under pressure.

But as the night deepened, a flicker of unease crept back in. "Adam, can I ask something?" I ventured, my heart racing. "What if we do this—what if we dive in and it all goes wrong?"

He turned to me, his expression serious, the glint of the moonlight reflecting in his eyes. "Then we learn. And if we're brave enough, we try again."

His words hung in the air, heavy with the weight of their implications. I felt a shiver run down my spine, a mixture of fear and exhilaration. This was more than just a casual fling; this was a commitment to something real, something that could change everything.

"Deal," I replied, sealing our unspoken pact in the twilight. "But you owe me cookies for the effort."

"Only if you promise to help," he countered, a playful glint returning to his eyes.

"Deal," I said, feeling a rush of excitement at the thought of what lay ahead. With laughter threading through the shadows, we leaned into the uncertainty, ready to embrace whatever challenges awaited us, two broken souls weaving a new story together in the dark.

The laughter still lingered in the air like the sweet remnants of a favorite song, wrapping around us as we strolled through the park. The sky deepened into indigo, and stars began to dot the canvas overhead, each one a distant promise of light in the vast expanse of darkness. Adam walked beside me, our shoulders brushing now and then, a subtle reminder of the closeness we were forging.

"What's next on your agenda? Baking lessons?" I quipped, glancing at him sideways. "Or do you save that for when you want to impress a date?"

"Hey, I'll have you know that baking is a lost art, and I'm on a mission to revive it," he replied, feigning indignation. "And as for dates, well, I'll be taking applications after I perfect my chocolate chip cookies."

I chuckled, and the lighthearted banter felt like a balm, soothing the tension that had simmered beneath the surface. "You know, I could help you with that. But only if you promise not to blame me when the cookies turn out more like hockey pucks."

"Deal, as long as you don't expect gourmet results," he shot back, his smile infectious.

The playful exchange shifted into a deeper silence, one that wrapped around us like a warm blanket. It felt almost too easy, the way our laughter had forged connections, a stark contrast to the sharp edges of our pasts. The shadows of doubt still loomed, but they began to feel less daunting in the glow of our shared moments.

"Tell me about the first time you baked alone," I prompted, curious to peel back another layer of his history. "Was it a disaster or a masterpiece?"

He hesitated for a beat, as if sifting through memories. "I was about ten, and my mom had left me in charge of making a birthday cake for my little sister. I thought it'd be easy, you know? Just mix some ingredients, throw it in the oven."

"Classic kid logic. How'd that go?"

"I ended up using salt instead of sugar," he admitted, rubbing the back of his neck in embarrassment. "The look on her face when she took a bite was priceless. She spit it out faster than I could say 'happy birthday.'"

"Your sister must have loved you for that," I teased.

"Oh, she did. I'm pretty sure I became her favorite punching bag that day," he said, laughing, but there was a wistful edge to it. "It's funny how the little moments stick with you, even years later."

"Not funny. It's endearing," I corrected, feeling a warmth spread in my chest. "You cared enough to try. That's what matters."

His gaze met mine, and for a moment, everything else faded. It was just the two of us, suspended in the vibrant tapestry of night. "And you? What about your first attempt at cooking?"

I grinned at the memory. "Oh, I was twelve. My mom decided to let me make dinner. I wanted to impress her, so I picked something ambitious—a stir-fry."

"Sounds innocent enough."

"Except I thought 'hot' meant literally burning it to a crisp. Smoke alarms, screaming family members—it was a culinary catastrophe."

His laughter filled the air, light and infectious. "It's good to know we're both in the same disaster club."

We continued to share stories, the laughter ringing out into the night as if we were the only two people in the universe. With each tale, each vulnerability revealed, the walls that had once seemed insurmountable began to crumble further. There was an undeniable chemistry building, something alive and crackling between us, but lurking beneath it all was a thread of apprehension, whispering warnings that echoed with the memories of our past.

As we reached the park's edge, the distant sound of music and laughter drew us toward a small outdoor festival. Strings of lights twinkled overhead, and the vibrant energy was infectious. A band played lively tunes, people danced, and the smell of food wafted through the air, a tempting invitation.

"Let's go check it out," Adam suggested, his eyes sparkling with excitement.

"Are you sure you can handle the thrill of a festival?" I teased, nudging him with my elbow.

"Just wait until I unleash my dance moves," he shot back with mock bravado, leading the way into the crowd.

The atmosphere was electric, filled with laughter and the warmth of camaraderie. We wove through the throng, my hand brushing against his in the bustling crowd, each touch igniting a spark that sent ripples of warmth through me. The rhythm of the music enveloped us, urging us to let go and simply be.

"Okay, you have to dance with me," I said, grabbing his wrist and pulling him toward the makeshift dance floor.

He hesitated, a sheepish smile spreading across his face. "I'm not much of a dancer, you know."

"Don't worry! Just let loose," I encouraged, spinning him into the fray. "No one's watching, I promise."

He laughed, the sound a mixture of disbelief and delight. "Famous last words, right?"

The beat pulsed through my veins as we began to move, and I found myself caught up in the infectious energy of the crowd. As the music swelled, I lost myself in the moment, laughing and twirling as Adam joined in, awkwardly at first but gradually finding his rhythm.

"See? Not so bad!" I shouted over the music, my heart racing from the exhilaration.

"Okay, okay, maybe this isn't the worst thing ever," he admitted, a broad smile spreading across his face.

As the night wore on, the atmosphere transformed into something magical. I felt a sense of freedom I hadn't experienced in years, the laughter and movement melting away the insecurities that had once tethered me. But just as I thought we were riding the high of this newfound connection, a commotion erupted on the edge of the crowd.

"Hey! Watch it!" someone shouted, their voice tinged with anger.

I turned, curiosity piqued, as a cluster of people began to gather, tension crackling in the air like static. "What's happening?" I asked, nudging closer to Adam, who instinctively placed a protective arm around my shoulders.

"I don't know, but let's check it out," he said, pulling me through the throng.

As we got closer, I caught sight of two men facing off, fists clenched, their faces twisted in anger. "You think you can just waltz in here and take over?" one of them barked, his voice harsh.

"Maybe I can, maybe I can't. But you're going to regret underestimating me," the other shot back, his tone dripping with confidence.

Suddenly, the crowd surged, and I found myself caught between bodies, the air thick with tension and uncertainty. Adam's grip tightened around me, his protective instincts flaring to life. "We should back off," he murmured, but the scene had captivated my attention, an inexplicable pull urging me to see what unfolded.

In that moment, as the confrontation escalated, something in me knew that this was more than just a squabble; it felt like a crack forming in the fragile world we had started to build. A voice deep within whispered that everything could change in an instant, and as I searched Adam's face, I saw a flicker of fear mirrored in his eyes.

Just then, a loud crash echoed through the crowd, and everything shifted—my heart raced, and as I turned to Adam to warn him, his expression froze. The moment hung in the air, suspended, a sense of dread washing over us like a wave, leaving us teetering on the edge of an unforeseen chaos that threatened to pull us under.

Chapter 23: "When the Past Returns"

Just when I thought we had finally found our rhythm, the past came crashing back into our lives. I stood in the kitchen, the aroma of freshly brewed coffee wafting through the air, intertwining with the scent of cinnamon from the pastries cooling on the counter. Sunlight streamed through the window, illuminating the tiny motes of dust dancing lazily in the warm glow. It was the kind of morning that made everything feel right in the world. I was just about to pour myself a second cup when I heard Adam's phone buzz from the living room, a sound I'd come to associate with either a trivial business alert or something that could turn our day upside down.

His voice echoed through the house, tinged with a nervous energy that prickled my skin. "What do you mean it's back? We settled that years ago!" A knot formed in my stomach as I instinctively set the coffee pot down, my heart quickening. I moved quietly toward the doorway, peering into the living room where Adam stood, his silhouette framed against the light filtering through the curtains. The tension in his posture was palpable, every muscle taut as he listened intently, his expression morphing from confusion to frustration.

The details of his past dealings had always been somewhat of a mystery to me. Adam had a way of keeping certain things close to his chest, as if they were secrets wrapped in velvet—soft to the touch, but ultimately impenetrable. It was part of his charm, I suppose, the allure of the enigmatic. But now, it seemed those secrets were clawing their way back into the light. I couldn't make out the words, but I could sense the weight of the conversation pressing down on him, and I felt a familiar rush of fear, twisting like a vine around my chest.

"Look, I need time to figure this out," he finally said, his voice strained. He ended the call abruptly, the silence that followed resonating with the echo of his anxiety. I stepped fully into the room, crossing my arms, as if I could physically shield him from whatever demons were creeping back into our lives. "What's going on?" I asked, trying to keep my tone steady despite the unease bubbling beneath the surface.

He ran a hand through his hair, a gesture I had come to recognize as his tell—a sign that something was deeply wrong. "It's a deal I thought was dead and buried. Some old investors are stirring up trouble, claiming I misled them." His gaze flicked to mine, searching for understanding—or perhaps reassurance. "It's all nonsense, but it doesn't matter. They're going to the press."

The world outside seemed to blur, muffled by the sudden weight of his words. I envisioned headlines flashing across screens, a public feeding frenzy over a story that could easily distort the truth. Adam's reputation, hard-won and carefully crafted, could be at stake. My heart ached for him, but I also felt a wave of frustration wash over me. "Why didn't you tell me about this sooner?" The words slipped out, sharp and accusatory, though I quickly regretted the tone.

He met my gaze, eyes stormy. "Because I thought it was over. I didn't want to drag you into my mess again." There it was—the familiar shadow of his guilt, lurking just beneath the surface. I could almost hear the unspoken plea: Don't let this ruin us. "I can handle it," I insisted, stepping closer. "Whatever it is, we'll figure it out together. You don't have to go through this alone."

A flicker of gratitude passed over his features, but I could see the worry still etched into the lines of his brow. "I can't let you bear the brunt of this. It's not just my name on the line—it's ours." The weight of his words hung between us, heavy and real, like an anchor threatening to drag us both down.

I took a deep breath, steadying myself. "We've faced storms before, haven't we? This isn't the first challenge, and it won't be the last." The warmth of my conviction seemed to fill the space around us, wrapping us in a shared resolve. "We're stronger now, Adam. You're not alone in this."

He nodded slowly, his expression softening as he reached for my hand. "You really believe that, don't you?" There was a hint of awe in his voice, a disbelief that made my heart swell. "I do," I said firmly, squeezing his fingers. "We'll navigate this mess together, just like we always have."

We spent the day devising a plan, surrounded by scattered papers and half-drunk mugs of coffee, trying to outsmart the storm that was brewing on the horizon. Each idea tossed around the table was met with enthusiasm and doubt, laughter punctuating the seriousness of our situation. But beneath the banter lay a thread of tension, a constant reminder of the impending chaos waiting to unfold.

As night fell, I watched Adam pace back and forth, his mind racing with possibilities. I could see the shadows under his eyes, the way he bit his lip as if chewing on his worries. "What if they twist my words? What if they spin this into a narrative that's completely unrecognizable?" His voice trembled slightly, and for a moment, I saw the boy behind the man, vulnerable and scared.

"Then we fight back," I replied, stepping closer, determined to ground him. "You have the truth on your side. Remember that." The warmth of his gaze met mine, and for a brief moment, the world outside faded into insignificance.

But the truth, as I soon learned, is often muddied by perception, and before long, the waves of past mistakes began to lap at our door, threatening to pull us under. And just as the tide surged, so too did the unrelenting tide of the media, transforming our lives into a headline and our love story into mere gossip. As we prepared to face the impending chaos, I realized that in the crucible of uncertainty, we were being forged anew.

The phone rang again, its shrill insistence slicing through the fragile silence that had settled over us. I watched Adam's eyes dart to the screen, a mixture of dread and determination coursing through him. "It's the PR team," he said, a grimace flashing across his face as he silenced the call. "Guess they're eager to get ahead of the story."

I leaned against the doorframe, arms crossed, feeling the weight of the world settle on my shoulders. "Do you think they'll want to spin it into a tragedy?" I joked lightly, trying to keep the atmosphere buoyant, though I could feel the unease coiling around us like smoke. "You know, 'Rags to Riches to Ruin' or something equally melodramatic?"

Adam chuckled, albeit briefly, a flicker of a smile teasing his lips before the tension resurfaced. "I'm just waiting for the 'scorned lover' angle to make its debut. You'll be featured as the woman who stood by me during my dark days." His attempt at humor fell flat against the impending reality, but it was enough to spark a momentary flicker of warmth.

We dove back into the chaos of our strategy session, gathering everything we could to combat the storm. The evening wore on, each hour stretching into the next, filled with papers scattered around like fallen leaves, our ideas taking shape among the clutter. I flipped through notes, trying to keep the mood light while my mind raced with the implications of what lay ahead.

"Okay, so here's the plan," I said, tapping a pen against the table to punctuate my point. "We need to control the narrative before it spirals. Let's get ahead of the media."

Adam paused, looking at me with an intensity that made my heart skip. "What do you suggest? A press conference? A heartfelt Instagram post?"

I feigned a gasp. "A heartfelt Instagram post? That would truly bring out the drama. I can picture it now: 'In the depths of despair, I found love in my coffee mug.'"

He laughed, the sound rich and genuine, echoing against the walls of our kitchen. "You're ridiculous."

"I prefer the term 'refreshingly honest.'" I winked, feeling the tension ease ever so slightly between us.

As we tossed ideas back and forth, the clock crept closer to midnight, the hours slipping away like grains of sand. The weight of uncertainty hung heavily over us, but our banter felt like an anchor amidst the turbulence. We plotted the approach to media inquiries, weighed the pros and cons of various PR tactics, and shared concerns that lay heavy on our hearts.

"Honestly, what if they twist my words? What if this spirals out of control?" Adam's voice softened, the bravado slipping away like a shadow.

I reached across the table, placing my hand over his. "You know your truth, Adam. They can't take that away from you."

His eyes held mine, searching for solace in the storm of doubt. "And what if my truth isn't good enough for them? What if it makes me look bad?"

"Then we lean into it," I said firmly. "You're not that person anymore. The people who matter know you, know who you are now. And I think they'd back you up."

He squeezed my hand, a flicker of relief breaking through the worry etched across his features. "You always know what to say."

"Years of practice," I replied, a teasing grin escaping me. "And maybe a touch of clairvoyance."

As we settled into a plan that felt solid enough to withstand the storm, my phone buzzed violently on the counter. Glancing at the screen, I saw a notification from a news outlet that made my stomach drop. "Oh no," I breathed.

"What is it?"

"Looks like they've already started reporting on it." My fingers shook as I clicked on the alert, a headline screaming at me from the screen: "Business Tycoon Faces New Controversy: 'He's Not Who You Think He Is.'"

Adam's expression shifted, a storm brewing behind his eyes. "They're already spinning this?"

I nodded, trying to catch my breath as I scrolled through the article. "They're dragging up all sorts of dirt from the past, painting you as some kind of villain."

His face paled, the implications settling like a heavy fog. "How can they do this? I thought we had settled everything."

"We might have to push back the narrative," I suggested, urgency creeping into my voice. "We need to prepare a statement, something strong that counters their claims."

But before we could strategize further, the phone rang again, this time blaring through the stillness like an alarm bell. Adam glanced at the caller ID, and I could see the tension spike in his shoulders. "It's my father."

"Do you want to take it?" I asked, sensing the weight of his hesitation.

He shook his head, the frustration palpable in the set of his jaw. "No, not right now."

The ringing stopped, replaced by an eerie silence that stretched like a taut string. A moment later, another notification pinged on my phone. Another article, another headline—this time more sensational. "Business Bad Boy Adam Blackwood: The Fall of a Golden Boy."

Adam slammed a fist on the table, his frustration bubbling to the surface. "This isn't just a story; it's a witch hunt!"

"I know," I said, voice steady despite the rising tide of fear within me. "But if we respond with calm and clarity, it might just work in your favor."

He let out a ragged breath, running a hand over his face. "What if it doesn't?"

"Then we adapt," I replied firmly. "Together, we adapt."

He met my gaze, and in that moment, I felt the weight of everything we had built together, the strength of our love melding with the resilience of our spirits. This would not be the end of us. It would be a beginning—a chance to prove not only to the world but to ourselves that we could weather any storm.

The night wore on, a relentless companion filled with the constant ping of notifications and the soft glow of screens illuminating our faces. The initial thrill of brainstorming our response had faded into an undercurrent of dread, each article I skimmed through another dagger aimed at Adam's reputation. "Look at this one," I said, my voice shaking slightly as I pointed at yet another headline. "They're calling you a 'falling star,' like you're about to crash back to Earth."

Adam rubbed his temples, a weary smile flickering for just a moment before the weight of the world settled back onto his shoulders. "I didn't realize I had risen so high to begin with. I thought I was just trying to get through the day without losing my sanity."

"Welcome to the world of fame, my friend," I replied, attempting to inject a bit of levity into the situation. "Next, they'll want to know what brand of toothpaste you use."

"Probably something that promises 'whiter teeth and a brighter future,'" he shot back, his lips quirking as he finally succumbed to a genuine laugh. The sound filled the room, a buoy in our turbulent sea, but I could sense the tension lurking just beneath the surface, ready to crash in at any moment.

We strategized late into the night, our living room transformed into a war room, papers strewn about like battle plans. I jotted down ideas while Adam paced, the creaking floorboards echoing his restless energy. "What if we go live on social media? Directly address the rumors?" he suggested, his brow furrowing in thought.

"Sure, let's give them a show," I said, unable to hide the sarcasm. "I can already see the headlines: 'Adam Blackwood Goes Off Script!'"

"Do you think they'd really bite?"

"Absolutely! They love a good spectacle." I leaned back in my chair, crossing my arms, contemplating the absurdity of our situation. "But how about we do it together? You and me, side by side. No dramatic solo performances."

He nodded slowly, considering the idea, but his hesitation was palpable. "What if I crumble under the pressure? What if I can't find the words?"

"Then we both crumble, and we pick up the pieces together," I said, my voice steady. "That's the whole point of this—facing it head-on. Besides, I've seen you handle tougher crowds."

"True," he admitted, a spark of determination igniting behind his eyes. "Let's do it."

We worked through the early hours of the morning, sketching out key points Adam wanted to make, focusing on transparency and honesty. Each time he doubted himself, I reminded him of the man I loved—the one who had fought to build a better life, the one who inspired me to be brave in the face of adversity. "You're not that person anymore," I urged. "Show them the man you are now."

Finally, we settled on a plan, and just as I felt a sense of relief washing over me, my phone buzzed again, jolting us both. I glanced at the screen, my heart sinking as I recognized the number. It was Adam's father.

"Do you want me to take this?" I asked, glancing up to see the storm gathering in Adam's eyes.

"No," he said firmly, shaking his head. "Not now."

We stared at the phone for a moment, the tension thickening as the ringing stopped, leaving behind an unsettling silence. "I'll handle my father later," he said, his voice taut with barely restrained emotion.

"Just remember, you're not alone in this," I reminded him gently, hoping to soothe the brewing tempest within.

As dawn broke, we finally settled into a semblance of calm, the first rays of sunlight filtering through the kitchen window, casting a warm glow over the remnants of our chaotic night. The air held a fresh scent, a mix of hope and possibility.

"We can do this," Adam said, his voice softer now, more assured. "With you by my side, I feel like I can face anything."

"Then let's do it," I replied, my heart swelling with love and determination. We shared a quiet moment, the weight of the world still pressing down on us, but now we were bolstered by a shared resolve.

We set up the camera in our living room, arranging ourselves in front of the softly lit backdrop. "Are you ready?" I asked, my heart racing.

"Not even close," he muttered, adjusting his collar. "But ready or not, here we go."

As the camera began to roll, I felt a surge of adrenaline. Adam's hand found mine, his grip firm and reassuring, and I looked into his eyes, ready to tackle whatever came next.

"Hello, everyone," Adam began, his voice steady, though I could see the tension lingering at the corners of his eyes. "I know there have been a lot of questions and rumors flying around, and I wanted to take a moment to address them directly."

We spoke together, the words flowing more easily than I'd anticipated, bolstered by our shared purpose. Adam was open, honest, and unapologetic, navigating the murky waters of public scrutiny with grace. I chimed in with supporting points, reinforcing his commitment to transparency.

But just as we started to feel a glimmer of control, a sudden alert chimed from my phone, a notification that felt like ice water down my spine. I glanced at the screen and froze.

"Adam..." I whispered, my voice barely escaping my throat. "You need to see this."

His brow furrowed as he leaned over, peering at the screen. The headline was as sharp as a knife: "Shocking Twist: Adam Blackwood's Business Deal Involves Corruption Charges!"

The words hung in the air like a dark omen, a chill sweeping through the warmth we had just begun to forge. Adam's face paled, the confident facade crumbling as the weight of reality pressed down upon him once again.

"Where did this come from?" he asked, voice strained.

"I—I don't know. It just popped up!" Panic flared in my chest as I scanned the article, each line pulling me deeper into a vortex of fear. "They're saying you're implicated in a scheme involving money laundering and fraud!"

Adam's expression morphed from shock to disbelief, a storm brewing behind his eyes. "That's impossible! I'm not involved in any of that!"

I felt a wave of uncertainty wash over me, mingling with the panic that had taken root. "Then we need to respond, and fast!"

His gaze shifted to the camera still recording, capturing every moment. "What if this is it? What if they've finally taken me down?"

"No," I said, fierce determination rising in my chest. "This isn't over. We will fight this. We'll clear your name."

But as I spoke, the doorbell rang, a sharp sound that cut through the tension, and I could feel the icy fingers of dread wrapping around my spine. The door opened, revealing a figure standing on the threshold—a figure I had never expected to see again.

"Hello, Adam," she said, her voice smooth and deliberate, a sly smile playing at the corners of her lips. "We need to talk."

In that moment, the room felt like it was collapsing around us, the foundation of everything we had built shaking under the weight of secrets long buried, now clawing their way back to the surface.

Chapter 24: "The Redemption"

The room buzzed with an electric tension, an unspoken war of whispers and speculation swirling in the air, thick enough to cut with a knife. As I stood at the back of the press conference, I felt the anticipation coil within me, a taut string ready to snap. The polished wood of the podium gleamed under the bright, unyielding lights, and the camera flashes went off like tiny fireworks, capturing the moment that would shift everything.

Adam stepped onto the stage, and the atmosphere shifted with him. Gone was the wary, reticent man I had first met—this was a man transformed. He wore a tailored navy suit that accentuated the broadness of his shoulders and the strength in his stance. His hair, usually tousled in that effortless way, was combed back, revealing the sharp angles of his jaw and the fierce determination in his eyes. He looked powerful, regal even, as he surveyed the crowd, his gaze sweeping over journalists and onlookers, each of them hungry for a morsel of scandal. But today, they were not going to find easy prey.

"Thank you all for being here," he began, his voice steady and commanding, echoing against the walls of the ornate hall. I leaned forward, my breath hitching, caught in the cadence of his speech. "Today, I stand before you not just as a businessman, but as a man who has made mistakes. Mistakes that have hurt not only myself but the people who believed in me."

My heart raced. This was the moment of truth, the moment that would define him—and us. I could see the muscles in his jaw clench slightly as he continued, "I take full responsibility for my actions. I have let the ambition and the drive for success cloud my judgment, and in doing so, I betrayed not only my company but also the trust of those closest to me."

The murmurs rose, but Adam remained undeterred, his eyes never straying from the podium. It was as if he drew strength from the very words he spoke, each syllable a step toward atonement. "To those I've hurt, I am deeply sorry," he said, his voice low but resolute. "I am committed to making things right. This will not be a quick fix; it will take time, effort, and the willingness to be vulnerable in front of you all."

The vulnerability in his statement resonated with me, wrapping around my heart like a warm embrace. I thought back to the man who had hidden behind his wealth and power, afraid to let anyone in, including himself. That man was still in there somewhere, but he was learning, evolving. I admired his bravery, the willingness to bare his soul before a room full of critics.

He paused, his eyes finally locking onto mine, piercing through the chaos of the room. In that fleeting moment, the world around us faded, leaving only the two of us suspended in time. I felt my pulse quicken, the connection between us palpable, charged with an unspoken understanding that transcended the scandal. He was fighting not just for his redemption but for ours, a chance to build something real amidst the ruins of the past.

"I have also been given a second chance," he continued, his voice breaking through my reverie. "A chance to reevaluate what truly matters in life." There was a softness in his gaze now, a glimmer of hope that flickered like a candle in the dark. "And for that, I must thank someone special—someone who showed me what it means to be vulnerable and open, to love and to be loved in return."

The room held its breath. I swallowed hard, the implications of his words sinking in. This was it—this was the moment where he could acknowledge me, not as the woman who had been embroiled in the scandal but as the one who had encouraged him to face his demons head-on.

"I owe much of my newfound perspective to a remarkable woman who believed in me when I didn't believe in myself," he said, his voice unwavering. "Her strength and courage helped me see the man I could be, and for that, I will be eternally grateful."

A collective gasp swept through the crowd, and I could feel the weight of their scrutiny pressing down on me. My cheeks flushed as I held his gaze, feeling simultaneously proud and terrified. This wasn't just about him anymore; it was about us, about the choices we had made, the paths we had taken.

As he finished his speech, his resolve seemed to invigorate the room, igniting a spark of hope amid the darkness of the scandal. "I promise to rebuild what I have broken and to earn back your trust. I will not shy away from accountability, nor will I turn my back on those who rely on me. Thank you."

The applause erupted, a thunderous sound that reverberated through the hall, filling every corner with renewed energy. I watched him step down from the podium, the uncertainty of the past still lingering in the air, yet now there was a glimmer of possibility. As he made his way through the throng of reporters and camera flashes, I knew he was seeking me out, navigating through the chaos with purpose.

When he finally reached me, there was no hesitation in his embrace. I melted against him, the warmth of his body grounding me in a world that had felt so out of control. "You did it," I whispered, my voice muffled against the fabric of his suit. "You faced them."

He pulled back slightly, his hands framing my face as he searched my eyes. "I couldn't have done it without you," he murmured, his breath warm against my skin. "You're my anchor, and I'm ready to fight for us."

In that moment, as the weight of the world shifted from our shoulders, I understood that redemption was not a destination but a journey we would navigate together. I smiled through the tears threatening to spill over, feeling lighter than I had in months.

Together, we would face whatever came next, hand in hand, ready to rewrite our story against the backdrop of a brighter, hopeful tomorrow.

The room buzzed with the remnants of excitement and tension, the echoes of applause still lingering like a sweet melody in the air. I clung to Adam's hands, our fingers intertwined as if forming an unbreakable bond amidst the chaos. The journalists, buzzing with questions, had begun to encircle us, their cameras flashing like lightning bugs in the dusk. Yet, in that moment, none of it mattered. I was wrapped up in the warmth of Adam's presence, a sanctuary from the storm that was brewing outside.

"Are you ready for this?" he asked, his voice low, carrying a hint of mischief that made me smile. His eyes sparkled with a mix of determination and playful defiance, a rare sight I had come to cherish.

"Ready as I'll ever be," I replied, squeezing his hand tighter, trying to suppress the flutter of nerves in my stomach. The aftermath of his speech would unleash a torrent of questions, and I had a feeling the media wouldn't be shy about their inquiries.

The first journalist, a sharp-eyed woman with a notepad poised like a weapon, broke through the crowd. "Mr. Langston, what specifically do you intend to do to rectify your past mistakes?"

"Would you like me to start with the time I thought I could outsmart my own conscience?" he quipped, a playful smirk tugging at his lips. The tension in the air dissipated slightly, and laughter rippled through the crowd.

But the reporter was relentless. "And what about your relationship with Ms. Sinclair? How does she fit into your plans for redemption?"

I could feel the heat rising to my cheeks, and I shot Adam a quick glance, ready to gauge his reaction. Instead, he took a step closer to me, his presence a reassuring wall against the onslaught of questions.

"She's not just a part of my life; she's the reason I'm standing here today," he said, his voice steady, laced with a sincerity that hushed the crowd. "Without her support, I would still be lost in my own arrogance."

I couldn't help but smile at him, pride swelling within me. His words rang true, but the acknowledgment also came with an unexpected weight. Being the center of attention—especially in a situation laden with scandal—was not something I had anticipated.

"Does this mean you two are an item?" another reporter called out, and a ripple of curiosity swept through the audience.

Before I could respond, Adam pulled me closer. "Let's just say we're figuring things out together. One day at a time."

There was a glimmer of understanding in his gaze that made my heart race. This was more than just a public statement; it was a commitment, a promise whispered beneath the clamor of flashing lights and probing questions.

As the media continued to bombard us with inquiries, I marveled at how effortlessly Adam navigated each question, his confidence evolving with every word. It was clear he had shed the skin of the man I had first met—the one who hid behind walls of wealth and prestige. This Adam was raw, exposed, and undeniably captivating.

Once the initial frenzy began to die down, we found a moment to breathe. I pulled him to a quieter corner of the room, away from the throngs of reporters, and leaned against a cool wall, my heart still racing from the adrenaline.

"You were amazing up there," I breathed, a giddy smile breaking across my face. "I mean, who knew you had such a way with words?"

He chuckled, his eyes sparkling with mischief. "Well, I've had a lot of practice pretending to be a charming billionaire."

"Oh please, don't sell yourself short," I replied, a teasing lilt to my voice. "I always suspected there was a real human in there somewhere."

The corners of his mouth turned upward as he took a step closer. "And you have this uncanny ability to bring him out, you know?"

Before I could respond, a commotion erupted nearby. The press had started to swarm again, eager to catch any whispers of scandal or a potential slip of the tongue from Adam.

"We should probably go before they discover our hiding spot," I suggested, glancing at the throng of reporters who were now glancing around like sharks sensing blood in the water.

"Lead the way," he replied, his tone light but serious, and I turned on my heel, heading toward the exit. Just as we neared the door, I felt a surge of warmth on my arm as he pulled me back, bringing me into the shade of a nearby alcove.

"Wait," he murmured, his voice dropping to a whisper, "I want to say something."

I looked up, curiosity piqued. "What is it?"

He hesitated, his brow furrowing as if he were choosing his words carefully. "I know this is all new for both of us—this relationship, this chaos—but I want you to know that I'm committed. To you, to us, to whatever this is."

His sincerity wrapped around me like a warm blanket on a chilly night. I could feel the weight of his words, heavy yet liberating, and I nodded, unable to find my voice for a moment.

"I want that too," I finally managed to say, my heart swelling. "But it feels like we're still wading through the aftermath of a storm."

"Every storm eventually clears, doesn't it?" he said, a wry smile gracing his lips. "And sometimes, a little rain is necessary for growth."

Just then, the moment was interrupted by a loud crash from the crowd, a scuffle breaking out as a couple of overzealous reporters jostled for position. Adam's grip on my arm tightened instinctively, his protective nature surfacing.

"Let's get out of here," he said, glancing back at the chaos. I nodded, my heart racing again—not from fear, but from the intoxicating mix of adrenaline and closeness that lingered between us.

As we slipped out of the venue and into the cool evening air, I couldn't help but feel a sense of hope rising like a phoenix from the ashes of our past. We had weathered the storm and emerged stronger, but the path ahead was still uncertain. In that uncertainty, however, lay the thrill of possibility, a landscape we could paint together, stroke by vivid stroke.

"Ready for whatever comes next?" Adam asked, his gaze fixed firmly on the horizon.

"Only if it includes a large pizza and a cozy couch," I replied, laughter bubbling up between us, dissolving the last remnants of tension.

"Now that's a plan I can get behind," he said, his laughter joining mine, a melody of shared joy and renewed promise as we stepped into the night, hand in hand, ready to face the future together.

The city stretched before us like a canvas brushed with the warm hues of twilight, the sky igniting in shades of orange and pink as the sun dipped below the horizon. I breathed in the crisp evening air, laced with the fragrant scent of blooming jasmine from a nearby garden. There was something magical about this moment, the laughter and banter between us creating an almost surreal backdrop against the reality we had just faced.

"Okay, so pizza and a couch it is," Adam declared, grinning as he held the door open for me to step into the car. "But I'll drive, just in case you try to sneak in a salad."

I rolled my eyes, feigning exasperation. "I was only suggesting a healthier option! You know, to counteract the emotional damage of being in the spotlight."

"Emotional damage is best healed with pizza," he countered, slipping into the driver's seat. "And I, for one, refuse to play into your attempts at healthy eating. This is a moment for indulgence."

As we drove through the streets, the city lights twinkled like stars, creating a comforting glow that enveloped us. I glanced over at him, my heart swelling with affection. He looked so at ease, a stark contrast to the man who had stood before a throng of reporters just hours earlier. The tension of that moment had evaporated, replaced by a lightness that buoyed us both.

"What's your pizza order?" he asked, a playful glint in his eye.

"Extra cheese, pepperoni, and definitely some olives. You can't have pizza without a little drama," I replied, leaning back against the plush leather seat.

"Olives? Really? You're a culinary risk-taker, aren't you?"

"Every bite an adventure," I teased, giving him a mock serious look. "You could learn a thing or two about living on the edge, Mr. Billionaire."

His laughter filled the car, rich and deep, and I couldn't help but feel like I was falling for him all over again. The vulnerability he had shown today, coupled with his light-heartedness now, made him feel more human, more real.

Before long, we pulled up to a cozy pizzeria tucked away on a quiet street, the kind with a warm, welcoming atmosphere and a hint of nostalgia clinging to the air. The bell jingled above the door as we entered, a cheerful sound that signaled the start of our unwinding evening.

"Two slices of your finest pepperoni and olive special, please!" Adam called to the counter, his charm disarming the staff as he flashed a winning smile.

The server grinned, likely accustomed to the whims of eccentric patrons. "Coming right up! And what can I get for you, Miss?"

"I'll take the same, thanks," I said, glancing at Adam with a raised brow. "Aren't we a couple of adventurous eaters?"

"Living dangerously," he agreed, his eyes sparkling with mirth.

We found a table by the window, the flickering candlelight casting soft shadows on the checkered tablecloth. As we waited for our order, the conversation flowed easily between us, bouncing from lighthearted teasing to deeper discussions about what had transpired earlier that day.

"Do you think they'll ever let this die down?" I asked, stirring the remnants of my soda absently.

He sighed, leaning back in his chair. "I hope so. But I'm not naïve. Scandals have a way of sticking around. Still, I'd rather face them head-on than hide in the shadows."

I admired his resolve, the courage he exuded even in uncertainty. "You're not that guy anymore. I mean, you did well out there."

He smiled, a soft, contemplative expression that made my heart flutter. "Thanks to you."

Just then, our pizzas arrived, steaming and glistening with cheese, a feast for the senses. The rich aroma enveloped us, and I felt my mouth water in anticipation. As we dug in, laughter bubbled up easily, peppered with playful jabs and shared stories, the kind that draw people closer.

"You know," Adam said between bites, "I didn't think I could enjoy something so simple after everything that's happened. But here we are."

"Sometimes, it's the simplest moments that mean the most," I replied, savoring the flavors bursting in my mouth.

He nodded, his expression shifting to something more contemplative. "That's true. I spent so much time chasing success, thinking it would fill the emptiness inside. But it's moments like these that ground me."

I felt a pang of empathy, understanding the weight of his past. "We all get lost sometimes," I said softly. "But it's about finding our way back, right?"

"Exactly," he said, leaning closer, his intensity drawing me in. "And I feel like I'm finding my way back to who I really am. With you."

The air between us shifted, the weight of his words sinking in. This was a pivotal moment, one where honesty hung delicately in the balance, and I wanted to tread carefully. "And who is that person, Adam?"

He opened his mouth, hesitated, and then closed it again, his brow furrowing slightly. Just then, the cheerful chime of the pizzeria door swung open, drawing our attention.

A figure entered, silhouetted against the light from outside, and the atmosphere shifted in an instant. The vibrant chatter of the restaurant dimmed as the newcomer stepped into view, a familiar face that caused my stomach to drop.

It was Clara, her sharp gaze scanning the room until it landed on us, a calculated expression on her face. My heart raced, a mix of surprise and anxiety flooding my senses. I had hoped to escape the tangled web of scandal and deceit for just one night, but here she was, poised to shatter the fragile bubble of happiness we had created.

"Adam," she called, her voice dripping with a saccharine sweetness that made my skin crawl. "Fancy running into you here."

He stiffened, his relaxed demeanor vanishing as Clara approached, her presence casting a shadow over our moment. "Clara," he acknowledged, his tone cool but edged with annoyance.

"What a lovely dinner date you've got," she remarked, her eyes glinting with an unsettling mix of jealousy and triumph.

I felt a rush of protectiveness surge within me, but I also sensed the tension radiating from Adam, as if he were bracing for impact. "What do you want?" he asked, his voice steady but firm.

"Oh, nothing much," she said, feigning innocence. "Just thought I'd check in and see how you're handling all this... publicity. I mean, it's not every day you make a public apology."

"Get to the point, Clara," he snapped, his patience clearly wearing thin.

A wicked smile curled her lips as she leaned against the wall, arms crossed. "I just wanted to remind you that I'm still very much involved in this little saga. And it might not be as easy to move on as you think."

The atmosphere turned electric, charged with unspoken tension. My pulse raced as I glanced between them, uncertainty swirling in my mind. It was clear Clara wasn't here to simply exchange pleasantries. She had an agenda, and it felt as if the ground was shifting beneath our feet.

"I'm not afraid of you," Adam said, his voice low and unyielding.

"But you should be," she countered, her smile widening. "You see, I have a little surprise that could change everything for both of you."

With that, the air thickened, the shadows closing in as uncertainty loomed on the horizon. The familiar warmth of the evening faded, replaced by an unsettling chill that hinted at storm clouds gathering just out of sight, and I could only hope that whatever lay ahead wouldn't tear us apart before we'd had the chance to truly find our way together.